Death &

A Victorian Sensation Novel

Carol Hedges

Little G Books

For Martyn, Hannah, Archie & Avalyn

About the Author

Carol Hedges is the successful British author of 16 books for teenagers and adults. Her writing has received much critical acclaim, and her novel Jigsaw was shortlisted for the Angus Book Award and longlisted for the Carnegie Medal.

Carol was born in Hertfordshire, and after university, where she gained a BA (Hons.) in English Literature & Archaeology, she trained as a children's librarian. She worked for the London Borough of Camden for many years subsequently re-training as a secondary school teacher when her daughter was born.

Carol still lives and writes in Hertfordshire. She is a local activist and green campaigner, and the proud owner of a customised 1988 pink 2CV.

Diamonds & Dust, A Victorian Murder Mystery, was her first adult novel. It was followed up by Honour & Obey. Death & Dominion is the third in the series.

The Victorian Detectives series

Diamonds & Dust
Honour & Obey
Death & Dominion
Rack & Ruin
Wonders & Wickedness

Acknowledgments

Many thanks to Gina Dickerson of RoseWolf Design, for another superb cover, and to my two patient editors for their invaluable help with this edition.

To those wonderful individuals who have urged me to give Stride & Cully another outing: Lynn, Terry, Michael, Ali, Ros, Jo, Val and so many others too numerous to mention. This book would not have been written without your encouragement.

Finally, I acknowledge my debt to all those amazing Victorian novelists for lighting the path through the fog with their genius. Unworthily but optimistically, I follow in their footsteps.

Death & Dominion

A Victorian Sensation Novel

"What we are said to perceive is usually a compound result, of which one tenth may be observation, and the remaining nine-tenths inference."

John Stuart Mill. A System of Logic, 1843

London, 1862. It has been a cold summer – the coldest on record, they say, and the autumn nights have come early and bitten hard. Wind batters the city, rattling the windows and inn-signs, whipping up the Thames into white-capped rage.

Wind whirls rooks into the sky like cinders. Wind prowls across narrow quadrangles and round unsuspecting corners, blowing dead leaves into nooks and stairwells. In weather like this, right-thinking people wrap up warm and stay indoors in front of the fire.

Not all of them though. Look more closely.

A tall man is making his way towards King's Cross station, his shoulders squared, tilting forward as he walks. He is darkly handsome, the sort of man who causes women's heads to turn when he enters the room. He knows this. His name is Mark Hawksley (though not all of the time).

As he reaches the entrance, a gust suddenly rocks him on his heels forcing him to make a half-step backwards. He takes a deep breath, the wind pummelling his face, the richness of the oxygen making him feel temporarily light-headed.

Steadying himself, the man enters the shadowy arch of the station and heads for a specific platform where a train is expected to arrive at any minute. In the station air, he can hear it coming, the sudden frantic chugging of a locomotive, a series of clanks as it passes over the final set of points, then a long exhalation of steam as it pulls alongside the platform and comes to a halt by the buffers. Instantly all is bustle and bedlam. Dogs bark, porters shout, and trolleys are hurriedly trundled towards the baggage carriage at the back.

Two respectably-dressed men alight from the front carriage of the train, turning to help down a small female figure, heavily-veiled and clad in deepest black.

They escort her along the platform, steering her carefully through the milling throng of passengers, the meeters and greeters, the mounds of luggage, and the cabbies touting for fares.

Reaching the barrier, they hand over three tickets and are allowed through and onto the forecourt. They glance around apprehensively, their faces clearing as Mark Hawksley steps forward into the light, lifting his top hat in a smooth elegant gesture.

"So here you all are at last," he says.

"Here we all are. Just as we telegraphed you," one of the men replies.

Hawksley gestures towards the heavily-veiled woman.

"May I?" he asks.

"Be our guest," the other man nods.

He lifts the thick veil, then steps quickly back, uttering a gasp of surprise.

"Amazing," he breathes. "She is exactly as you described her in your letter. You might almost believe … But come, we need to get our guest to a place of safety before she is recognised."

Mark Hawksley steers the little party to where a line of cabs is patiently waiting. He signals to one driver, gives him careful instructions, then bundles the group into the rear of the cab. He closes the door. The driver whips up the horse. As the cab rattles away into the night, Hawksley's handsome, chiselled features break into a wide smile.

"Oh yes," he murmurs. "You will do nicely. Very nicely indeed."

***

But this is not the only arrival tonight in the greatest capital city in the world. Even as the hired cab is pulling away from King's Cross station with its mysterious cargo safely stowed aboard, another cab is pulling up outside one of the white stuccoed houses in Cartwright Gardens, Bloomsbury.

The rear door opens and a small dainty foot booted in slightly shabby kid leather extends itself cautiously, followed by a discreet section of shapely leg, and then the rest of the cab's occupant, who turns out to be a young person with emerald-green eyes, a red mouth, determined chin and hair the colour of falling Autumn.

She gives the cabman instructions to "Follow on with my box, if you please," with a toss of her head that makes the feathers on her straw bonnet bob and dance merrily.

Having issued her orders, she mounts the steps to the front door, where she raps out three short knocks on the brass lion-headed knocker and waits to be admitted, looking around with an expression of satisfaction on her pretty face.

The door opens and the young person hands the snooty-looking maid her card. She announces, "I am expected," and is ushered into the black-and-white tiled hallway. The maid carries the little pasteboard square into the drawing room.

Miss Belinda Kite has arrived in London.

But is London ready for her? A question yet to be answered.

An hour later, Miss Belinda Kite, dressed in a very becoming grey silk gown, trips down the staircase and enters the dining-room. Here, the master of the house, Josiah Bulstrode (of Bulstrode's Boots and Shoes, Leeds), is seated at the head of the table, solemnly carving slices from a joint of beef.

He is a well-built man in his late thirties, with a high complexion and Macassar-oiled hair and moustaches. His actions are being observed from across the table by a young lady. She is his sister, and Belinda Kite has arrived to be her paid companion.

The young lady reminds Belinda of a watercolour painting done by someone who had not much colour but a lot of water, giving off the impression of not only being colourless, but rather damp.

"Now then, Sissy, one slice or two?" Josiah says to the pallid one, holding the carving fork aloft.

Miss Kite clears her throat, ever so lightly, to indicate that her presence requires noticing. The master of the house waves her to a seat with the fork, and continues cutting the meat.

"Well, Miss Kite," he says. "Here you are at last. Dinner is on the table and we are ready to eat it."

He places a slice of beef on a plate and passes it to the pale one.

"I trust you have found everything to your satisfaction, Miss Kite. You take us as you find us. As I said in my letter, I'm a bluff, no-nonsense northerner. My sister Grizelda here is the younger sister of a bluff, no-nonsense northerner. And that's the long and short of it."

"Oh indeed," Miss Belinda Kite murmurs, unrolling her napkin and placing it upon her lap. "Only, if I may correct you – my name is pronounced '*Keet'*, as in the French manner. My father*, le Marquis,* was always most particular about it."

And she opens her emerald-green eyes very wide, and smiles sweetly at the bluff, no-nonsense northerner, who harrumphs and nearly drops the carving knife on the floor.

"Well, would you listen to that, Sissy … we have French nobility dining with us!" he says, handing the noblewoman a plate of beef.

The pale lady smiles wanly.

"I know you come highly recommended, Miss *Keet,*

or I studied your references carefully, and they was excellent. I only hope you can cheer up poor Sissy over there, for she has had a very hard time since the Unfortunate Incident which I believe I mentioned briefly to you, and she needs a companion to entertain her and take her about a bit."

"Oh, I'm sure I shall be delighted to do so," Belinda Kite says, smiling at nothing while cutting up her meat. Both her little fingers are crooked daintily.

Boiled beef and potatoes are soon consumed – though Sissy merely picks at hers – and are swiftly followed by a cherry tart, which Belinda Kite enjoys very much, rolling her eyes and declaring that cherries are her favourite fruit.

She actually has a second piece, after which she indicates that the long journey and the cold weather have quite sapped her energy, and if the company would excuse her, she'd like to retire to her room.

Belinda Kite mounts the stairs to the nicely-appointed first-floor bedroom, where a few hours ago her box was deposited. She sits at her dressing table and begins to unpin her hair, wondering what the Unfortunate Incident endured by Grizelda Bulstrode really was. No details have been furnished, as yet.

Belinda has endured several Unfortunate Incidents in her young life. She has no doubt that there will be many more. Except that now she is going to make sure that they occur to other people. As for her references, she knows that they are excellent. And so they should be, for she wrote them herself.

***

It is next morning, and Detective Sergeant Jack Cully, whom we last met cat over boots in love, is on his way to work. He is later than usual due to a misunderstanding over crumbs.

Marriage has brought Cully many advantages and blessings, but it has also provided him with many puzzling dilemmas – the spilling of crumbs being one of them.

Now he hurries towards Scotland Yard, keeping his eyes open for gangs of villainous individuals. For ever since July, when Hugh Pilkington, MP, was accosted by robbers who choked him and stole his watch, London has been in the middle of a garrotting panic.

The press, eager to seize upon any minor news event, especially during a slow summer when most of the Court remains in mourning for Prince Albert, and the Queen is in total seclusion at Windsor Castle, has been making hay with the story. Articles have appeared almost daily, referring to the *Race of hardened villains* who inhabit the seedier sections of the city. So scared have people become, that innocent citizens walking home in a foggy evening have been set upon by other innocent citizens who believed them to be potential garrotters.

Cully has seen gentlemen sporting a spiked 'anti-garrotte' device – a fearsome object that looks like a cross between a medieval instrument of torture and a clergyman's dog-collar. Fortunately, the investigations are in the hands of the uniformed police, thus freeing the Detective Division for other matters.

Cully enters the portals of Scotland Yard, nods to the desk sergeant, and runs a quick eye over those waiting on the Anxious Bench for news of their nearest and dearest. He can never pass it without recalling the small slope-shouldered figure of Emily Benet (now Emily Cully) as she sat forlornly waiting for news of her murdered friend, Violet Manning.

Currently the bench is occupied by a well-dressed man in a tall top-hat. He sits in the customary pose of hands clasped, head down, eyes staring at the floor. Cully passes him by without giving him a second glance. A man waiting for news is nothing remarkable.

Entering Detective Inspector Stride's office, Cully is surprised to find his boss hard at work. Papers are being scanned and moved from one pile to another, with alarming alacrity.

"Morning, Jack," Stride says gloomily. "Incredible how all this paperwork mounts up."

He crumples a sheet of paper clearly labelled *Important* and bowls it overarm into the wastepaper basket. "Most of this stuff isn't for reading, it's for having been written."

"Early start?" Cully observes.

Stride rolls his eyes upwards.

"Mud," he says obliquely, following this by, "new drugget in the hallway. The wife has taken it into her head that all muddy boots must now be removed on entering the house and placed by the front door. Never done it in my life. Not going to start doing it now. Thought it best to get out of the house early to avoid further discussion on the subject."

Cully nods. Now that he has joined the ranks of the married men, such topics have taken on a whole new resonance.

Stride shuffles a few more papers. Then he looks at Cully.

"Right," he says. "Did you notice a man sitting on the Anxious Bench? He's been there some time. Apparently, he claims that somebody is trying to poison him. Fetch him in, would you, and let's see what he has to say."

***

No crumbs are being spilled in the dining room of

the white stuccoed house in Cartwright Gardens, Bloomsbury, where Joseph Bulstrode (boot and shoe manufacturer and bluff, no-nonsense northerner) is tucking into a laden plate of bacon and scrambled eggs.

Toast and hot coffee sit at his elbow. Chops and kedgeree await his attention in silver chafing dishes on the mahogany sideboard. All the ingredients of a good London breakfast are here in abundance.

A slightly more modest repast is being consumed by Grizelda Bulstrode, who conveys tiny squares of buttered toast into her mouth with the cautious apprehension of one posting letters.

Halfway through the meal the door opens to admit Miss Belinda Kite, clad in a slightly soiled cotton morning gown, her hair newly released from its curling papers. She looks as fresh as a daisy, having slept all night in newly laundered sheets. She eyes the breakfast table, a smile hovering at the corners of her small red mouth.

"Morning, Miss Keet," Bulstrode says. "Sit you down. Mary is all ready and waiting to serve your breakfast, as you can see."

"Thank you," she murmurs.

She lowers her eyes, lowers herself into her seat, and unrolls a starched linen napkin. A hovering maid places a plate in front of her, pours some coffee into her cup, offers bacon and eggs, toast, marmalade, breakfast rolls. Miss Kite smiles and dimples, and helps herself lavishly.

"Now then, Sissy," Bulstrode remarks, "there's a breakfast to set a lady up for the day ahead. I hope our simple English fare is to your taste, Miss Keet – after all, you've been brought up different, have you not?"

Belinda Kite, her mouth full of hot buttered toast, inclines her head graciously. For it is true – she is not accustomed to such fare. Hitherto, her fare has been distinctly unfair.

"Ladies," Bulstrode says, rising and brushing crumbs from his waistcoat, "the world of business calls, and cannot be ignored. I have buyers to see and shops to visit. I shall leave you to get to know each other. Sissy, do not forget you have an appointment with the dressmaker after luncheon. I expect Miss Keet will be able to enlighten her as to the latest Paree fashions."

He crumples his napkin upon the table and strides out of the room.

Grizelda plays with the crusts on her plate. She shoots Belinda a couple of nervous glances, opens her mouth a few times as if she is on the point of imparting something, but in the end, says nothing.

The maid enters with a tray and begins to remove the breakfast things.

Belinda Kite paints a pretty smile onto her face.

And so it begins, she thinks.

***

Mr Frederick Undercroft, lawyer, perches unhappily on the chair opposite Stride's desk. He is a lean-featured man in his early fifties, clean-shaven, his greying hair worn slightly long and touching his high starched collar at the back.

He presses his thighs together, presses the bones of his knees, then reaches down and picks a scrap of thread from the hem of his trousers.

Stride waits patiently.

"I've been feeling a little seedy for quite a while, Inspector," Undercroft begins. "I couldn't put it down to anything specific. Then, after supper the other week, I retired to my study with a glass of my favourite port. When I picked up the glass, I noticed there was some cloudy substance like chalk at the bottom of the glass. I poured the port away and threw out the bottle."

As he speaks, he fiddles with a button on his pink waistcoat.

"I thought nothing of it at the time. Some days later, again after supper, I noticed a dish of chocolate creams on the sideboard. I am partial to chocolate, very partial indeed, so I helped myself to a couple of creams. The first one I bit into had a metallic taste. I spat it out at once, but a short while later I began to feel extremely unwell. I mentioned it to my wife, who ate a couple of the creams herself, but she said she could taste nothing unusual."

Stride glances up from the notes he has made.

"Bad food and drink happen to all of us. I agree that is unfortunate, but I hardly think …"

"No – wait, Inspector, let me finish, please. You have not heard the full story. On Monday morning, a small box wrapped in brown paper was delivered to the house. It was addressed to me personally. My wife opened it and discovered several pieces of cake. We happened to be going out after I returned from work, so she handed the box to a servant to take down to the kitchen. In our absence, one of the maids helped herself to a cake from the box."

He pauses.

"The poor girl immediately became violently ill and took to her bed. We sent for our local private physician. This morning, she died. The physician thought the girl may have been poisoned, and that her death should be reported. Given the incident with the chocolate creams and the port, I felt it desirable to come straight here."

Stride sets down his pen slowly. He places the tips of his fingers together and observes Undercroft thoughtfully.

"Do you have any enemies, sir?"

"I am a lawyer by profession. I specialise in dealing

with Wills and Probate. I hardly think that is conducive to making enemies – certainly not the sort who would try to poison me."

Stride nods.

"And beyond the legal profession?"

"I belong to a Club. I have friends. I am fond their company and they of mine. I believe I am known generally as a convivial fellow."

Stride nods.

"Thank you, sir. As soon as I am able, my sergeant and I will come and view the body. We shall then want to question your servants. Please make sure the room in which the woman died is left untouched. I don't suppose you have kept any of the cakes … or the chocolates?"

Undercroft shakes his head.

"Cook put both on the fire."

"That's a great shame, sir. Without evidence, it might be hard to prove that anybody is trying, as you suggest, to poison you."

"One of my servants has just died!" Undercroft exclaims, his face flushing unpleasantly. "Isn't that evidence enough?"

"When we have viewed the body, I'll arrange for it to be brought to Scotland Yard for a post-mortem investigation," Stride responds calmly. "We need to ascertain the exact cause of death before we proceed any further. Doctors have been known to get things wrong before now."

He rises.

"Thank you, sir. If you'd care to leave your card with my sergeant, we'll be in touch very shortly. Oh – if any more parcels of cakes arrive, or you notice anything unusual at table, I'd advise you to keep hold of it and let us know at once."

Cully ushers the lawyer out, returning a short while

later carrying a small card, which he places it on Stride's desk.

"Downshire Hill, Hampstead. Very salubrious," Stride remarks.

"What do you make of his story?"

"Nothing. Yet. We shall have to wait for the post-mortem results."

"You believe what he said about having no enemies?"

Stride's eyes narrow.

"If what he says turns out to be true, it tends towards the opposite way of thinking. Only an enemy, and a very bitter and vengeful one, would stoop to poison. Something does not quite add up here, Jack. But we shall work out what it is eventually."

***

Meanwhile a cab is making its way down Hackney High Street. It slows, then halts outside a small red brick-built terraced house. The driver alights from the box, and opens the cab door.

Two people emerge and step down: a man and a heavily-veiled woman. They traverse the gravel path. The man (still called Mark Hawksley) rings the bell. A brass sign next to the door reads *Edward May, Portrait Photographer.*

The couple are ushered into a small parlour that doubles as a waiting area. There is a strong smell of chemicals overlaid with beeswax. They sit on unmatching chairs, in silence, until the door opens and a small bustling individual hurries in. He has uncombed hair, discoloured fingers, and a jacket stained with unidentified substances. He stands in the doorway, staring at the veiled woman.

"Ah," he says. Then repeats, "Ah," but slightly more

warily.

Hawksley steps forward.

"No questions, remember."

He slips his hand into his waistcoat pocket. There is the jingle of coins.

"Quite. Yes. Indeed. So, would you like to come this way, sir ... and madam." The photographer's voice hesitates on the final word.

They follow him into a well-lit back room. Boxes, metal stands, tripods and trays of paper occupy most of it. By the window there is a high-backed chair, draped in crimson velvet. Fake pillars have been placed on either side.

"I thought maybe a side view – as being more appropriate?" May suggests.

"Whatever you think best."

The woman is placed on the chair. Her hands are arranged in her lap. Then the veil is lifted and folded back to reveal her face.

"Oh, my goodness!" May gasps.

Hawksley shoots him a warning look.

The photographer blinks, swallows, then sets up one of the cameras on a tripod. He places the black cloth of the camera over his head.

"Please sit exceptionally still." His voice is muffled.

The woman does not move a muscle. It is as if she has been carved from alabaster. She remains absolutely motionless, until May emerges from under the cloth, rubbing his hands.

"It is all done."

Hawksley nods in a satisfied manner. The woman replaces her veil.

"I shall require a few days to get the photographic likeness printed," May says.

"You wrote that you wanted a hundred *cartes-de-visite,* is that correct?"

"And some posters. To begin with, yes. Obviously, if all goes well, I may require more in time."

The photographer inclines his head. Looks expectantly. Hawksley dips into his pocket. Money changes hands.

"I shall let you know when everything is ready," May says.

"Thank you. And remember – absolute secrecy. As we agreed."

Hawksley beckons to the woman. She rises and they leave the studio, quit the house and get back into the waiting hackney cab. Not a single word has passed between them the entire time. Nor does it at any time during the return journey.

***

Mr Frederick Undercroft, lawyer, lover of pink silk waistcoats and chocolate creams, walks out of Scotland Yard into the grey drizzle of a London autumn morning.

He decides to seek some diversion before returning to a home which was, when he left it earlier, a chaos of wailing servants and his whey-faced wife. It will probably still be so on his return, with the addition of members of the Detective Division of the Metropolitan Police.

Mr Undercroft adjusts his black top-hat (best quality silk Paris nap, lined in white silk and made by his regular hatter, Daniel Digance & Company) and heads towards the Strand.

If you were to ask him about his pleasures and pastimes, Mr Undercroft would inform you that he is, and always has been, an avid reader and great supporter of authors.

However, if pushed, he might reveal (to the

appropriate interrogator) that he derives much of his reading matter from certain specialist bookshops in Holywell Street, and it is thence that he now directs his footsteps.

***

Let us pause at this point, and consider Holywell Street, that double affront to Victorian propriety: site of obscene and pornographic literature and Jewish old-clothes dealers. It is labyrinthine, made up of tall old-fashioned buildings whose crumbling upper storeys extrude over the narrow-pavemented street.

Behind them, warehouses and dark fetid alleys lead to dirty backyards containing printing works, and shabby lodgings which are rented to numerous families by the room or floor space.

Marginally affected by the 1857 Obscene Publications Act and subsequent police razzias upon its shopkeepers, Holywell Street is stagnant, quaint and corrupting, a picturesque symbol and survivor of old London. It is a great dark spider at the centre of the web of obscenity.

Nowhere is the web more tangled, or the spider more scuttling, than at number 39 Holywell Street. Situated next to a small barber's shop advertising *Shampooing, Cutting, Shaving and Hats Ironed*, number 39 is the domain of Edwin Gregious, bookseller and printer. Or, as he prefers to describe himself, *niche bookseller specialising in expensive and exclusive limited editions.*

Undercroft arrives at his destination to discover the usual crowd of Hogarthian street-types lounging in front of the shop window, attracted by the pavement baulks of cheap books and prints.

A few young women also linger, staring in horrified fascination at the semi-nude prints of cavorting nymphs and generously-endowed satyrs displayed in the flyblown windows.

He brushes past the gawpers, mentally noting one rather attractive young woman in a pretty blue-ribboned bonnet. They exchange a quick glance before the woman lowers her eyes modestly, a becoming flush appearing on her cheeks. Undercroft smiles as he enters the dark shop. He enjoys the piquancy of a brief erotic encounter.

"Ah, Mr Undercroft, how good to see you once more," Gregious murmurs, coming out from behind the counter. He lifts up a book. "And how timely is your arrival. I have just obtained a brand-new edition of *The Wedding Night, or Battles with Venus.*"

He holds the book, stroking it with his fat white fingers.

"Lovely binding," he breathes. "Take a look. It is lavishly illustrated too."

Undercroft takes the proffered volume and turns the pages. It is indeed lavishly illustrated. He peruses the illustrations carefully for some time, then hands it back to the bookseller, nodding his approval.

"A nice copy, as you say. I shall purchase it."

A short while later Frederick Undercroft takes his leave, a brown paper parcel tucked under one arm. He walks briskly to the Strand where he hails a cab, giving the driver instructions to take him to Hampstead.

As the cab bowls through the lunchtime traffic he thinks about the events of the past week. Undercroft knows he is considered by his male acquaintances, and members of his Club, to be a thoroughly nice bloke. It's disconcerting to contemplate that somebody out there in the teeming metropolis seems not to agree.

When he arrives back at the smart Regency townhouse overlooking the Heath, it is to find the two detectives from Scotland Yard already at work. Stride is waiting in the drawing room, seated on a hard chair amidst the dark gleaming furniture. He looks about as comfortable as the collection of stuffed birds who perch uneasily under a bright glass dome.

Seated opposite is Mrs Georgiana Undercroft, the lawyer's tightly-corseted, tightly-reserved, tight-lipped wife. Anybody can see that she must have been beautiful once: she still has a clear complexion and large blue eyes, though time has caused her chin to sag and her lips to grow thin and feathered.

She glances up as her husband enters the room, and her eyes flick towards the brown paper parcel. Her expression subtly changes.

"Detective Inspector," Undercroft says smoothly, placing the parcel on a side table and sliding into a chair. "I apologise for not being *in situ.* A slight delay ... But I am here now, and ready to answer any questions you may wish to put to me."

Stride produces his notebook, licks the end of a pencil and begins.

Meanwhile, two floors up, Jack Cully (who has drawn the short straw) is standing in the servants' attic bedroom. He has viewed the body, made copious notes, and is now questioning the other housemaid, who stands in the doorway, small and downcast of expression, pleating the edge of her apron.

"We were in the kitchen helping Cook with the clearing up after breakfast when the parcel was delivered," she tells him. "It was a small box wrapped in brown paper. The mistress brought it straight down to the kitchen and said: *'Cook, somebody has sent round some cakes for Mr Undercroft as a gift. As we shall be out today, I wonder if you could put them somewhere safe until we return.'* So, Cook put them on the window ledge.

"There were three cakes: a cheesecake, a piece of

gingerbread and a slice of plum cake. They looked very nice and fresh, as if they'd just come out of the oven. Later that morning, while we were having a break from our work, Molly said: *'I don't think the master will eat all that cake, and Mrs Undercroft never touches sweet stuff. Shame to waste them.'* Then she opened the box and helped herself to the gingerbread."

"Just Molly had some cake?"

"Oh yes, sir. Just Molly. The rest of us wouldn't take any. But Molly was …" she pauses, bites her lower lip. "Mr Undercroft was particularly fond of her. Molly always used to bring his shaving water to his dressing-room in the morning. Nobody else was allowed to."

"What happened next?" Cully prompts.

"She ate the whole cake. Then a short while later she said: *'I don't feel well.'* She said her throat was burning. Then she began to rub her stomach and started shaking. Next thing, she was sick. And Cook said: *'I think there must be something wrong with those cakes, best get rid of them,'* and she threw them and the box they came in into the fire. By now, Molly was white as a sheet and crying out in pain. We helped her up to bed but she kept on being sick, even when there was nothing left inside her to bring up. It went on all night. This morning, she died."

Tears begin to run down her pleasant pink face.

"It could have been me," she gulps. "I nearly ate the plum cake. I was very hungry and we never get any cake; the master always eats it all."

Downstairs, Stride is making slow progress with the Undercrofts. Trying to elicit anything useful out of them is like wading through treacle. No, Mrs Undercroft tells him, she did not recognise the handwriting on the box.

There was no note in the box with the cakes. They had never received parcels of cake through the post before, although they regularly got groceries delivered from Fortum & Mason and wine from Justerini & Brooks. No, she didn't think it unusual.

Undercroft seems bemused by the whole interview process – Stride guesses he is more used to asking the questions than answering them. He merely corroborates everything his wife says with a curt nod.

Eventually, when the men arrive to remove the body to the police morgue, Stride decides to call it a day. He has elicited as much as he can. He tells the Undercrofts he will be in touch when the autopsy report has been written, and rejoins Cully in the hallway.

"Mark my words, there's certainly something strange going on," Stride says as they step out into an afternoon whose sky is tawny and lucid with incipient rain. "Neither of those two were saying anything significant."

"Then how do you know?"

"Because they weren't saying it loud and clear," Stride tells him. "But I shall get them to tell me what they're not telling me. Sooner or later."

"It certainly looked like some sort of poisoning to me," Cully remarks as they retrieve their hats from the rosewood hat stand in the hall.

Stride waves a dismissive hand.

"First rule of detection, Jack: assemble the facts. Then digest the information and consider the implications. We're not jumping to any conclusions until we have read the police surgeon's report. I've heard of flour being contaminated accidentally. Chances are it was something on those lines."

"Then shouldn't there be other cases?"

"There may well be. Perhaps they just haven't been brought to our notice. Yet."

***

As the two detectives make their way back to Scotland Yard, and the rain starts falling, a slender figure alights from an omnibus and walks with a determined step towards Cartwright Gardens, Bloomsbury. She carries a covered wicker basket on her arm.

Under the neatly-trimmed bonnet you may recognise the face of Emily Benet, now Mrs Emily Cully. Since we last saw her on the arm of Jack Cully, Emily Benet's life has undergone many changes. She is a wife, and a housekeeper of rented rooms in Kennington.

But more importantly, she now runs her own small dressmaking business. Once, Emily and her friend Violet Manning had dreamed of owning their own dressmaking business, sewing gorgeous gowns for ladies in high society. When Violet was brutally murdered, that dream died with her.

Yet, miraculously, it has risen from the ashes. And now, Mrs Emily Cully, private dressmaker, is shown into the parlour where two young women are seated side by side on a chintz sofa.

One of the women has a long pale-complexioned face that reminds Emily of the horses she sometimes sees trotting in the park on a Sunday afternoon. Difficult to find a colour that flatters, she thinks.

As the young woman rises awkwardly, Emily also notes that she is thin, flat-chested, and angular, her bony wrists protruding from her sleeves. *Difficult to fit, too.* Her companion, who has not risen, catches the edge of her expression, and, as if reading her thoughts, smiles knowingly.

Emily Cully looks away. She is here to measure for a dress, not to have any opinion, verbal or non-verbal, or to show any complicity. Nevertheless, as Grizelda

Bulstrode falters her way through the opening politenesses, she steals a glance at the pretty young woman introduced as 'my companion Miss Keet'.

The glance encompasses the nicely-made grey silk gown the companion is wearing. Emily's professional eye takes in the intricate lace detailing of the collar and cuffs and prices it up.

She wonders how a companion could afford a day dress like this. A closer glance reveals that the dress, though clearly new, looks as if it were originally made for a slightly larger person. It doesn't sit quite right around the neck and on the shoulders.

There is an anomaly here, but now Grizelda Bulstrode is asking her opinion on styles and colours, so Emily quickly shelves her thoughts away and concentrates on the lanky young woman.

She opens her basket and takes out pattern books and swatches, lays them on the table and begins to explain the various options and designs available.

Part of the dressmaker's art is tactfully steering her customer away from the rocks of recklessness and towards the shore of safety. By the time she leaves, Emily has gently persuaded her gauche client that a soft lavender colour would suit her delicately pale complexion far better than the bright pink or garish purple that she initially wanted.

The design chosen, measurements taken, and a delivery date arranged, Emily repacks her basket and takes her leave. She will now pay a visit to one of the big department stores in Regent Street, where her best friend Caro, who is in charge of the sewing room, will quote her a good price for the material, laces and thread. Then she will distribute the work amongst her little team of home workers.

Emily is pleased with the day's business. A new client, two dresses ordered and a deposit put down. She decides to spend some of it on a nice piece of meat for her husband's supper and sets off to find a butcher's shop, temporarily dismissing from her thoughts the enigma of the smirky companion in the ill-fitting silk dress.

***

So who is Miss Belinda Kite, daughter of a French *Marquis* and now companion of the lacklustre Grizelda Bulstrode? You may be surprised to hear that she does *not* have any aristocratic connections.

Her origins are far more prosaic. In reality, Miss Kite's father was a dancing master who married, far too young, a very pretty but ultimately flighty French ladies' maid who fled the matrimonial home shortly after Belinda's sixth birthday.

Left on his own with a daughter to raise, Mr Kite accepted a post at a girls' boarding school in North Street, Brighton. This establishment consisted of seven teachers and thirty-three girls ranging in age from eight to eighteen. Its purpose was to teach the girls, who came from aspiring middle-class families, how to turn up their noses at domestic chores and to pass their time elegantly with the sort of drawing-room accomplishments that indicated they were gentlewomen.

Thus, graduates of the school knew about the uses of whalebone, the making of umbrellas, the names of several kings and queens, and had a smattering of Italian and French – qualifications essential to sitting in parlours awaiting suitable marriages.

This elite establishment admitted the very young Miss Kite as a boarder in part payment for her father's services. And it was here, as she slipped into young womanhood, that Belinda Kite learned how to deceive, perfecting her secrecy and skills for subterfuge.

Then, three days short of her seventeenth birthday, Belinda's life was suddenly turned upside down once again. Her father, in the tradition of flighty Kites, unexpectedly eloped with Miss Venetia Veneziana, the pretty young language teacher, leaving his daughter alone in the world.

Once the furore had died down, Miss Belinda Kite took stock of her situation. It seemed to her that she was no less attractive than her contemporaries, and she was certainly a lot brighter than most of them.

All she lacked was money, and a way to insinuate herself into society. So, she bided her time, reluctantly teaching the younger girls French, helping out with sundry household chores, and putting up with the withering scorn that young ladies with privileged lives, nice clothes and pocket money tend to pour upon those less fortunate. Meanwhile she secretly waited an opportunity to escape.

The opportunity came one Christmas Eve. While the school and teachers were celebrating the feast with a party, Belinda crept into the headmistress's office and took some headed notepaper and envelopes. Then she slipped into the dormitories and helped herself to sundry articles of jewellery and a couple of pretty silk dresses that she'd had her eye on for some time.

After assembling her purloined loot, she packed her trunk, bade an unfond farewell to North Street and did a moonlight flit up to London on the night coach. She found lodgings, and the next morning left her references at a number of reputable employment agencies. No more teaching and skivvying. It was time to stand on someone else's feet.

And here she is now in the Bulstrodes' drawing room, fiddling with a piece of embroidery – because a young woman must look busy at all times. Dinner has been consumed in varying amounts, and now the three diners are occupying themselves usefully until it is time for bed. Outside, the rain tap-taps against the glass.

Grizelda is engaged in a sensation novel, an occupation which entails stooping forward in her chair and squinting at the pages in a rather unattractive fashion. Her brother leafs through the newspaper, pausing occasionally to read some titbit aloud. Every time he does this, Belinda instantly drops the embroidery onto her lap and fixes her large green eyes upon him with rapt attention.

"Now then, ladies," Bulstrode says. "Listen to this: *An opportunity exists for a shrewd man of business to invest in a Brand-New Enterprise that cannot fail. The Dominion Diamond Mine Company, newly formed by an Expert in the South African Mining Business, will be opening its doors to investors at the Golden Cross Hotel, Charing Cross, this Friday at 10 am. Potential shareholders will be able to view plans and maps, and read endorsements by several notable persons. Ladies welcome. Refreshments.*"

He lowers the newspaper. "What do you think of that? Should you like to invest in diamonds, Miss Keet? Should you like to be rich?"

A church clock strikes the hour, hazy with distance and rain.

"I should like it very much."

All the churches of the city, talking of money, Belinda Kite thinks. She recalls the children's rhyme:

When will you pay me? say the bells of Old Bailey.
When I grow rich, say the bells of Shoreditch.
When will that be? say the bells of Stepney.

Bulstrode throws back his head and laughs.
"So should I, Miss Keet. And that is why I shall

present myself at this Golden Cross Hotel on Friday morning. And I should like it very much if Sissy and you were to accompany me."

Grizelda Bulstrode's head jerks up from her book. Her eyes widen in horror. Her mouth opens to protest.

"Now, Sissy, you can't stay in this house for ever, you know. It is time to start getting over the Unfortunate Incident. That is why we are here, remember? I'll be with you, and Miss Keet will be with you – and it'll be a chance for you to wear that new dress I've heard so much about."

He returns to his newspaper. Grizelda Bulstrode gives her companion a panic-filled glance, but is met with an indifferent stare. Belinda Kite is already mentally running through the contents of her meagre wardrobe to determine whether she possesses anything suitably becoming for her first foray into London society.

Later, alone in her room, Belinda undresses in the dark. A gas lamp throws a flickering light in from the street. She catches a glimpse of herself in the mirror. The voluptuous curve of her hips, the swell of her round high alabaster-white breasts, the shadow of her hair.

She is Belinda Kite, young and vital. The wonderful world, alive with strange chances and unexpected opportunities of every kind, is within her grasp.

You have to trust these people, she thinks. Because you need money. You need it, even though you hate it. And with money, trust is everything.

***

Trust is also the basis of the small group known as The Gathering of The Select & Apocalyptic Brethren, which meets every Thursday after supper above a music publisher's shop in Charles Street, Soho.

The group is led by the Senior Prophet About, author of the pamphlet *On the Philosophy of a Divine Revelation by Means of Inspired Writings, also Containing An Humble Attempt to Account for the Apparent Discrepancies and Contradictions in the Literal Sense of the Word of God.*

Conciseness is not one of Mr About's virtues.

It is a Thursday evening, and Senior Prophet About mounts the raised platform and grips the sides of the lectern. His dark eyes under their swooping grizzled brows survey his audience, which consists of ten middle-aged or elderly men, two women, one small boy and a Jack Russell terrier. They instantly cease their chatter (or scratching their ear with a hind leg), and sit more upright, an expectant expression upon their faces.

About's expression becomes focused, inward looking. He pauses, brushes back a straying lock of grey hair from his forehead, strokes the side of his bushy beard. The group await. They do not have to await long.

"Brothers and Sisters," he intones sonorously, "Last Night I walked the Streets of this City of Shame and Desolation and I have seen the Wickednesses and the Aberrations that Flourish in every dark Corner."

There is a rapt indrawing of breath.

"There Is Fornication in Every Street," About announces. "Harlotry and Vice go Hand in Hand down Each Thoroughfare. Yeah – even in those Places sanctified to the Lord and to His Mighty Work, have I seen Evil being done!"

There is a gasp from the women in the audience, who get out their pocket handkerchiefs and fan themselves.

"Yes, dear Sisters in Christ, you may well faint; you

may well be appalled, but I tell you it is so. And what is our so-called Police force doing to stop all this Vile Filth from being flaunted openly under the very noses of our innocent children?"

He pauses for dramatic effect.

"Nothing! That is what they are doing. Absolutely. Nothing!"

"How truly shocking!"

"Indeed, Sister. That is exactly what I thought. And thus I asked myself: what does the Lord require of me – of us? I sought Him on my knees in the watches of the night. And I believe He has spoken and He has said: *Go forth, My brothers and My sisters – for all who do My work shall be called My brothers and My sisters – go forth into the highways and byways of this Iniquitous Place, this Habitation of Harlots, this City of Sin, and spread the Word that unless you repent of your Wicked Ways, I, the Lord will visit such Tribulation and Suffering upon you that your bones will crack and your flesh will shrivel and waste away.*"

He pauses, glances around the room. Every eye is fixed upon him, every mouth is slightly ajar (except for the dog, who has found a flea).

Mr About's gaze falls upon the small boy. He fixes him with an intense stare. The small boy stares back. They exchange a glance of understanding.

"What sayeth the Infant Prophet? Speak …"

The small boy, who has long blond curls and is clothed entirely in white with a white sash tied round his waist, closes his eyes, rocks a little in his seat, then intones in a piping childish treble:

"I see Fire descending out of Heaven. I see Angels in Bright Chariots riding on the Clouds. I see all the Wicked People tumbling into a Burning Pit of Fire."

A collective sigh runs around the room.

"Lovely, innit," one of the women whispers to her

companion.

"Could listen to him all day, I could," the companion replies, rolling her eyes ecstatically.

Senior Prophet About raises a hand. The small boy lapses into silence.

"The Infant Prophet has spoken. Brothers and Sisters, let us hearken to his words. The Lord has sent us a warning of what is to be. Shall we close our ears? We shall Not! Then let us seek Him in prayer and meditation and learn what is His Mighty Purpose in this Matter."

About shuts his eyes, the congregation close their eyes, and the dog gives a loud yawn. This is the signal for us to seize the moment, and tiptoe silently from the hushed upper room, for the Senior Prophet's communication with the Deity can last for an hour or more, and we do not have all night.

Instead, let us go down the musty staircase, quietly open the creaky wooden side door at the bottom, and enter the intoxicatingly seductive night-time world of the city.

***

London at night. Fantastic and magical, a dazzling transmogrification through myriad brilliant points of gaslight that illuminate the main thoroughfares of the city like lines of fire.

The shops present a glittering gallery of visual desire, as images and goods pass by the strolling *flâneurs*. Here are point lace and kid boots, Talma and parasol, feather fans and stationery, and seductive linens.

The Holborn branch of Moses & Son, Tailors, lights up the night sky with many thousands of gas-flames, forming branches, foliage and arabesques of light, and sending forth so dazzling a blaze that that it is visible at a distance of half a mile.

Stroll down the Strand towards Charing Cross with its lighted lamps, its statue of King Charles the First, and the gleaming windows of Northumberland House. Cabs and buses roll by you in quick succession. Lamps run down each side of the way. A chemist's shop throws crimson, violet and green lines of colour across the street.

The lights are especially bright outside the entrance to the Golden Cross Hotel, where a cab has just pulled up to collect a passenger. A tall man emerges from the doorway. It is Mark Hawksley, elegant in full evening dress. He is on his way to one of the many clubs. He stubs out a cigar and gets into the cab.

As it rattles away, he runs a hand through his hair and thinks about what will happen tomorrow. The roads to riches and to ruin both begin with a single step. He does not intend to find himself stepping onto the wrong road.

***

Day dawns, a fine autumn morning, the kind to make a man happy to be alive. And probably the man would have been happier to be alive. He is in fact dead. And to Dr Erasmus Beard, eminent private physician, who has been urgently summoned, his death looks remarkably similar to a case he attended a short while ago.

Dr Beard has arrived at the Queen's Square home of rich City banker Mr Osborne to find it in mild uproar. A manservant has been taken ill the previous evening. His sufferings have continued unabated throughout the night, ending only in the early hours, when he fell into a coma and died.

As Osborne describes the symptoms of the poor unfortunate man (a burning sensation in the throat and stomach, followed by violent purging and vomiting), Beard becomes more and more convinced that once again, arsenic has been at work.

His suspicions are confirmed when he learns that the Osbornes were in receipt of a small box of cakes which arrived via the parcel post yesterday at six-thirty.

"As we had already eaten our evening meal, I ordered the parcel to be taken to the kitchen," Osborne tells the good doctor. "This is the tragic result. Cook says she left the box of cakes in the larder. James drove me out later to meet a couple of friends. When I came back, the rest of the kitchen staff had retired for the night. He must've gone to the larder and helped himself. Cook says there was only one cake left this morning."

Dr Beard makes a mental note of this.

"I'm afraid to say that this occurrence is not the first that I have had to deal with recently. Another family has experienced an identical event with an equally fatal outcome."

"Another family? Who? Where?"

Dr Beard demurs.

"I am not sure that I should divulge the name of a patient. Confidentiality, and all that."

Osborne's face darkens.

"To hell with it! You will tell me, Doctor. And at once."

Dr Beard weighs up the consequences of sharing private patient information. The Osbornes are valued clients. Regina Osborne and her daughters are always going down with some minor ailment that demands his services. They pay on time and they do not quibble the bill. He would be sorry to lose them.

Also, Osborne is well-known for his vicious temper.

Beard has heard him raging at his staff, and at his son George, on many occasions. He is an influential man in the city, and his good opinion, once gone, could lose Beard other rich patients. Whereas he is rarely called to the Undercroft home. And they still haven't settled their bill from his previous visit.

"A family by the name of Undercroft also received a box of cakes," he says. "And one of their servants died after eating one. It is my opinion, based upon what you have told me, and my preliminary inspection, that your manservant also died as a result of poisoning. This must be confirmed by a post-mortem examination, of course, but I think in the light of the similarities of the two deaths, that you should alert the Detective Police at once. They will want to examine the body, and then arrange for it to be taken to the police mortuary. And they will want to test the remaining cake as well."

Osborne stares at him in disbelief.

"The *Undercrofts?* Fred and Georgiana? Live in Hampstead? But we know them well. Are you saying that somebody is trying to poison them too?"

Dr Beard says nothing.

"My God," Osborne exclaims, staggering back. "What is the world coming to?"

Again, the good doctor remains silent, such matters being beyond his remit.

Dr Beard steps out of the Osbornes' lavishly-decorated hallway and into the street. He has never, in his long medical career, encountered an incident of what looks like deliberate poisoning. Now, he has attended two in a very short space of time. He adjusts his spectacles and hurries away, hoping there will be no more cases in the near future.

***

Pale autumn sunshine filters through the grimy windows of Scotland Yard, where Detective Inspector Stride sits at his desk. It is starting out as a perfect day. He knows it will soon be an imperfect one, but just for these few minutes, it is possible to believe that it won't.

A knock at the door heralds the entrance of Jack Cully and a cup of black coffee.

"The autopsy report on the Undercrofts' servant has just been sent over," Stride says.

Cully places the coffee on Stride's desk.

"Have you read it?"

Stride shakes his head. He picks up the folder, which is on top of a pile of other folders that he also hasn't read, and pages through it, skimming past a long introductory section on the various types of chemical analysis available for the detection of corrosives, irritants and other poisons. The police surgeon's love of extraneous verbiage is notorious.

He also skim-reads a long discursive section debating whether it was possible to ascertain that the cause of death could be solely attributed to one specific ingestion of a corrosive or irritant substance, followed by a detailed description of the post mortem appearance of the dead body, concluding with the various tests applied to the internal organs. Finally getting to the last page, he finds, as he expected, the surgeon's verdict.

"Arsenic poisoning," Stride says, clapping the folder shut. "Just as I suspected."

Cully, who has been standing patiently by the desk, forbears to mention that as he recalls it, this was exactly what Stride had not said.

"So what happens now?" he asks.

"Now," Stride says, rising and reaching for his hat, "we shall pay a second visit to Mr Undercroft and his good lady to relay the news. I want to question the servants again to see if anybody in the household knows where those cakes could have come from. Maybe someone baked them, but chances are, if they were fresh, they were bought locally."

"We can now say it is definitely a murder inquiry?"

Stride pauses on the threshold.

"Looks like it, Jack. And a very nasty one. What sort of a person would deliberately put arsenic into cakes? Cakes! It's almost beyond comprehension."

***

Meanwhile, a short distance away in Charing Cross, a line of carriages is parked outside the Golden Cross Hotel. For today is the launch of The Dominion Diamond Mine Company, and a lot of eager investors have read the puff in the newspapers, and are waiting to buy shares.

Standing in the crowd on the pavement are three familiar individuals: the two Bulstrodes – he is staring at the competition, she is staring at the pavement, and with them, Belinda Kite, wearing her grey dress and short coat.

At the appointed time, the doors of the hotel are flung ceremoniously open by two liveried flunkies. The crowds push and jostle their way into the richly-carpeted atrium, where a notice directs them to one of the function rooms on the ground floor.

Here, under a sparkling crystal chandelier, are set out rows of gilt chairs facing a raised dais, upon which sits a darkly handsome man in his thirties. He is flanked by two other men, both dressed in business suits.

On either side of the stage is a board with large poster, bearing the name of the company and a head-and-shoulders photograph of a woman with protruding pale eyes and slightly flabby cheeks. She is wearing a black silk gown and widow's bonnet. Her face, thanks to the postal service and certain food items, is familiar to every member of the audience.

In one corner, four hotel maids stand behind a white-clothed table laid with cups and saucers and plates of biscuits. In the other corner is a desk, with a big leather-bound ledger and a clerk with a set of quill pens, a cash box and a serious expression.

Bulstrode places his little group in the middle of the second row, right in the eye line of the central figure on the dais. Grizelda Bulstrode immediately looks down and begins fiddling with the clasp on her reticule. Belinda Kite, having surveyed her surroundings and ascertained that she is the youngest and by far the most attractive woman in the room, turns her gaze to the handsome man on the dais.

She notes with satisfaction his dark brown eyes, straight brows and chiselled saturnine features. He has black hair with just a tiny touch of grey at the temple. He sports side-whiskers, but his chin and upper lip are clean-shaven.

His complexion is good and his thin mouth has a sardonic twist to it. Byronic. He could have stepped straight out of the pages of a romantic novel.

Belinda Kite stares in rapt fascination, recalling her time at school when the novels left by her errant mother were her sole escape from drudgery, and candles were her one luxury. She read only after all were asleep, in the secrecy and privacy of the night.

Back then she burned two, even three candles at a time. In winter, she wrapped herself in a cloak against the room's chill. She read about love, about passion, about the delicious shivery things men and women got up to with each other in bed in the dark. She would lick a finger, turn the page …

Now one of the men rises and the room stills in

eager anticipation. Faces turn towards him. He clears his throat.

"Good morning, gentlemen ... and not forgetting the ladies, of course. Welcome to this first public meeting of the Dominion Diamond Mine Company. I am William Ginster, one of the backers of this fabulous enterprise.

"On behalf of myself, and Oswald Pyle, my fellow backer, I have the very great honour to present to you the Owner and Chairman of the Dominion Diamond Mine Company, Mr Mark Hawksley."

There is a ripple of polite applause as Hawksley gets to his feet. He is taller than Belinda imagined. And unlike Bulstrode, whose ample stomach bulges over the waistband of his trousers, he is lean and spare; there is not an ounce of fat on him.

His broad shoulders fill the well-cut dark wool suit. He has long legs. A gold chain straddles the waistcoat. He glances round the assembled company, his gaze coming to rest momentarily upon Belinda. For a second, their eyes meet. Then he advances to the edge of the dais and addresses the crowd.

"Gentlemen, I stand before you not only to offer you the opportunity of a lifetime – the chance to be part of a great adventure – but I also stand before you as a devoted son, mourning the death of one of the finest fathers a man could have."

He pauses. A murmur of sympathy is heard from the audience.

"It was my father, Herbert Hawksley, a chief government mining engineer, who discovered the Dominion Diamond Mine deep in the South African bush. He was enacting business in that far-off land for our beloved country when he stumbled upon it by chance. The story he told me was that he had made camp with his servants by a river, and in the morning, going to refresh himself, he saw something sparkling in the water. This, gentlemen and ladies, is what he found …"

The man digs into his trouser pocket and produces a black velvet pouch. From it he draws a large sparkling diamond. It winks and glitters seductively in the artificial light of the room. He holds it up, to gasps from the audience.

"I have had this stone cut and polished by a top diamond merchant in Amsterdam, and he tells me it is priceless. My father had no time to do more than make a map of the area, locating the source of the diamond to a cave in a rock, where he believed the river originated. Sadly, he died shortly afterwards of a fever, leaving his papers to be returned to his grieving family."

Another pause. Another murmur of sympathy.

"This map is now in my possession – and can be seen on one of the tables. It was my dear father's dying wish that the mine should be opened and the diamonds that he was sure lay deep beneath the earth should be dug out, to be cut and polished so that they might one day adorn the necks of many beautiful women, like the lovely ladies I see sitting in front of me."

He pauses. Once again, his dark eyes come to rest upon Belinda Kite – this time with a look of predatory interest. He continues, "Gentlemen, by purchasing shares in the Dominion Diamond Mine Company today, you are not only making a shrewd investment that cannot but return an enormous dividend, you are also helping to fulfil the last dream of a dying man. Your generous contributions will enable me to follow my dear departed father's footsteps, to sail to South Africa, there to hire the diggers and equipment needed to open that mine and extract the diamonds, just waiting to be plucked from the earth."

He gestures towards the promotional posters.

"When I told the tale I have just told you to the lady whose picture you see before you, and whom I'm sure I don't have to name, she had no hesitation in allowing her portrait to be associated with our enterprise. I think that tells you everything you need to know. If the Dominion Diamond Mine Company is good enough for her, how can it not be good enough for each and every one of you? Thank you."

He pauses again. Puts the diamond back into his pocket. Produces a handkerchief and applies it briefly to his eyes. Then, to tumultuous applause, he sits down, which is the signal for everybody to make a rush for the desk at the back, where the clerk has opened the ledger in preparation.

Bulstrode steers his two female companions to the tea-table. Giving instructions to Belinda to see that Sissy has all she wants, he turns on his heel and joins the mêlée around the desk. Grizelda Bulstrode gives his retreating back a desperate look, then stands with her arms stiffly at her side.

Belinda requests two cups of coffee, hands one to Grizelda, and sips daintily from her own.

"That was very interesting, wasn't it?" she remarks. "Especially seeing a real diamond. I have never set eyes on one before. Wasn't it beautiful?"

Grizelda Bulstrode bares her teeth in a lacklustre smile. Belinda thinks that she looks for all the world like a horse about to bolt. Suddenly she is aware that somebody is standing behind her.

She feels warm breath on the back of her neck, the sensation of heat. Belinda looks round. It is Mark Hawksley, the owner of the beautiful diamond. He is so close that she can smell the intoxicating scent of his cologne. Her heart beats fast. Dry-throated, she swallows, averts her eyes from his face.

He bows low.

"Ladies, I hope you are being attended to?"

Grizelda Bulstrode gives a whinnying little laugh. Her face flushes unbecomingly. She gives him a coy look from under her colourless eyelashes.

"You are, of course, here with your husbands?"

The question is addressed to Grizelda. His eyes, however, watch Belinda closely.

"Oh, no," Grizelda replies. "I am here with my brother. This is my companion."

He nods, and opens his mouth to reply just as Bulstrode elbows his way through the crowd and joins them. He is clutching a piece of official-looking paper and is beaming all over his face.

"Ah, there you are, Sissy and Miss Keet. Mr Hawksley – pleased to make your acquaintance, sir. I have never heard so good a speech as you gave back then. You should come up to Leeds and speak to us manufacturers. We are in want of good speakers like you."

He flourishes the piece of paper.

"As you see, I have just purchased shares in your company, sir. A lot of shares. I believe in your company. YOU made me believe in your company. Sissy, Miss Keet, you see before you a man after my own heart."

Bulstrode leans forward, drops his voice.

"So you have actually met Her Majesty? I've seen her picture on the stamps, but that's not the same, is it? My, I'd pay good money to see her in the flesh, as it were. Not that I ever will … She's taken it bad, hasn't she – her husband dying suddenly like that. We noticed all the people in mourning as soon as we arrived in London, didn't we, Sissy?"

He gets out his card-case.

"We are currently residing at Number 11 Cartwright Gardens, Bloomsbury. Only renting it, until we go back home, but if you are not too busy, I should be honoured to see you at my table one evening. I'd like to hear all about when you met the Queen."

"I should be delighted to accept your kind invitation," Hawksley replies, his eyes still on Belinda.

"We dine at six – no ceremony, just simple fare, as befits simple people. Come and share a bit of northern hospitality." Bulstrode leans forward. "Though I must point out that Miss Keet, my sister's companion, is the daughter of a French Mar-kee. A Mar-kee, eh! Now then – what do you think of that!"

"Really? Is she now? *Eh bien, mademoiselle, je suis très honoré de faire votre connaissance.*" Hawksley smiles, his dark eyes dancing.

His accent is not good, but both Bulstrodes stare at him in open-mouthed admiration. Hawksley lifts Belinda's small gloved hand to his lips. His eyes offer a challenge: *Are you what they say you are?*

Belinda Kite gently withdraws her hand. Then she thanks him, in perfect French, for his salutation. Expresses her gratitude to Bulstrode and his sister for giving her a job, in perfect French, and finally wishes him the best of luck with his forthcoming enterprise. In perfect French.

Bulstrode claps his hands.

"Well done, Miss Keet. Jolly bong, as they say in Paree, I've no doubt."

Belinda's red lips curve in a secret smile of triumph. Her emerald eyes saucily return Hawksley's challenge. For a second they stand facing each other, locked in mutual admiration. Then William Ginster touches his elbow.

"Excuse me, Mark – your presence is required elsewhere."

Mark Hawksley raises his hand to the brim of his hat, bows again and walks away.

Bulstrode stares after him.

"Now then, Sissy – there's a fine figure of a man for you! Rich too. And coming to dine some time soon. Maybe you should purchase another pretty dress in honour of the occasion, eh? What do you think, Miss Keet?"

Belinda Kite murmurs something vaguely appropriate. Privately, she thinks it will take a lot more than a new dress to make Grizelda attractive in any man's eye.

"Now, I fancy a spot of luncheon," Bulstrode says as they step over the hotel threshold. "Doing business always gives me a keen appetite and I am sharp set after this morning. Let's see if we can find somewhere nice to eat."

He takes his sister by the arm, and they walk towards Regent Street. Belinda follows a few paces behind, dawdling as she passes tempting shop windows full of lovely things she cannot afford.

One day, she promises herself, she will have her own carriage and a pair of ponies. She will wear beautiful diamonds like the one she has just seen, and own a wardrobe stuffed with beautiful dresses. She will enjoy every luxury known to womankind. One day.

***

Meanwhile Alfred Monday, poet and dilettante, emerges into the street as the noonday bells are chiming across the city. He rents a small room on the first floor of a baker's. It is a room with a view but few amenities. The view, especially in wet weather, consists of a dirty pavement, which has a dry patch in the middle, thanks to the underground bake-house.

Per contra, the stifling smell of new bread comes steaming up the stairs from five o'clock in the morning, when the baker and his journeyman arrive to light the ovens ready for the first delivery of hot breakfast rolls, and the floury black beetles march up with it in such squadrons that Alfred Monday has contemplated keeping a hedgehog to deal with them.

That he does not shift lodgings is in part due to the low rent he is charged, and the notion that a poet *should* suffer for his art. And starve. Though Alfred Monday is slightly ambivalent on the latter score, preferring to write on a full belly.

With this end in view, he sallies forth to see whether he can find a nice little meal and some gullible person to buy it for him. Making his way up Regent Street, his eye is taken by a trio of individuals promenading in the opposite direction.

A stout man with a pale unattractive woman on his arm, and, walking just a step behind, but clearly one of the party – oh, what a vision! A beautiful young lady with a heart-shaped face and russet curls peeping out from under a pert blue bonnet.

As she walks along, her crinoline sways in a way that sets his poetic heart a-beat. Monday looks, he sighs, he feels the stanzas rise. He retraces his steps, keeping the trio in sight.

They enter Caldwell's Coffee House. He enters also. They choose a table, and he slides into a seat close enough to overhear their conversation. From this he gathers that the gentleman has been buying shares in some company, and that the beautiful young lady is not his wife.

Inspired, Monday extracts a penny notebook from his soiled velvet frock-coat, licks the end of his pencil and begins to write. The gentleman orders coffee and buns for the ladies, and a plate of cold meat and bread and butter for himself, after which he picks up a newspaper and buries himself behind it.

Monday writes a few more lines. Then catching the eye of the beautiful young lady, he bows low. Upon her nod of acknowledgement, he rises and goes over to their table, addressing them in the affected drawl that has caused several of his close friends to snigger that *Monday can't tell his Rs from his elbow.*

"Fair ladies," he says, "You see before you Alfwed Monday, a humble poet. Bowled over by your beauty, and captivated by your charms, he has huwwidly scwibbled down the following lines."

He clears his throat, adjusts his frayed cuffs and declaims:

"Shall I compare you both to a Summer's day?
You are both more lovely and more temperate.
Wuff winds do shake the darling buds of May
And Summer's lease has all too short a state."

He pauses. Looks up from the notebook. Two pairs of eyes are staring at him intently. The plain woman sighs. The pretty one smirks. The fat man lowers his newspaper.

"Very pretty, Mr ...?"

"Monday, sir. Alfwed Monday. A mere London poet. A lowly witer of verse. I hear by your accent that you are not fwom these parts."

"Indeed, I am not. I am Josiah Bulstrode, owner of Bulstrode's Boots and Shoes Factory in Leeds. Would you care to join us, Mr Poet? It's not often Sissy and I have the privilege of meeting a poet. Nor of having a poem written for us. No, indeed it is not."

Alfred Monday needs no second invitation. He pulls out a chair and seats himself between Grizelda and Belinda, upon whom he bestows his nicest smile.

A second plate of meat and a side plate of bread and butter is ordered. When it arrives, Monday falls to with most unpoetic zeal. It has been some time since he has eaten.

While he eats, Bulstrode regales him with several anecdotes about lasts and leathers, a subject on which, as a factory owner, he is extremely conversant. Grizelda picks the currants out of her bun and peeps at the poet from under her pale eyelids.

Belinda Kite, however, having taken careful note of the state of his linen and the condition of his coat and shoes, pays him not a whit of attention, merely raising her eyes from her plate every now and then to glance round the room thoughtfully.

When every scrap of food has been consumed, Monday reaches for his non-existent wallet, but the gesture is brushed aside.

"My treat, Mr Monday," Bulstrode says, signalling to the waiter.

Bulstrode settles the bill. Monday bows, smiles his thanks, tears off the piece of paper with the poem, and presents it with a flourish to Grizelda, who accepts it with a simpering little smile.

He eyes Belinda hopefully, but she is busy tying the strings of her bonnet.

As they make their way out of the coffee shop and back into the noisy thronged street, Belinda Kite has already forgotten the poet and the encounter. She remembers only the hungry expression on Hawksley's face. The way his dark eyes appraised her. The way it made her feel inside.

Something is beginning, she thinks, though what it might be she does not yet know. Maybe it is simple desire, not like love, nothing so complicated. Or perhaps it is like a first love. Like an obsession.

***

We last met Police Constable 'Taffy' Evans patrolling his beat in Regent Street. Since then, honesty and integrity have proved their own reward. Now he is a sergeant in the Metropolitan Police. He wears the distinctive dark blue coat and black stovepipe hat. He has a new leather belt with a snake-type clasp.

Some things remain, though. He is still engaged to the lovely (if volatile) Megan, and now has high hopes that his recent promotion, bringing with it clouds of glory and an increase in salary, will finally enable him to marry her.

She certainly hopes so, and has dropped epistolary hints to that end several times. And also hints of what might happen if he fails to honour his promise.

Sergeant Evans is proceeding, as they say in police parlance, to Drury Lane, whence he has been summoned by one of his beat constables. An 'incident' has occurred. No surprise to anyone in authority: the area is notorious for its filthy alleys, lodging houses and pubs where vice and criminality breed and flourish.

Prostitutes and beggars throng the streets, and Sergeant Evans has taken the precaution of being accompanied by a couple of constables, because even though he has patrolled this area in the past and knows its little ways very well, you can never be too careful.

He turns into Shelton Street, where a small crowd of assorted citizenry awaits his arrival.

"Oi, P'liceman," a woman in the crowd shouts out as he approaches.

The crowd parts, giving Sergeant Evans his first view of a derelict brick-banded building, one of the many common lodging houses that line the filthy street. Someone has painted, in large red letters, somewhat trickly in places, the stark words *Den of Theeves* on the front door.

"Wrote it on number 24. And number 30," one of the

men says, nodding at the door. "Shockin', innit?"

Accurate, though, Sergeant Evans thinks to himself, recalling who generally rents rooms in this street.

"Oh, indeed it is shocking," he agrees setting his facial expression to suitably shocked.

"An' that ain't all," the woman says, stepping forward, her massive uncorseted bust quivering with indignation. "You wanter see what they painted on Mrs Carmine's door. None too happy, she woz, when she saw it."

"What did they paint?"

The woman leans forward, emitting a strong smell of onions, armpits and unwashed clothes.

"Filthy Fornicators."

A small child, clinging to her skirts but barely visible, pipes up,

"Wossa forn'cater, Aunty Flo?"

"It's a kind of machine," Sergeant Evans says smoothly, giving the woman a quick look.

The child nods.

"Aw. I nivver seen no machine up there, only them ladies wot wears dresses showing their bubbies."

Sergeant Evans takes out his notebook.

"Have any more properties had their doors painted?"

"There's summat on the chapel door in Little Wild Street."

"Show me."

The man leads the way. The crowd tags along hopefully, in the way of any crowd anywhere. On the wooden doors are the red-painted words:

God sees You. Repent From Your Wikked Ways.

Now Sergeant Evans is really shocked. He was brought up Chapel, and vestiges of his Bible-based Welsh childhood have never left him, despite the attempts of the heaving teeming city to drive it out.

He sucks in a long breath.

"This is an abomination upon God's house."

"You're right there, officer," the man agrees. "And whoever done it can't spell properly either."

His words strike a chord. Sergeant Evans eyes the red obscenity and begins to think professionally. *Must be someone local, else how would they know which doors to write on? Also, someone small in height – the letters are only five foot or so off the ground. Must have been done in the very early hours.*

"Where might one obtain a pot of paint and some brushes around here?" he asks.

The crowd goes into a huddle. Various names and locations are suggested for consideration. Finally, a small man steps forward. He has a small unhappy face, prominent at the forehead, receding towards the chin. His mouth is pursed in an expression of permanent disappointment.

The small man gives it as his opinion that the nearest hardware shop to buy paint is in New Oxford Street, though whether *this exact* paint was purchased there, he really couldn't say.

The crowd agrees, and seeing that Sergeant Evans has now closed his notebook, indicative that nothing more exciting is going to happen, begins to melt away into the courts and alleys that lead off Sheldon Street.

Sergeant Evans casts a final look at the chapel door, shakes his head in nonplussed incomprehension, and sets off for New Oxford Street, where he will find the paint shop, but not the red paint – red being a colour not popular with the upmarket clientele that frequents the establishment.

He will eventually return to Scotland Yard, where he'll discover that more important events have taken over in his absence, meaning that his conscientiously-written report will lie on Stride's desk, unread, for many days.

***

The lights have been dimmed in the Golden Cross function room. The crowds have dispersed, the biscuits and coffee have all gone. The clerk has been sent on his way. There only remains Mark Hawksley, his two companions, and a cash box stuffed with cheques and notes.

"A very good day's business," Ginster remarks.

Hawksley agrees. He opens the cash box and dashes them each a fistful of notes.

"Expenses, gentlemen. Enjoy it. There will be plenty more where that came from. And I have another idea – it came to me earlier when I was speaking to one of our good investors."

His companions regard him curiously, but Hawksley waves them away.

"Let us agree to meet at the Albion this evening," he says. "By then I will have finalised my plans and will be able to tell you more."

They walk out of the hotel. Ginster and Pyle set off in different directions. Hawksley watches them depart with a smile of satisfaction. Then he gets out the sparkling diamond and throws it up in the air. He is careful to catch it as it falls, for he knows that if it reaches the ground, it will splinter into tiny fragments.

He needs this 'diamond' for other days. As he strides away, he turns over Bulstrode's business card in his pocket, and remembers a pair of green eyes, a shapely figure and an innocent yet insouciant air. Other days, and other pleasures. It is all turning out even better than he planned.

***

Sergeant Evans' return to Scotland Yard coincides with the delivery of the dead footman to the police morgue. While Stride and Cully have been spending a fruitless morning (though it has not been without cake) visiting local confectioners in the Hampstead and surrounding areas, the dead man's body has been viewed by another pair of detectives, who have questioned the Osborne family and their servants.

Now the body, plus the remaining cake still in its delivery box, are with the police surgeon. Stride and Cully hurry across the yard to the cold, clinical, white-tiled autopsy room that smells of chemicals and mortality and unhappiness.

The police surgeon, like all pathologists, is no respecter of men. To him, heroes and whores, leaders and laggards are all mere meat on a slab. Alive, they might have been somebody. Dead, their secrets pour out as blackened livers, inflamed hearts. Their brains exposed in the bowl of their skull.

He greets Stride and Cully with his usual air of lugubrious satisfaction.

"Good morning, gentlemen. Did you know that according to recent studies, each human brain differs according to sex, age, consumption of alcohol and disease?"

"Very interesting," Stride says flatly.

"Oh indeed, Detective Inspector. Very. It would be even more interesting, would it not, to see if *language* made any difference. Say, the brain of a French female compared with that of her English counterpart. What would we discover, I wonder?"

"That they were both dead?" Stride suggests.

The surgeon rolls his eyes and tutts.

"You have no imagination, Detective Inspector."

"I have a job to do. That's why I'm here."

"Indeed you are. And what I have is one case of death by poisoning, immediately followed by another. Or rather, a strong presumption of it. Lucky I didn't put my equipment away, isn't it?"

He gestures towards a large wide-mouthed glass jar and a series of smaller ones lined up on the wooden bench.

Stride looks at the jars. They are glass-stoppered, clean, and very empty. He attempts not to think what they might have contained. What they are about to contain. He tries not to let his thoughts show on his face, but fails.

"Ah, Inspector, I see you are displaying your usual distaste for the fascinating autopsy processes. I guess you are not intending to stay and watch the evisceration of this poor unfortunate, then?"

"I'll leave it to you, shall I?" Stride grunts. "After all, you're the expert."

The police surgeon smiles complacently.

"Indeed so. I leave speculation to the professionals like yourself. Though in this case, it is more a question of verification rather than deduction, as we have an actual uneaten example of the last food this man ingested."

He smiles and starts rocking gently on his feet – the sign that a lecture is about to be delivered. Stride braces himself.

"Unlike strychnine or cyanide, that both work to a strict timetable, arsenic is a mysterious and shilly-shallying poison, Detective Inspector. It has to be absorbed into the bloodstream before it can have its fatal effect."

"Have you found evidence of it in the cake?" Stride asks, trying to keep the impatience out of his voice.

"I have indeed tried a few chemicals upon the

sweetmeat, and I can say with complete confidence that should you have attempted to partake of even a mouthful, your future would very quickly be a thing of the past. And what a tragic loss to policing that would be, eh?"

Stride wills himself not to display his irritation. The long-winded and idiosyncratic nature of the police surgeon has been a source of annoyance ever since he joined the Detective Division. But the man's skill is second to none. He reminds himself of this now.

"So you found evidence of poison?"

"Oh, indeed. The cake was laced with arsenic. It could have been by chance, for it might have occurred before the baking process. Or maybe not. That is for you to discover. But either way, there is clear evidence of admixture."

"Have you got the box that the cakes came in?" Cully asks.

"Indeed I have retained the item, as I expected that you would wish to examine it. It is on the bottom shelf, under the table."

"We will show this box to Mr and Mrs Undercroft," Stride says. "Perhaps one of them might recognise the similarity."

The police surgeon nods.

"Do so. I shall now attempt an anatomical exploration of the body itself. Did you know, Detective Inspector, that is it not the ingestion of the poison itself that causes the ultimate demise of its hapless victim, but the strain upon the heart which generates a complete system collapse. To the victim, of course, the point is somewhat academic."

The surgeon's hand hovers over the set of gruesome dissecting knives laid out in their blue-lined rosewood case.

Stride winces, feeling his gorge rising.

"Come on Jack," he says spinning on his heel. "Nothing to be gained standing around here. We have two murders on our hands now. Let's go to my office and see what avenues we need to go down to find the poisoner."

***

The Albion Tavern has known days when stagecoaches clattered into the cobbled yard and passengers descended to stretch their legs and partake of refreshment before continuing their journey.

The coming of the railway, however, has put paid to those glory times, and now The Albion Tavern is a public house serving the bustling area around King's Cross Station. For this purpose, the bar has been refurbished with new gas lighting. The floor has been freshly sanded and the half-dozen compartments provided with new oilcloth-covered tables and wooden benches. But the drinkers are transient, the place anonymous. It is the sort of bar where nobody knows your name.

The black-framed prints of naval engagements and men o' war that ornamented the dark painted walls have been replaced by bright mirrors, so that it is impossible not to meet yourself at every turn of the head, each sighting being a source of doubt or vanity.

Look more closely. In a back booth, Hawksley and his two companions Ginster and Pyle are regaling themselves with boiled beef, potatoes, and tumblers of brandy and water. Hawksley has spread a map upon the table, and they are all studying it intently. A pretty young barmaid in a slightly stained apron stands within summoning distance, awaiting their pleasure. Earlier she and Hawksley reached an agreement for when the meeting ends, where the pleasure will hopefully be mutual.

"It is decided," Hawksley says. "You two will travel to the West Country, to Bath, Bristol and Exeter. You will seek out a suitable venue in each town – after which you will place an advertisement in the local papers for the dates we have agreed and using the names I have told you. Write to me when all preparations are complete, and I shall be with you on the earliest train."

"And what will you do in the meantime?" Ginster asks.

Hawksley smiles. "I shall remain here in London, the home of our beloved monarch, who rarely ventures out of her castle gates, but who may be making an appearance at a couple of very select gatherings."

The two men stare at him.

"For a very large amount of money, of course," he continues smoothly. "You cannot expect a Queen to attend a champagne supper for under a thousand pounds a head."

Pyle whistles under his breath.

"I take my hat off to you, Mark," he grins. "I thought you just wanted her for the photographs, nothing more. If anybody deserves to be rich, it is you, and that's for sure. How do you come up with these schemes?"

"I just listen to what the public want. And then I give it to them. They want to see the Queen – so they shall see a Queen. It will not be the one who currently hides herself away in Windsor Castle weeping and wailing for her dear departed Prince Consort, but they have never seen *that* Queen, so they won't know the difference."

***

London at night. The restlessness of a great city,

tumbling and tossing before it can get to sleep. A late-night cab rattles by. The last veritable sparks of flickering life, worn out by the night's entertainment, trail away and the city finally sinks to rest.

Two cloaked and hooded figures are walking the streets under the pattering rain. Through the interminable tangle of streets they go, ducking into doorways to avoid a solitary policeman on his beat, while the rain drip drips from ledge and coping, splash-splashes from pipes and waterspouts.

The shops are all shuttered, the theatre lights are extinguished. The figures pass Newgate, grim and black, touching its rough stones, imagining the prisoners within its walls sleeping in their cells and dreaming of green fields and endless horizons. They pass cemeteries where the dead sleep, but do not dream. They hear the spreading vibrations of church clocks striking three.

At length, the two reach their destination, where they pause, and set to work. By the time they have completed their task and started on their way back home, the gaslights will be extinguished, light by light, like pearls spilled from a curved rope, as day arrives. The first straggling workpeople will be out and about, and the first street-corner breakfast sellers will be lighting their fires.

***

Detective Inspector Stride is known for his *sang-froid* and his ability to be master of his emotions in any situation. Very little, it is said, can surprise him. And yet here he is, seated behind his desk, stunned into total and uncomprehending silence.

The reasons for this are standing not three feet away: Clamp, chief reporter on *The Morning Post,* and

Dandy, ditto on *The Inquirer*. The two journalists appeared in the outer office first thing, managed to elude the desk constable, and have now thrust their unannounced selves into Stride's office.

Dandy leans forward and thumps an ink-stained fist on Stride's desk. A pile of paperwork shifts uneasily.

"What are the boys in blue going to do about this, then?" he snarls. "Because it's a bloody disgrace!"

Clamp agrees. He is rotund, wearing a loud tweed suit, and sweating slightly in the heat generated by the office fire.

Stride eyes them both thoughtfully, and in silence.

"I'm telling you, Stride, we aren't going to stand for it."

Stride nods his head slowly.

"Let me see if I have this correct: you say that someone painted words on the doors of *The Post* and *The Inquirer* last night and it's a police matter? Really?"

"It ain't the words, it's what the words say."

Stride raises an eyebrow.

"And what do they say, Mr Dandy? I am agog."

"*Liars and hypocrites,* that's what they painted on our doors," Clamp butts in. "Big red painted letters for all the passing world to see and gawk at."

"*Spawn of Satan & Purveyors of Filth* on ours," Dandy says.

Stride smiles thinly.

"That's certainly an interesting, and some might say valid, point of view."

Dandy glares at him.

Stride meets the glare levelly and shrugs.

"Everyone's a critic nowadays."

"Something tells me you aren't taking this seriously, Stride."

"Detective Inspector Stride, Dandy, as I'm sure you

know only too well. And yes, I am taking it very seriously. I have broken off an investigation to listen to you. And now I have heard you out, I should like to return to it, if you don't mind."

"So you're not going to do anything?"

"Has anybody died? No? Then I suggest you get a bucket of hot soapy water, some turpentine and a scrubbing brush, and scrub whatever was written *on* your doors *off* your doors. If you are still worried, you might consider employing a night-watchman. Maybe he'll catch the criminals *red-handed*."

He rises to his feet.

"Good day to you both, *gentlemen*."

There is a pause while the two reporters consider their options, one of which is clearly to remain exactly where they are until Stride changes his mind. When it becomes evident after a few leaden minutes have slunk by that he isn't going to, Dandy folds his arms, narrows his eyes and glares.

"You ain't heard the last of this, Stride," he exclaims. "By God you ain't!"

Grabbing his hat, he stalks out, closely followed by Clamp.

Stride goes straight to the window and opens it as Jack Cully enters.

"I've just passed two very angry men in the corridor. They were swearing like troopers. Was one of them who I thought it was?"

"It was. He has gone, and in a minute the scent of his foul cologne will follow him. Good riddance to them both."

"What did they want?"

"Some matter about paint on their walls. So, of course, they come straight round here, shouting the odds and expecting me to investigate it. As if I have nothing better to do than listen to their trivial gripes and grievances."

Stride gestures at his desk.

"There are reports on here that go back to last week and I haven't had time to even open them yet. We have an unsolved double murder on our hands. And I'm expected to drop everything for some minor incident of vandalism? I think not."

***

Meanwhile, Georgiana Undercroft, wife of Frederick Undercroft, lawyer, sits at her dressing table mirror staring dully at her reflection while the maid prepares her for the day ahead. As the brush moves rhythmically over Georgiana's thinning hair, she thinks about the past.

She was sixteen when she first became acquainted with Frederick Undercroft. They had met at the home of a mutual girlfriend, where eligible young men and marriageable young women frequented the many musical evenings and supper parties organised by her friend Regina's generous parents.

In those days, Georgiana was an acknowledged beauty. She had bright blue eyes, lustrous chestnut hair and a slender waist. She was kittenish and gossipy, a lively flirtatious girl who knew the effect she had on the numerous young men that sought her out on social occasions.

Frederick Undercroft was an up-and-coming young lawyer, handsome, suave and charming, tipped for the top of his chosen profession. His manners were impeccable, his clothes fashionable, and everybody who witnessed their courtship nodded and predicted them both a long and happy life together.

She gets up from the chair and opens the wardrobe door. Clothes flutter against her cheeks like the wings of giant moths. When did it start to go wrong? How did she end up here, so far from that happy loving future she expected?

Once, he vowed could not wait to spend time with her. He wrote her little *billets-doux,* bought her presents, complimented her on her face and figure. Once, their evenings were full of shared conversation, their nights of lovemaking – which she soon got used to, after the initial shock.

She selects a grey wool dress, the colour of fog, of smoke. Of ghosts.

They must, she thinks, have seemed a glamorous young couple when they appeared at balls and dinner parties. But within the four walls of the house it was soon a very different story.

How long was it before she realised that he was unfaithful? And had always been unfaithful, even back in the days of their courtship? How soon before she discovered that the sprightly young lover who whispered sweet words into her ear and sent her loving messages had a mistress, a pile of debts, and his eye on her inheritance from Papa?

How humiliating to have to acknowledge that the missed meals and unexpected absences and late nights in chambers were, in reality, times spent in other women's company and in other women's beds?

She remembers notes on pressed paper, discovered carelessly crumpled in his waistcoat pockets almost as if he *wanted* her to find them: *"Darling One ... how I long for your sweet sweet caresses"* and that Italian bitch with her *"Caro mio"* and dismissive references to *"La Sposa".*

If only she'd been able to bear him children, perhaps that would have kept him by her side. But after several miscarriages and one pathetic little scrap who only lived a few hours, that door closed as firmly as the one he has had installed between their two dressing rooms. The door he keeps locked from his side.

She lets the maid dress her, arrange her hair into two bunches, pin her back hair into a bun. The lines from her nose to her chin seem more pronounced than ever, her skin has a scraped rawness. Light is a white sheet at her window, a dull white sheet that is folded away every evening and hung out again next dawn.

The final indignity, only a few months ago, was the delivery of a diamond and turquoise bracelet. A mistake of the jeweller's. When she opened the parcel, saw the exquisite piece, read the letter that accompanied it, she felt the final string of her heart give way. Since that day she has been just an empty shell of herself, hollowed out by pain and humiliation.

As she reaches the wide staircase the doorbell sounds. She waits for the parlour maid to answer it. She hears a male voice, the maid's reply. Then the girl is in the hallway looking up.

"Detective Inspector Stride and Detective Sergeant Cully to see you, ma'am."

Georgiana feels a comet's tail of fear run down her spine, but years of marriage to Frederick have schooled her in the art of hiding her emotions. She draws herself upright and slowly descends to the ground floor.

"Yes, can I help you Inspector?"

Stride greets her politely. She scans his face for any indication that he brings news that she does not wish to receive. There is no indication. She leads the way to the drawing room.

"I regret to inform you," he tells her, "that a similar tragic incident to your own, also involving a box of poisoned cakes, has happened just recently. We have come into possession of the box. I was wondering, if it isn't too much trouble, whether you could take a look at it and say if you recognise the handwriting on the label."

Stride hands her the box, watching her attentively.

"The name and address seem to be written in capital letters."

"Even so – does the handwriting look familiar at all?"

"I am sorry, Detective Inspector, I do not recognise it, I'm afraid. In any case, I only saw the box very briefly before handing it to the maid."

"Maybe your husband ..."

"Frederick is at work. I deal with all the private correspondence that arrives at the house."

"I see."

There is a pause. Stride waits politely for her to continue.

Georgiana Undercroft's face shuts down even further.

"This box of cakes was delivered with no accompanying note," Stride continues. "Your own box of cakes was also delivered with no accompanying note, is that correct? Did you not think it odd at the time?"

Her thin shoulders lift imperceptibly

"I did not think anything of it at all, Inspector. My husband's business has led to gifts being delivered here in the past. Grateful clients like to show their appreciation."

"Would not they like the recipient to know how much they appreciated them by including some sort of signed communication?"

She does not reply.

Stride waits for her to answer. He is sure she is hiding important facts from him. He is unsure how to uncover them.

"Is there anything else you'd like to tell us about this matter? Anything you say will be treated with the utmost confidence."

She shakes her head.

"There is nothing, Inspector."

"You have been most helpful," he lies.

She gives him a polite cold smile that does not reach her eyes.

The maid shows the two detectives out.

As soon as they have gone, Georgiana takes down her mantle and bonnet from the hall stand and steps out of the front door. A carriage awaits her in the street. She gives the coachman instructions and climbs inside.

A short time later the carriage pulls up outside the town house of Regina Osborne, who has summoned her for an urgent meeting. Georgiana descends and rings the bell. A parlour maid shows her into the dusk-rose papered drawing room where Regina stands waiting.

The two ladies greet each other politely. Normally Regina Osborne is only At Home after 3 pm, spending the morning writing letters or ordering the servants about. She does not ever deviate from her set routine. But now she has.

"How are dear George and Violet?" Georgiana inquires, after the maid has served her tea in a tiny porcelain cup and gone out of the room.

"George? He's fine. Violet is not well at the moment – you heard she was …" Regina leans forward and nods significantly.

"I think I did. And Eliza and Harriet?"

"They're both down at the Adler-Chinstraps, hunting."

Georgiana inclines her head. The whereabouts of Regina's adult offspring is of no interest to her whatsoever, but the necessary formalities must be waded through before the matter in hand is dragged kicking and screaming into the limelight.

"Now then, Georgy," Regina says, stirring her tea briskly. "Enough chit-chat. We heard you had a box of cakes delivered, as we did ourselves. A box of *poisoned* cakes. These boxes of cakes … what are your thoughts?"

"Oh … I …" Georgiana stutters.

"Let's not mince words. We are women of the world and we know each other's situations too well, don't we? Do you think it is one of Them?"

"Them" is the term Regina Osborne uses to describe the females associated with her husband and with Frederick Undercroft. The ones neither wife is supposed to know about. But of course, they do. Osborne, much to Regina's chagrin, has also been chronically unfaithful throughout their married life.

Not that Georgiana cares about Regina's feelings. Regina introduced her to Frederick in the first place. And when, one evening a few years ago, she arrived on Regina's doorstep in floods of tears, clutching a few personal belongings and saying she could bear it no longer, Regina abruptly turned her away, telling her she would not interfere in another woman's marriage.

Since then, Georgiana has come to believe that everything wrong with her life that cannot be laid at her husband's door is Regina's fault or the fault of Regina's husband. But mainly Regina.

"I don't think …," she begins hesitantly.

"Well, start thinking. I have made a list of all the ones I know about, and my purpose in inviting you here was so that you could do the same. If we find the same name on both lists, we shall go at once and confront the filthy sluts!"

"It might not be one of Them."

"Nonsense, who else would it be? Both our husbands like to eat cake. And who else knows that our husbands like to eat it? Who else would want to hurt them?

Assuredly it is some strumpet seeking revenge, you can count upon it."

"If that is the case, should you not allow the detective police to investigate the matter?"

"Let some grubby little men poke around in one's private business? And then see whatever they find splashed all over the newspapers for the whole of London to gawp at? Is that what you want?"

Remembering the earlier visit from Stride and Cully, Georgiana flinches.

"I thought not. Because that is exactly what will happen if we don't deal with it ourselves. Remember poor Lady Sarah Gibson – forced abroad by the scandal. Whereas her philandering husband is living quite openly with that vile woman, and nobody blinks an eye or says a word."

She goes to the rosewood bureau and opens it.

"Here is paper and pencil. Write!"

Georgiana frowns, fidgets with the pencil. Then begins to write in flowing copperplate. Regina Osborne watches in grim silence.

Finally, Georgiana looks up.

"These are all I can recall."

She hands the list and pencil to Regina who scans it rapidly.

"Aha! There are names here that I recognise."

She ticks off a couple of names.

"Leave it with me. I already know where one of the whores is. I shall find out the address of the other one and let you know. Then we will sally forth and extract the truth."

**

It is a mere hop, skip and a jump (though not literally) from Regina Osborne's townhouse to the brightly-lit porticoed shopping paradise that is Regent Street. And here are Sissy Bulstrode and Belinda Kite just getting down from a hansom and walking into Dickins & Jones. They have come to look at lace collars. Possibly gloves. Maybe fans. Certainly shawls. Though only one of them will ultimately take the looking process forward into a purchasing one.

For Belinda, the outing is a welcome break. She has been Sissy's companion for only a short time, but already it feels like a lifetime. She has never met anyone so lacking in energy and spirit.

It isn't that she dislikes Sissy – there is so little about her to like or dislike, but this is London: the greatest city in the world! Excitement and adventure are here for the taking. Or the leaving, which is what her febrile companion seems determined to do.

Belinda knows Bulstrode will eventually return to his factories in the north of England, taking Sissy with him. She visualises the north as a bleak, black-chimneyed place full of smoke and smut and sad-faced people. Once they depart, her future is uncertain. Now is all she has.

Yet Sissy seems content to while away the hours waiting for her brother's return reading novels, or working on pieces of needlework. She shows no interest in carriage rides, taking tea at one of the fashionable little West End tea rooms, or visiting the many attractions of the great city. The furthest they have ventured so far on their own is a walk around the neighbourhood.

It has taken all Belinda's ingenuity to get her to leave the house today, but here they are at last, making their way up to the second floor where the women's clothes and accessories are located.

As soon as they arrive Sissy is greeted by a smiling shop assistant, who quickly assesses the hierarchy, and ushers her to a seat by the counter. Belinda is left to stand, her mouth watering as pair after pair of lovely coloured gloves are laid on the shiny wooden counter for Sissy to try on.

After Sissy has made her choice, the gloves are swept away, to be replaced by indoor caps of cotton and linen, then by delicate lace collars, pinned to a board. It is as much as Belinda can do to keep her hands by her sides, but she manages to model the perfect companion: feasting her eyes upon the lovely things while murmuring a few words of judicious advice.

After the exhausting process of choosing and then arranging for the things to be sent to the house in Bloomsbury, Belinda suggests a cup of tea to fortify them for the journey home. To her surprise, Sissy agrees. They visit the marble-decorated rest room, then find the restaurant where they are shown to a small corner table.

"This is a lovely shop," Sissy whispers, after Belinda has given the waitress their order. "I have never been inside a big department store before. Back home, we only have small shops with far fewer items. I have never bought so many things before. I hope Josiah will not be displeased."

Belinda blinks. This is the most she has ever heard Sissy say since her arrival.

"I am glad you enjoyed it," she replies.

"I expect this is nothing like as grand as you are used to," Sissy continues, as the waitress places their cups and saucers on the table.

Belinda smiles deprecatingly.

"What was it like, to live in Paris?" Sissy asks.

The smile fades slightly.

"Oh … it was … very like here, but everybody spoke French."

Belinda buries her face in her teacup, resolving to spend a little more time working on her back story.

"How sad to have fallen upon hard times," Sissy continues. "I cannot imagine what it must be like."

I bet you can't, Belinda thinks grimly. You have a rich brother who spoils you. You only have to open your mouth, and you get money to spend. In time, despite your lack of looks, you will receive a proposal of marriage from some rich man. You will never have to lift a finger in your life.

"Oh, truly, I hardly think about it," she lies, rolling her eyes to the ceiling.

Tea drunk, they retrace their steps and arrive back on Regent Street once more. Alas, while they have been enjoying themselves, it has started to rain and Regent Circus has a lock.

A pattern of umbrellas spins through the growing host of rain-soaked vehicles, none of which can move until the others do. People are cutting in like Christmas dinner. Whips are being liberally applied.

Belinda and Sissy stand on the pavement outside Dickins & Jones regarding the shouting, neighing, swearing, steaming mass of horses and humanity with dismay. How can they get across to the other side, where the cab stands are located? How will they get home? Sissy furls and unfurls her umbrella, biting her lips and breathing loudly.

"Oh, how I wish Josiah were here," she cries.

Sadly, the doughty factory owner is not here. But somebody else is. Just as Sissy is about to collapse into a hysterical fit, a tall broad-shouldered man in a well-brushed top hat steps up to them. It is Mark Hawksley.

"Ladies," he says, raising the hat. "May I be of assistance?"

Sissy turns to him, relief plastered all over her face.

"Oh, Mr Hawksley, is it you? Oh – we are in such a

plight. We cannot reach the cab rank and we need to go home. My brother will be waiting for us."

Hawksley eyes Belinda, who is deliberately averting her eyes.

"I happen to have a cab waiting around the corner," he says. "May I offer to escort you both?"

Sissy's expression brightens instantly.

"Oh, that would be so kind of you."

He offers her his arm. She grabs hold of it as if it were a log in a fast-flowing river. He does not offer his other arm to Belinda, who is forced to push her way through the crowds on the pavement, trying always to keep them in sight.

Hawksley steers Sissy into a side street, and there, just as he said, is a cab. He opens the door and helps her inside, seating her on the single seat with her back to the horses. Then he holds out a gloved hand to Belinda.

"Thank you, but I can manage," she says, tossing her head.

Hawksley smiles down at her. He stands slightly aside to allow her to enter and once again, she feels his breath on the back of her neck, is aware of his strong powerful body, smells his exciting cologne. He gives the driver instructions, then seats himself next to her.

The carriage moves off. Sissy closes her eyes. Belinda stares out of the window, seeing nothing but the blur of rain and the fractured glimmer of gaslight. Suddenly she feels the sensation of Hawksley's leg against hers. She gives him a quick sideways glance but he is staring straight ahead, his face expressionless.

She moves her own leg, but she is already sitting close to the carriage wall. His leg finds hers again, presses gently against it. She feels its firmness, the warmth of it. She does not pull away.

Later that evening, when her brother returns and they

are seated at the dining table, Sissy hesitantly relates the events of the afternoon to him.

"By God – that man did you a good turn," Josiah says, pushing half a potato into his mouth. "I have a mind to write and thank him. Indeed, I shall write and thank him. And I shall invite him to dine with us – what do you think of that, little Sis?"

"Whatever you say, Josiah," Sissy says, blushing.

"Aw – I can see you're pleased with the idea. A new love to drive out the old, eh?"

Belinda pauses, a forkful of food suspended in mid-air. She stares fixedly at Sissy, who is simpering at her brother in a slightly foolish way.

"See, I told you you'd soon forget that great booby of a farmer once we got to London. And wasn't I right? Mr Hawksley – who'd have thought it? A fine figure of a man. Elegant, good-looking. Owner of a diamond mine to boot. Rescuing my little sister!"

He throws down his cutlery with a clatter.

"Damn it! I'm going to write to him now! Strike while the iron is hot. Dessert can wait."

He pushes back his chair and strides noisily out of the room. Sissy averts her eyes from Belinda's gaze and fixes them on her plate instead. She pushes her food around, a secret smile lurking at the corner of her lips.

It is none of my business, Belinda reminds herself, returning her attention to her supper also. So this was, presumably, the Unfortunate Incident – some 'great booby of a farmer' back in Yorkshire had jilted her. Somehow, she is not surprised, given Sissy's unprepossessing face and figure and her diffident personality.

She recalls the warmth of Mark Hawksley's leg pressed against hers in the carriage. The way his eyes brightened and crinkled at the edges with wry amusement as he helped her down from the carriage, holding her small hand in his just a little longer than propriety demanded.

One didn't have to be a mind-reader to know which of the two of them he preferred. *But he is not going to marry you,* a small voice inside her head reminds her. *You may have far better looks, but you are only the hired companion. You have nothing and you are nothing.*

Belinda Kite turns her attention back to her dinner, which she finishes in silence.

***

Meanwhile Frederick Undercroft, who has a fondness for the company of women who are not his wife, is spending the evening with his lovely friend Hectorina Rose. They have spent many evenings together over the years, either dining out, or sitting next to each other on the sofa in the tiny house he rents for her in Maida Vale.

Hectorina Rose has very black hair, likes very showy jewellery and has the full-bosomed figure that men of Undercroft's vintage find most alluring. She also wears stylish silk dresses. Some of them have been bought and paid for by Undercroft. Some have not.

Tonight, they have supped at Cromerty's Restaurant – a discreet little place where a gentleman can entertain a member of the opposite (or the same) sex and no eyebrows are raised. Oysters and French champagne have gone down a treat. Now a small silver bowl of hothouse red grapes is placed on the table. Hectorina Rose picks up the fruit scissors and cuts a stem of grapes from the bunch.

"I think I'd like a grape too," Undercroft says.

She pushes the bowl across the table.

"Help yourself."

He leans forward. "Oh, let's do it properly."

Hectorina Rose knows the routine. She dutifully picks up a grape, and offers it to his waiting mouth. Undercroft smiles. To him, this simple manoeuvre is so much more than a mere sharing of food. It is as if the woman is symbolically offering herself to him. Which, a short while later, she will do, in one of the small upstairs rooms that smell of old cooking and stale sex.

But even as he is working away on top of her, with Hectorina Rose dutifully writhing and groaning beneath him, as befits a true professional who knows where her silk dresses come from, Frederick Undercroft cannot escape the dark thoughts that lately seem to have attached themselves to his life like limpets.

As he climaxes, too soon and unsatisfyingly, he feels shapeless words rise to his mouth and stay there, unfinished and uncertain.

By the time he leaves it is past midnight and the streets are cleared out of rain and people. Undercroft walks to the main thoroughfare, where there are always cabs to be hired, at whatever time of day or night.

As he turns a corner, a man hurrying in the opposite direction bumps into him. He is carrying what looks like a pot of paint in one hand, and a brush in the other.

Undercroft pushes him off with an exclamation of annoyance. The man mutters something that could be an apology, could be a mouthful of profanity, and vanishes into the anonymity of an adjacent alley.

Only when he is seated in the cab does Undercroft notice that there are drops of red paint on his shoes. Like blood spots. All the way home he stares hypnotically at them, wondering whether they could be an omen.

In what is left of the night he lies awake, the inside

of his head shiny with the clarity of sleeplessness. It's hard to contemplate, in the grey hours of the darkness, that possibly the only reason someone would come to your funeral would be to make sure you were dead.

***

A fine golden bowl of an autumn morning, and it is standing room only in the outer office of the Detective Division. The Anxious Bench has metamorphosed into the Angry Bench, and is currently packed with the kind of people who live in the separate world that exists behind the respectable facade of the city.

The noise is deafening, the smell of cheap scent and unwashed bodies is overpowering, and the duty constable is struggling to maintain some sort of order as Jack Cully pushes open the door.

He is immediately mobbed by a group of men who all try to talk at once, each raising their voice to be heard above their fellows. Cully sends the constable a *What-the-hell?* look. The constable shakes his head and shrugs his shoulders.

"Gentlemen," Cully raises a hand. "I can't attend to all of you at once."

He scans the group, picking out one man whose face seems vaguely familiar.

"You, sir – would you care to accompany me to a quiet room, where you can explain what this is all about."

"It's all about vandalism," a voice at the back of the room calls out shrilly. "Desecration of the vilest and basest kind."

Cully can't make out the speaker, but he recognises the voice as belonging to Reverend Micah Eliphaz, the vicar of St Xavier the Charitable. It is a very High Anglican church and the vicar has a voice to match.

Over time Cully has had to deal with numerous formal complaints from him about ragged street children sheltering in the porch, or beggars sitting outside the gate.

"Words," shouts a florid-faced woman sitting on the bench. "Someone painted rude words all over our door."

"And on ours," another woman echoes.

"And on my Boarding House for Respectable Young Professional Ladies," a third adds.

"*Red* words," the first woman says significantly, nodding her head at Cully as if the colour is somehow implicated in the crime.

"Step this way," Cully orders the familiar-looking man, who dutifully follows him to one of the sparse whitewashed rooms that are used either to house criminals temporarily or to interview suspects. A small group of supporters gathers outside the door.

"Name?" Cully asks.

"Edwin Gregious, city bookseller."

Ah, now Cully remembers. Mr Gregious has a shop in Holywell Street. The police had conducted a razzia upon his and several other warehouses, carrying off masses of obscene books, photographs and prints. Jack Cully prided himself on being broadminded, but even he was shocked by some of the confiscated material.

"Can you tell me what has happened?" he inquires.

"When I went to open up my shop as usual this morning, somebody had torn down the shutters in the night and covered all over the window with red paint."

Mr Gregious' moustache quivers with indignation.

"I have my regular customers. What will they think? Then there's the passing trade. I had just put a whole new selection of pictures in the window too. Classical and Roman themed. Very tasteful."

Cully recalls some of the 'Classical themed pictures'

seized on the last raid – they consisted of stark naked women lying down with their legs wantonly open, and priapic satyrs or bulls standing over them in various states of arousal.

"So what are the police going to do about it?" a voice from the half-open doorway interrupts, followed by a chorus of disgruntled citizenry.

Cully attempts to build a barricade against the rising tide of ire.

"If you would all like to give your names and addresses to my desk sergeant, I will make sure an officer attends each incident and takes a statement from you," he says.

There is the muffled sound of boots moving out of the way and Sergeant Evans enters the room, making it seem suddenly much smaller.

"I am sorry to interrupt you, Detective Sergeant Cully," he says in his lilting Welsh accent, "but I have just been talking to some of the ladies in the waiting room, and I wondered whether the person, or persons, unknown who perpetrated these acts of vandalism could be connected to the red painted doors that I saw in the Drury Lane area, as mentioned in my recent report?"

Only Sergeant Evans would refer to the bedraggled army of elderly whores working on their decline as 'ladies', Cully thinks wryly.

"You wrote a report?"

Evans draws himself up with pride.

"I placed it upon Inspector Stride's desk myself."

Oh damn, Cully thinks. Someone should have warned the young sergeant about placing things on Stride's desk without telling Stride that they had been placed. The report was probably sitting under a vast pile of unread paperwork. And Stride himself was currently in a meeting with the Home Secretary.

"You mean there's been other properties painted and the police ain't investigated it yet?" Mr Gregious exclaims.

Cully curses inwardly.

"I'm sure the police are doing all in their powers to catch the criminals," he repeats, reaching for the automatic response that worked nine times out of ten.

Sadly, this is the tenth time.

"So we aren't the first after all?"

"I shall make sure I look into it personally," Cully says.

Another stock phrase. That doesn't work either.

Mr Gregious' air of righteous indignation is so tangible you could strike matches on it.

"I find this very hard to hear, officer. Very hard indeed. You were quick enough to come down and raid my premises and confiscate my stock on the mere hearsay of a couple of magistrates. Now it appears that when I am the innocent victim, you can't be bothered."

"Nobody said that," Cully replies in what he hopes in a reasonable tone of voice. But Mr Gregious is currently not at home to Mr Reasonable.

"Let me give you some free advice, young man," he huffs.

Jack Cully groans inwardly. In his experience, free advice often turned out to be expensive.

"I pay my taxes, so I am entitled to protection under the laws of this land. As are all those good people in your outer office. And if we don't get it – well then, we shall just have to take the so-called *law* into our own hands! So there!"

Having uttered this anarchical threat, Mr Gregious rises, glares at the two men and stomps out of the room, where his aggrieved voice can be heard sharing his opinion of police incompetence to the waiting crowd.

"Oh dear. I'm so sorry, Detective Sergeant Cully," Sergeant Evans says, his expression woebegone.

"Not your fault, lad. You weren't to know. Now, let's get that mob out there calmed down and pacified before they really do riot. Then I suggest we head for Detective Inspector Stride's office, find your report and start looking into things."

***

Meanwhile in a smart hotel room off Bath's beautiful Regency Crescent, a man stands in front of a mirror, tying his cravat. Shortly, he will make his way to the Assembly Rooms where he will give a presentation to the good citizens of that fair spa town.

In the presentation, which has been widely advertised and will be standing room only, he will invite his audience to purchase shares in his company, which has been founded to re-open his late father's diamond mine, loaded with priceless gems just waiting to be dug out.

The name upon the poster is one he has chosen specifically for this event. It is not the name he uses in London. He has learned early on that if you want to get anywhere in this world – and he decided right at the start that he wanted to go as far as it was possible to go – you wear names lightly, discard them when appropriate, and seize the advantage anywhere you can.

And you move around a lot. You do this because most people do not. Change your town and your name, and if you have the right clothes and the right manner, the whole world is your lobster. So to speak.

He finishes tying the silk cravat, brushes a few imaginary threads from the lapel of his well-tailored black jacket, and smiles confidently at his reflection. He looks every inch a gentleman. Every inch a charmer. He turns from the mirror and hooks his top hat from the stand. Curtain up. It is time to charm some more golden guineas out of some more gullible pockets.

***

It is a day's coach ride from the elegant Assembly Rooms of Bath to the more mundane Lily Lounge, a discreet and pleasant tea-room. Located in Flask Walk, a narrow lane off the fashionable Hampstead High Street, it was initially opened to serve female shoppers with a choice of teas and delicious homemade cakes.

Now, with the advance north of the railway, the subsequent extension of the housing stock, along with the arrival of some more nice little shops, the Lily Lounge has branched out into also offering light lunches.

The lunch period is well under way when the door is pushed open to admit Regina Osborne in a severe tailored coat and an uncompromising bonnet. She is accompanied rather hesitantly by Georgiana Undercroft.

The two women are greeted politely by the tea-room owner, a lady of similar vintage but far finer beauty. She is wearing respectable shop black, her abundant dark hair coiled up and covered by a becoming lace cap. She offers to show them both to a table.

Regina plants her feet firmly and glares at her.

"You are 'Mrs' Lilith Marks, the owner of this … establishment?" she says, waving a dismissive gloved hand in the direction of the customers.

"I am indeed."

"I do not suppose you know who we are?"

"I do not suppose that I do," Lilith responds equably. "Would you like to see the luncheon menu?"

Regina Osborne tosses her head.

"Certainly not. We are not here to see the menu. We are here to see YOU!"

Georgiana Undercroft plucks her sleeve,

"I really think we should keep our voices down, Regina," she murmurs. "There are people staring at us."

"Nonsense, Georgy," Regina Osborne booms. "Everybody has the right to know who this woman is."

"Everybody knows that I am the owner and manager of this tea-room," Lilith informs her.

"Ah – but you were not always such, were you?" Regina sneers.

Light dawns on Lilith's face.

"Yes, I once *was* somebody different," she says quietly. "I presume you are referring to that time. But I left those days behind me a long while ago."

"Oh, I doubt that. Once a whore, always a whore."

Georgiana shifts her feet and looks uncomfortable.

"Is there some reason why you have entered my tea-room, other than to insult me?" Lilith asks, acid etching every syllable.

"You know the reason all too well," Regina spits. "We have come to confront you and tell you that we know all about your evil plans to poison our husbands by placing arsenic in your cakes and IT WILL NOT WORK! Now then – what do you have to say to that?"

Lilith stares at her as if she were mad.

"Aha! I see you have nothing to say in your own defence," Regina's voice rings out triumphantly.

"On the contrary, I am saying nothing because I do not have a clue what you are talking about."

"We have it on good authority that you were … *acquainted* with both our husbands in the past. And the connection may still be present."

"As I told you: those days are long gone. This is my

76

business now."

"But you sell *cakes* – I see *cakes* all around me. And it was by *cakes* that the poison entered our houses."

"I supply my customers here with cakes, which I bake myself. I do not sell them to anybody else. Whatever may have happened to you, it is nothing to do with me. Now please leave my premises, or I may have to summon the police and have you ejected."

Georgiana tugs urgently at Regina's sleeve again.

"For God's sake, Regina. It is clear that this woman knows nothing of what has taken place. Let us go at once."

Regina Osborne glares at Lilith venomously, then at the customers, who are listening avidly to every word of their exchange while pretending to be fascinated by the contents of their cups or the pattern on the table clothes.

"Very well Georgiana. If you insist. But we have done the right thing in confronting this woman. All such polluters of the sacred marriage bed must face up to their actions, either now or before a Higher Presence."

Lilith's face is a study as she walks to the street door and holds it open. Her parting words are uttered in a voice intended to carry to the far corners of the room.

"Good-bye ladies. Oh – and always remember I did not invite your husbands to my bed. They came of their own accord, probably because they weren't happy in yours."

And having delivered her parting shot, Lilith slams the door shut and crosses the floor of her tea-room, head held high.

As soon as the two women are in the street, Georgiana rounds on her companion furiously.

"How could you behave in such a reckless manner, Regina?" she exclaims. "I recognised many of my own friends and neighbours sitting in there. Now I will never be able to face them again."

"Nonsense," Regina replies defiantly. "It had to be done!"

"No, it did not! You could have written a letter, or waited until the shop closed. Instead you have subjected me to a humiliating and degrading episode that may well be related back to Frederick. I am so ashamed. And it was all for nothing! Of course that woman didn't send those cakes. It was quite obvious from the start."

"Oh? Did she not?" Regina turns to face her former friend, eyebrows raised in inquiry. "How can you be so sure, Georgiana? Is there something you haven't told me? Tell me at once!"

But Georgiana does not reply. The days of girlish confidences have long passed. Pressing her lips tightly together, she spins on her heel and walks off down the hill in the direction of home as fast as her legs will carry her.

***

Letters are also the topic of conversation around the Bulstrode supper table. Or rather, a specific letter, delivered earlier this evening. It is from rich, eligible, diamond-owning, damsel-rescuing Mark Hawksley.

In the letter, he thanks Josiah for his own letter, apologising profusely for not responding immediately – regretfully he was called away to the West Country to visit his sick mother.

He goes on to express his gratitude at being invited to partake of the simple fare offered at Number 11 Cartwright Gardens. He informs Bulstrode that he will accept his invitation to dine the following Thursday, and indeed is looking forward to becoming more acquainted with both Josiah and his delightful sister.

No mention of Belinda Kite. Or her leg.

Picking over the letter has been the sole source of interest for the whole of the meal.

"There, Sissy," Josiah says, triumphantly after a fourth re-reading. *"Delightful sister* – here it is in black and white. Now if that don't bring the roses to your cheeks and a sparkle to your eyes, then I'm a Dutchman!"

As he clearly isn't a Dutchman, Belinda glances across the table at Sissy, who looks very much the same as she ever does: pallid and unsparkly.

"So, Miss Keet, we are to entertain a guest," Josiah says, turning to her. "What shall we offer him? I don't think Mr Hawksley is the sort of man who'd fancy frogs' legs and snails, like you eat in Paree, eh?"

He laughs uproariously at his own joke.

"I'm sure that whatever you serve will be quite delicious," Belinda replies, keeping her features strictly neutral.

"I think a side of prime English beef is what's called for," Josiah declares. "Can't go wrong with good wholesome English food. I shall order it from the butcher tomorrow first thing. Sissy, you can choose a pudding – sweet stuff is more a lady's thing."

"But who will prepare all this food, Josiah?" Sissy asks, frowning. "I cannot be expected to cook it, and I don't think the current cook is good enough for a fine dinner party."

Bulstrode waves a dismissive hand.

"Oh, I shall hire a proper chef. And someone to wait at table properly. We don't want Mr Hawksley to think we northerners can't do London style and copy London ways, do we?"

Belinda breathes a silent sigh of relief. For one terrible moment, she feared she might be prevailed upon to prepare the feast. What she knows about cooking could fit on the back of a postage stamp and still leave enough room for the front page of *The Ladies' Fashion Weekly.*

"Just you make sure you're looking your best, Sissy. We want to make a good impression upon Mr Hawksley, after all, *he has met the Queen,"* Bulstrode lowers his voice and utters the final five words in a tone of hushed awe.

"I shall wear my new lavender dress. The dressmaker said the colour suited me."

Belinda Kite stares down at her plate, upon which she has deposited some bottled cherry stones from her half-finished dessert. She counts them in her head, silently reciting the old familiar rhyme from childhood: *Tinker, tailor, soldier, sailor, rich man ...*

If only, she thinks. She pictures Mark Hawksley's handsome, sardonic face. The image comes to her as something desirable, painfully clear. There is a tightness in her chest, a spreading excitement.

She wants to see him again. But not just him: she wants to see the life he has surrounded himself with. The people who inhabit it. Those who have money are afraid of nothing, she thinks. They no longer have any reason to be afraid.

***

One o'clock in the morning is a territory as much as a time, and Marianne Corvid is a long-term resident. She lies in bed, painting the past onto her eyelids. She is not awake, nor asleep, but trapped in between.

She listens to the sound of blood beating upward from her heart. There is a sensation hovering at the edge of her mind, near understanding. She reaches for it hard, and in doing so, feels herself beginning to wake.

After a few minutes have passed she gets up, more wakeful now, clear-headed, nocturnal. She goes downstairs to the rosewood writing desk and places a sheet of notepaper in front of her. Her eyes feel as though they are sinking into her head. There is no fire in the room, and it is as cold as Candlemas.

A church clock strikes the hour. As it does every night. Marianne Corvid wraps her shawl more tightly around herself. She is a pale woman, quite short, with dark hair and dark eyes – twin darknesses that serve only to emphasise the pallor of her skin.

Her hands hold on to the sides of the desk and she steadies her breath. It feels unreal, the smooth rapidity of events. As if she is standing outside her life, seeing it happen to another person. She stares out of the window at the patched sky, her mind churning like a piece of machinery she cannot switch off.

Marianne Corvid dips her pen into the ink pot, and writes:

Dearest,

I have been so unhappy since my last letter to you. I feel I can't go on without writing once more. I do not know whether you received my last letter – the postal service is not reliable, as I know to my cost, having not received any letters from you recently. I would have thought that you might have replied.

Every time I recall how we met – how the sudden death of my husband brought us together, my heart skips a beat. How wonderfully strong and supportive you were at that time. And then, when the desire for sensualities so long denied me began to glow again in my blood with renewed appetite, how ardent and persistent. How you warmed me with your kisses!

It is all dust and shadows. I have seen you in the

street. You passed me by without recognition. Another probably has your heart and is even now being warmed by those sweet caresses, as I once was. And I, who loved you more than life itself, am left with nothing but the precious memories of our secret times together.

All I ask is for one more meeting. One more chance for me to look my last upon the face of the man I once loved, but have now lost. I need to see you. Please grant me this, my final request.

The candle flickers. She signs her name, blots the signature and slips the letter into an envelope. Tomorrow she will post it. Marianne Corvid picks up her candle, and mounts the stairs. She returns to her bedroom and goes to her dressing table.

For a few seconds, she stares into the mirror, studying the reflection of her face. It is ghostly in the dim light, like a skull. The eye sockets are hollows of darkness. She looks like someone who has not slept peacefully for a long time.

Marianne Corvid lifts the lid of a small jewel box, from which she draws out a diamond and turquoise bracelet. Slipping it onto her wrist, she turns her hand in the dying flame of the candle.

She thinks of what she has done for love. What she has lost. How she has always been unlucky in time, too early, too late, her hope of desire always temporary. The jewels wink and glitter, reflecting light, deceiving.

***

A foggy morning in London. Buildings shadowy with it, the river an oozing stinking miasma of low-tide mud. Grimy pavements. No shade lighter than slate-grey. Faces barely distinguishable. Hoofbeats hollow in the fog. The smell of shit everywhere, settling into the stitch of clothes, and the pores of skin and stone.

At Scotland Yard, the newspapers have just been brought into Detective Inspector Stride's office by one of the desk constables. The shit is metaphorically about to hit the desk.

By the time Jack Cully arrives at Scotland Yard, a little late as he has had to help Emily pack up a couple of dresses for immediate delivery, Stride is in a state that might reasonably be described as apoplectic.

"See this, Jack?" He exclaims, stabbing a finger at the pile of papers. "Bloody Dandy and his crew have been at it again!"

Cully surveys the front page of *The Inquirer*, which bears the banner headline:

Mysterious Red-Hand Gang Terrorise City! Riot & Anarchy Follow in Their Wake!!

Under this, in slightly smaller letters is written:

Detective Police Refuse to Investigate.

"I thought it was just a few religious individuals with a Bible, a pot of paint and rather too much time on their hands," Cully says.

"Ah – that's where you're wrong, Jack. According to our good friends in the popular press, we are on the verge of revolution and anarchy. As Mr Dandy points out: the French Revolution began with slogans painted upon walls."

"I hardly think this is the same thing."

"The Bastion of the Common Man thinks it is. And where the Bastion goes, the mob follows. No Jack, I'm afraid we will have to take this silly painting lark seriously. Arrange for the night patrols to be doubled."

"I've already got some of the day constables to talk

to everybody who has had their property painted," Cully says. "There seems to be no links. No common thread – other than the words themselves."

"Then let's focus on the words. If this is some strange religious sect, somebody must know who they are, where they meet and when. You want to start asking around some of those small chapel places. I wouldn't put it past one of them to be at the bottom of this. Always seem a bit suspect to me," Stride says, the concept of religious tolerance being some hundred years in the future.

"I may take Sergeant Evans with me in that case," Cully says. "I believe he goes to one of those places every Sunday."

"Does he indeed? He seems like a very normal young man to me."

"I'm sure he is."

Stride grunts.

"Do whatever you think best, Jack. Only let's get on top of this painting nonsense, before it runs away with us and we really do have a riot on our hands."

***

Frederick Undercroft wakes in the green-papered bedroom he does not share with his wife. A Soho apothecary has prescribed him tincture of opium. The label on the blue glass bottle informs him that it is *to allay pain, relax spasms and procure sleep.*

Every night, Undercroft counts out ten drops into a silver spoon and swallows them with water. He sleeps, but his dreams are so vivid and violent that they leave him exhausted.

The instant before he wakes he experiences a moment of luminous terror, such as a man falling over cliff edge must feel, somersaulting through insubstantial air. He wakes up with bloodshot eyes and a strange bitter taste in his mouth.

A knock at his door heralds the arrival of the maid, carrying his hot shaving water in a jug. She is the replacement for Molly, and has been chosen by his wife. He does not know her name. He does know that she is fat, plain, and bovine of expression.

No more fun and games, no sly fondling. Molly had a small strawberry-shaped birthmark high on her upper thigh. On a good morning, she would let him look at it. On an even better morning she would allow him to kiss it.

The new maid slops water into the blue china bowl, mutters something, and goes out. Frederick Undercroft slides his bony shanks from under the bedcovers and prepares for the day ahead. He has clients to see. Wills to be read to disappointed family members. Dressed, he descends to the dining room where his wife is buttering a piece of toast. She glances up, her expression hardening.

How unattractive she is, he thinks. How unlike the gay giddy girl he courted all those years ago. His mind wanders back to that time. Then to other times and other gay girls. He could have done so much better for himself. He should have waited. Not sold himself so quickly.

"Are you feeling well this morning, Frederick?" his wife greets him dully.

He reaches for the toast rack, finds himself holding the cold blackened slice of bread up to the light, as if any poison accruing to it might be visible to the naked eye. Seeing nothing unusual, he places it on his plate.

"I am perfectly fine. I shall be out for most of the day, possibly in the evening also," he says.

"As you wish."

He has taken to going out, staying out, eating out.

The club, the bookshops along Holywell Street, the women, the friends he knows, the friends he once knew and now regards with faint suspicion. *Is it you?* his mind constantly asks, while he searches for clues, little 'tells' that might reveal who is trying to dispose of him.

He gulps down a cup of bitter black coffee, finishes the toast and gets up from the table. He does not ask Georgiana what plans she has made for the day, for her life is of no interest to him whatsoever. Which is just as well, for she has made no plans.

Since the ill-fated visit to the Lily Lounge, Georgiana has not ventured further than her own hallway, fearing the stares and whispered comments of her neighbours if she so much as sets a foot outside the front door.

She hears Frederick exchange some words with the parlour maid, hears the girl giggle, then the door slams. Relief settles upon her like a comforting blanket. She is just about to ring for more toast, when the parlour maid enters, carrying a silver salver.

"The letters have just arrived, ma'am. Shall I put them on the master's desk in his study?"

"No, Susan, leave them with me. And bring me some more hot toast."

Susan hands her the letters, bobs a curtsey and departs.

Georgiana rifles through the post, her heart thumping. Any day, any delivery, there might be something from one of the people in the tea-room who saw her and Regina, who heard Lilith Marks' dreadful parting words.

Three letters. All addressed to her husband. One is clearly from the Law Society – probably an invitation to a dinner. One, in a plain brown envelope, feels like a catalogue of some sort.

And the third? She stares at the small, sloping

feminine handwriting, turns the envelope over, her eyes narrowing, mouth hardening into a straight line. Then in a quick, decisive gesture, she reaches for a clean butter-knife and slits it open.

***

Lunchtime finds Jack Cully and Sergeant Evans sitting on a bench in one of the public gardens. They are enjoying a ham sandwich and the hazy autumn sunshine. From the trees, a drift of small red leaves has collected, like confetti, at the foot of the bench.

An interesting morning has been spent calling in at a few of the more esoteric places of worship in the city, culminating with a visit to the Wesleyan Chapel in Commercial Road, a square-fronted, unornate brick building that reminded Cully more of a workhouse than God's house.

In each location, the two officers have stood and listened while serious men in a variety of strange clothing gave them an outline of the group's beliefs. These have varied from vegetarianism to nudity.

They have been invited to attend various meetings. They have had pamphlets pressed upon them and have been informed earnestly and sincerely that in *no way* would *any* member stoop so low as to deface a public building, any building, with red paint.

In front of the bench a flock of sparrows have gathered, their feathers puffed against the cold. Cully watches their ragged hopping, then throws them the remains of his bread. As they feed, the little birds appear to dance between his feet.

"Hymn-writing weather," Evans says, repeating the parting words of the Methodist minister.

"Indeed."

They sit awhile in companionable silence.

"May I ask your advice, sir?" Evans says.

"Just plain Jack will do."

"Oh. Well. Right then, Mr Cully." Evans lowers his voice. "It's like this: you are a married man, aren't you?"

Cully nods.

"You know all about women, don't you?"

Cully pulls a wry face. He knows about one woman, his wife Emily, but what he knows is that he knows very little. Every time he thinks he has her worked out, she wriggles free, slipping out of his mental grasp like a little silver fish.

"What do you want to know?"

Sergeant Evans heaves a sigh that comes from somewhere deep inside his large, honest, manly chest.

"It's my Megan, see. The young lady I have been engaged to for some time. She has written me a letter saying that if I do not name the day for our wedding, she might have to marry Harry Todd the blacksmith instead. Now, this is my question: if she wants to marry another man, should I not step aside and let her?"

"Does she love this Harry Todd?"

Sergeant Evans stares ahead and cogitates.

"I don't think so. He is known for liking his drink. And he has a nasty temper. But he is there and I am here, so to speak."

He turns his face to Cully, his expression woebegone.

"Me and my Megan have been sweethearts ever since we were children. But I have been away from the valley for a long time, and I think she is getting tired of waiting for me to come back and settle things. And I cannot blame her. Women want to be married, don't they, Mr Cully? They want a little home and children and a husband to care for them. And here I am stuck in London, and poor Megan is in Cardiff, and I do not see how it is to be brought about."

"When are you due your next leave, lad?"

"Not for many weeks. It has been cancelled twice, and it may be cancelled again."

Cully's heart goes out to the young man. He remembers how desolate he felt when Emily Benet, as she then was, vanished from his life and he thought he'd never see her again.

"Leave it with me," he says, laying a comforting hand on the young sergeant's shoulder. "I'll put in a good word for you with Detective Inspector Stride. He'll make sure you get your leave brought forward, and some added on to make up for what you've lost. Then you can write to your girl and fix the day."

Sergeant Evans' face is one big radiant beam of joy.

"Thank you, sir, Mr Cully. If I could only write to my Megan with a bit of good news at last, why, I reckon that'd sweeten her heart."

"I'm sure it would. Then it shall be done."

Cully also makes a mental note to inquire about future job vacancies in the Cardiff Police. Loth as he'd be to lose the young man, who has proved his worth on several occasions, he can see that Evans is not cut out for life in London.

Sergeant Evans is clearly unhappy, and (in Cully's experience) an unhappy officer soon becomes a resentful one. His skills would be better utilised closer to home.

Cully gets up, brushing the last of the crumbs from his clothes, and consults his list.

"Right lad. Onward and upward. The Bible Believing Brotherhood of Bethel. Know anything about them? No, me neither, but I'm sure we will by the end of the day. And I bet we'll have a pamphlet or two to take away with us as well."

***

A dinner party is a serious matter. It should not to be entered into unadvisedly, lightly, or wantonly, but reverently, soberly and in the fear of God. Which is pretty much how Josiah Bulstrode and his sister Grizelda have gone about the preparations for their dinner party. Etiquette books have been consulted, recipes considered, caterers and florists obtained, table-waiting staff hired.

Now it is the actual evening of the dinner. In the kitchen, the finishing touches are being put to the meal. Soup is being salted, the sirloin is being garnished, and the hired staff are being harangued by the hired chef.

Upstairs in the parlour, Josiah (in rather tight evening dress and starched cravat) and Grizelda (in her new lilac creation, her hair freshly curled) sit nervously side by side on the overstuffed chintz sofa. They are awaiting the arrival of their guest, Mark Hawksley.

Belinda Kite sits to one side. She is dressed in the nicest of her purloined finery – an ivory satin gown, which she has painstakingly taken in at the seams, its original owner having had a tad more hip, and a tad less hooray than its current one. Her stomach is rumbling. It has been a long time since luncheon.

At 6.30 precisely, the front doorbell peals. Josiah shoots to his feet, to be restrained by Grizelda.

"Remember what the book said, brother: the servant will let him in and announce him."

Sure enough a few minutes later, the door is opened, the hired footman enters, and "Mr Mark Hawksley" is announced. He wears immaculate evening dress, tailor-made and fitting him like a glove.

A waft of delicious cologne emanates from him as he solemnly shakes Josiah's proffered fingers and bends low over Sissy's violet-gloved hand. He gives

Belinda a stiff little bow of acknowledgement (as befits her lowly status as companion), before seating himself in one of the easy chairs. He stretches out his hands to the welcoming fire.

"A cold night," he observes.

"Indeed so," Josiah agrees. "But here is warmth and good fellowship. We are delighted to welcome you at our table, are we not, Sissy?"

Grizelda Bulstrode picks at her gloves and smirks.

"And we are hoping that you will tell us all about your audience with our Noble Queen."

"I shall be deeply honoured to do so," Hawksley says solemnly.

The hired footman announces that dinner is served.

"Then let us dine," Bulstrode says, offering Belinda his arm.

Hawksley offers his arm to Grizelda and thus they proceed to the dining-room, where the table is set with ornate *épergnes* of hothouse flowers. Cut glass sparkles, candles flicker and shine, and the sideboard groans with silver-domed serving platters and steaming tureens.

Belinda is seated on Bulstrode's right. She slips off her gloves and slides the crisp linen napkin onto her lap. Looking up, she sees Hawksley watching her. His thin lips curve in a smile, his dark eyes send an unsaid compliment.

The soup is served. She sips daintily from her spoon, trying not to notice the slurping of her dinner companion, nor Griselda's nervous chinking of her spoon against her soup plate. Wine is poured. She lets the bitter bright red liquid fill her mouth, feeling its warmth sliding down her throat.

She takes no part in the conversation, which is all about stocks and shares, mines and minerals. Every now and then Bulstrode asks Grizelda for confirmation of something, or remarks that "of course, we can't expect the ladies to understand this, bless them."

Sherry is served, followed by the main course. Belinda picks up her knife and fork, cuts small pieces off the thick slices of meat, is helped to vegetables. A different wine is poured. Across the table, Hawksley tries to engage his dinner companion in conversation, responding to each answer as if Grizelda has uttered something incredibly witty.

Meanwhile Bulstrode attacks his dinner as if it is a foe that needs to be subdued and conquered. Nobody pays Belinda any attention. She is only the paid companion after all. She sips some more wine and wonders whether this is how dinner parties are meant to be.

Eventually, when mine host has scraped up the last drop of gravy, he turns to her and asks:

"Enjoying yourself, Miss Keet?"

Belinda rolls her emerald eyes up towards the ceiling.

"Oh, very much," she lies.

"I expect where you come from, they do these things somewhat differently eh?"

Belinda recalls the long unpolished dining-room table, the ferocious hierarchy of who sat nearest to the headmistress. The plain china plates and lumps of mutton congealing in their own fat. The way the rich girls' eyes would slide over her, pricing her much-mended clothes, the sneering expressions, the dismissive remarks uttered just loud enough for her to hear: *Oh, she's only the dancing-master's daughter.*

She smiles in a way that indicates whatever the recipient of the smile wishes to infer.

Bulstrode sets down his knife and fork with a clatter.

"Now then, Sissy, we can't let you monopolise Mr Hawksley for the whole evening, even though I'm sure he does not wish to tear himself away from your company, but Miss Keet and I want to hear all about Her Majesty."

Sissy smiles simperingly and looks coyly at Hawksley, who in return glances across the table, his glance flitting from Josiah to Belinda.

"Indeed, you do," he says. "Delightful as Miss Bulstrode undoubtedly is, it would be even more delightful to talk about our great Queen."

"Then go ahead, sir!" Josiah exclaims. "I for one cannot wait to hear you on the subject."

"But before I embark upon my experiences at Court, I have a very special proposal." Hawksley leans forward in his seat and lowers his voice. "It might be possible – for a certain sum, and only for a select few of your special business associates – that an audience could be arranged."

"With the Queen herself? In person?" Bulstrode gasps, his eyes round like saucers. "I read in the newspapers that she never goes out in public any more."

"She has been confined to Windsor Castle, it is true, but when she was told of her subjects' unhappiness at her long absence from public view, she declared that she might be prevailed upon to appear – only briefly – at a few select private functions. It was suggested that many of her loyal subjects do not have the immense honour to live close to her in London, and would very much appreciate a visit in their own part of the country."

"Like a Royal progress? I've read about them."

"Precisely. She has already favoured some of her subjects in the West Country with a brief private visit. I was fortunate to attend – she is the patron of my little enterprise after all – and it was a truly delightful occasion. I shall never forget it. Of course, it was only a very short visit, as she is still officially in deep mourning. And then, on the train back to London, I thought of you and your business contacts in the north."

Josiah's whole face is one big O of astonishment.

"You could arrange this?"

"Together, I'm sure we could bring it about," Hawksley says with a smile. Then he continues smoothly, "But let us save this conversation for later. For I am sure our two delightful dinner companions are far more interested in details of what the ladies were wearing on my visit."

He gives Bulstrode a knowing wink and embarks upon a lavish description of Court fashions.

Grizelda listens enraptured. Belinda frowns and plays with the fringe of her shawl. She recalls reading that the whole court had immediately gone into full mourning upon the death of the Prince Consort.

He is making it up, she thinks. Though he is doing it convincingly well.

Eventually dessert is served, accompanied by Madeira, after which Bulstrode rises, throwing his napkin onto the table.

"Now, Sissy and Miss Keet, you will have to excuse us gentlemen for a while. We have business matters to discuss in my study. Come, Mr Hawksley, if you please."

Hawksley bows, and follows Josiah out of the dining-room. Belinda feels her shoulders slump. The room seems suddenly empty without his presence, as if all the life has been sucked out of it. She takes tiny sips of her wine, savouring its sweetness. Across the table, Grizelda smiles to herself, pleating the edge of her napkin. They sit in silence for a while. Finally, she bursts out:

"Mr Hawksley is a very fine man do you not think?"

Belinda stares at Griselda's flushed cheeks, her rather overbright expression, recognising the combination of rather too much wine and rather too little self-awareness.

"Your brother seems to think so."

"Oh, Josiah is always a very good judge of character. As soon as he met … a certain person, he knew that he was not a good man."

"And wasn't he?" Belinda asks innocently.

"No, he was not!" Grizelda declares emphatically. "He was a cad and a bounder and a trifler with female affections. But I am not to think about him anymore," she adds. "Nor shall his name ever be uttered in this house."

Shame, Belinda thinks. These tiny, tantalising glimpses of the Unfortunate Incident only serve to whet her appetite for the whole tale.

"So, what does your brother think about Mr Hawksley?"

"That he is a good business man. A man after his own heart – I have heard him say as much."

"And you like him?"

Griselda's face turns bright pink. A colour that doesn't match her dress.

"Who could not like him? He is so handsome. Such a noble figure. Such fine brown eyes. And his manners are impeccable. He reminds me of Dorian Le Grange from *A Country Romance.* Does he not you?"

Not having read this worthy tome, Belinda cannot say. And despite agreeing with Griselda's description, she also senses something rather mysterious about Mr Mark Hawksley. There is more to him than meets the eye. Though what does meet the eye is certainly very agreeable.

"He is a pleasant gentleman," she replies, carefully keeping her voice and expression neutral.

Grizelda smiles foolishly.

"I think I shall just go upstairs and tidy my hair and change my cap," she says. "I will return before the gentlemen rejoin us."

Belinda Kite finishes her Madeira and indicates to the servant that she'd like a refill. Which she polishes off in record time. She is just contemplating a third glass when the door opens, and Mark Hawksley appears, wearing his street clothes. She gets (slightly unsteadily) to her feet.

"I came to bid you fair ladies adieu," he says, crossing the room. "I must leave. Business summons me, even at this late hour, and I cannot delay."

He stands so close that the scent of him fills her nostrils. She feels the heat from his body. Her heart thumps in her breast; her legs almost give way under her.

"What is it you desire, Miss Belinda Kite?" he murmurs, his dark brown eyes seeking and holding hers.

"Nothing."

He laughs softly, stretches out his hand and teases a curl of her hair with one finger.

She cannot move. She can barely breathe.

"Nothing? You lie. London is full of thousands and thousands of people, all wanting something. Want loves want. It is the human condition. It grows and breeds. Why should you or I be any different?"

She does not answer. She cannot answer. She doesn't have the words.

"Shall I tell you what I want, Miss Belinda Kite?" he whispers, bending so close that his face is almost touching hers, his breath warm upon her flushed cheek.

"Now then, Miss Keet," Josiah Bulstrode calls from the open-doored hallway, "don't keep our guest standing about. His cab is waiting in the street."

She hears heavy footsteps approaching.

Hawksley steps back hurriedly. Then he touches his top hat to her and walks quickly away.

Belinda Kite takes a long breath. Then another. She feels giddy, shaken. Barely has she time to gather her scattered wits when Grizelda comes flying down the stairs, eyes wild, cap askew.

"Oh no, where is he?" she wails. "I heard the front door close. Has he gone?"

"He has gone, Sissy. He has matters that require his attention. But we have agreed that he will be joining us shortly on a trip back up north. I am to write to Arkwright & Tambling to arrange a fine dinner at which Her Majesty will be present! You and I will be travelling by train with Mr Hawksley to attend the occasion. Now, what do you think of that?"

Sissy claps her hands in delight. Belinda Kite listens as Bulstrode outlines the proposed excursion. At no time is she invited to input into the conversation, which revolves around old acquaintances to be called upon, and the effect of Mark Hawksley's presence when they do.

Indeed, the initial phrase 'you and I' did not suggest the presence of a third person anyway. She presumes that she is to be left behind.

"By the time we return to London, well, who knows what may have transpired," Bulstrode says, giving his sister a significant wink. "A handsome young man, a beautiful young woman ... the right opportunities ... eh, Sissy?"

Grizelda blushes and lowers her eyelids.

"I'm sure I don't know what you mean, brother."

"Ah, but I bet Miss Keet does, though? You observed Mr Hawksley at dinner, did you not, Miss Keet? Did you ever see a man so smitten?"

Belinda stares straight ahead, unable to frame a

suitable response that does not involve out-and-out mendacity. Fortunately, Bulstrode is too far gone in his scheming to notice.

"I reckon by the time we return to London, there'll be a ring on your finger, Sis. Or at least the promise of one. You see if I'm not right. And Miss Keet will be dancing at your wedding in the Spring. Oh yes, she will. I'd put money on it. I would indeed."

***

Money is also the focus at The Gathering of The Select & Apocalyptic Brethren, taking place in its usual venue above the music publisher's shop in Soho.

Senior Prophet Xavier About, having warmed up the followers by a long verbal exegesis upon some of the more abstruse Levitical laws, has now moved on to his favourite topic: Sin and the City.

He stands on the temporarily-erected lectern, swaying to and fro as if moved by some internal gale. The followers (tonight minus the Jack Russell who is on ratcatching duties elsewhere) sit in rapt silence and watch him.

"Brothers and sisters, let it be known amongst you that I, the Lord's Servant, together with the Infant Prophet, have begun the good work to drive Iniquity from our midst. Yeah – even as The Lord did at Belshazzar's feast in the days of the Prophet Daniel, we have written upon the walls of the whores and concubines and the walls of the worshippers of gold and silver. We have declared Truth on the walls of the proclaimers of lies and the sellers of filth and depravity. They have been Weighed on the Scales and found Wanting."

"We saw the headlines in the papers," somebody interjects brightly from the back row.

About fixes his glittering dark eyes upon the commentator, and lowers his voice.

"Brother – do not say in this Holy Gathering of God's People that ye have succumbed to the vileness and wickedness that is sold on our streets every day?"

"Umm … I just saw it on a board … as I was passing by …. very quickly."

About's eyes narrow. He stares hard at the man. There is an awkward silence during which the congregation shuffles its feet and tries to look as if it is nothing whatsoever to do with the recalcitrant sinner.

About sighs, and switches his gaze to the Infant Prophet, who immediately pipes up in a shrill treble,

"Nobody shall drink wine from the goblets of the unrighteous. Nobody shall partake of the passions and pleasures of the lovers of the flesh. Nobody shall eat of the foods sacrificed to idols, for Lo! Is it not written?"

"It is written," the congregation intones, relieved to have found themselves shifted to safer ground.

"Brothers and Sisters in The Lord," About resumes, "do not be afraid. The Lord knows your deeds, your hard work and your perseverance. He knows you cannot tolerate Wickedness and that you WILL not grow weary."

He stands on tiptoes, surveying them from under his grizzled brows.

"Who will do The Lords' Work? Who will write what they have seen, what is now and what will take place later?"

"When you say 'writing' …" a man's voice pipes up cautiously, "you mean writing *Bible words*?"

About inclines his head.

"It's alright to write *Bible words* on things, is it?"

"If the Lord says so."

"What if we can't write the words quite properly? Some of them Bible words is awfully long and curly –

will The Lord punish us?"

About tries not to let his impatience show in his expression. They are after all his followers, even if some have never really mastered pen and ink and still sign their name with a letter X, which they probably spell wrong. They are his holy sheep – though many of them have about the same level of intelligence as a real one.

"The Lord will guide your hand, my Brother."

"Oh, that's alright then. Only I wouldn't want to upset Him. Didn't do much writing when I was growing up you see and …"

About cuts in quickly,

"The Lord commands us to write. Will. You. Write?"

A murmur of willingness runs round the gathering. Suddenly everyone wants to be a writer.

"Then go forth into the highways and byways of the Great Babylon. Arm yourselves with paints and brushes from Brother Murdoch's shop and let your words so appear before men that they may repent of their Wicked Ways. Be found Worthy of the Robe and Crown that awaits you in these Last Days, dear Brothers and Sisters. Be. Found. Worthy. Let us now seek Sanctification for our Great Endeavour."

About breathes in. Closes his eyes. Rocks backwards and forwards a few more times. The candles hiss and sputter. Somewhere in the distance a church clock strikes ten. The congregation sits, eyes closed, and waits for the Almighty to make further contact.

While the members of the congregation are thus preoccupied, let us take a moment to consider the small blond-curled white-clad phenomenon that is The Infant Prophet, currently picking his nose in the front row.

He is the son of Senior Prophet About – a late and unexpected addition to a household barren of offspring until he was born. However, the 'Infant' is actually a boy of some ten years, though his small stature, long blond curls and piping voice gives him the appearance of a child much younger than his actual age.

The Infant Prophet has led an unusual life. He was born to older parents who, at the time of his birth, rented rooms in Montague Place, near the entrance to the old Reading Room of the British Museum. His father worked as an engraver nearby.

Both saw his arrival as a miracle, and being of a religious persuasion (during the long pre-Infant period, the couple attended a small moderately normal chapel close to St Paul's), parallels were drawn to Abraham's wife Sarah, who also conceived a child when well past childbearing age.

The events that set the family's footsteps firmly on the visionary path were thus: One night the erstwhile engraver read the passage in the New Testament where the infant Christ informs his parents that He *must be about His Father's business.*

That night he dreamed he saw an Angel wearing white robes and carrying a flaming quill, who pointed to these very words carved in burning letters on a large rock. When he awoke, it was with the conviction that he had received a personal prophecy.

Henceforth, he informed his wife, over coffee and toast, his name would no longer be Millbank Tendring but Prophet About, as he had been commanded to be *about* His Father's business.

All this meant very little to the child, who grew up subject to the usual killer diseases of childhood, which he survived. However, change arrived one fateful day when he was four.

The boy was sitting on the floor, turning the pages of a picture book bought to teach him to read (a process that was proving fraught with difficulties), when he suddenly pointed to a picture and said in a piping treble: "God".

The picture was actually of a dog, but Prophet About immediately recognised this as a sign that the boy had been touched by the Finger of the Lord – the concept of word-blindness being completely unknown in 1856.

From that day onwards, the child became known as the Infant Prophet. His hair was never cut and he wore only white, evidencing to the outside world that he was a rare member of God's Chosen.

It took some dedication and ingenuity to kit out a small boy in white clothes in a city where sooty smoke covered most washing in grey smuts within minutes, but such was About's conviction of his son's holiness that it was achieved.

By the time he was eight, the Infant Prophet had absorbed by rote chunks of the more obscure books of the Bible and the Apocrypha, which at a given signal from his father, he could spout parrot-fashion and at random.

Sometimes he conflated different passages, but as the congregation's Bible knowledge ran the gamut from basic to non-existent, it only served to enhance his status.

Now, with the meeting ending and the flock dispersing to their various haunts, Senior Prophet About and the Infant Prophet lock up and make their way through the misty glimmering streets of the city.

"A *good* meeting," About declares, nodding sagely.

The Infant Prophet says nothing. He is thinking about the hot supper that will be waiting for them on their return. He hopes there will be fish and baked potatoes.

"I am relying on you to tell me what the Lord wants us to write, my son."

The Infant Prophet pulls a face which, luckily for

him, is hidden in the darkness. He knows, because it has been dinned into him from an early age, that God has chosen him. But the responsibility lies heavy on his young shoulders.

Sometimes, especially when he has to leave the house to perform an errand for his mother and in doing so encounters the jeers and catcalling of the local youth, he can't help wishing God would go and choose somebody else for a change.

***

Night wears on. Upstairs in her small Islington house, Marianne Corvid lies between her sheets waiting for the sleep that does not come. Instead, she passes through the familiar phases of sleeplessness known only to the true insomniac: the sly hallucinations, the endless settling of bones, the beating of her heart, so loud that it seems to fill the bed and resonate round the room. Her head feels empty, like a volute of a shell.

She loses all sense of time, hears the passing watchman call the hours as if on some other planet. She recalls kisses, words of rapture, a body hovering over hers. A touch that both consoled and devastated her. She strains to picture her lover, but although she can recollect individual features, the whole face eludes her.

For a space of seconds, she is left with nothing. Not awake, not asleep, but trapped in between. There has been no reply to her letter. To her several letters. The pain of rejection is raw, unhealed.

Eventually she rises, opens the shutters, letting in a slab of paler dark. She fumbles with the window catch, hears herself sobbing. She throws a cloak over her night-gown and goes downstairs into the small back garden.

London seems more beautiful at night. The best of it is lit and the worst is glamorised by darkness. It can also seem less dangerous, though this is a deception. The air is sweeter. The moonlight is kinder.

Once again, she experiences that small shock of being outside, the small hardening of whatever had softened, opened as she lay alone in her bed. She pulls her cloak about herself, breathes the cold air. The houses on either side are sleeping.

Marianne's mind is boiled down to the hardness of facts: her life has fallen away into itself without plot or premonition. Now she lives in the shadow of former pleasure. She digs her fingernails into the soft flesh at her wrist, greedily seeking the pain. She stares at the small red crescents, tears sliding down her cheeks like spilled wax.

***

Sunday morning. The din of the working week is dimmed. Shops are shut. Bells summon the faithful and the recalcitrant to worship. For Emily Cully, however, Sunday is just another working day. Here she is spreading woollen cloth on the clean parlour floor and laying a paper pattern upon it.

And here is Jack Cully in his shirtsleeves, released from police duties to act as pin-passer and wife-encourager, roles he is only too glad to take on.

"That's nice material," he observes. "I like the coloured green squares."

Emily Cully gives him that amused sideways glance of wives everywhere whose husbands are trying, thought not succeeding, to comment appropriately.

"It is very nice, dear. And the design is called tartan. It is Scottish and much favoured by our Queen."

"Oh? So now you're making dresses for Royalty. I

am impressed."

She smiles.

"It is for that new customer – the one I told you about. Miss Bulstrode is her name. She is currently visiting London with her brother. The dress is for a trip up North. It will be cold at this time of year, and I shall have to line it."

"Nobody better than you, Em," Cully says.

"She pays what I ask, and seems pleased with my work. That is the main thing. Although I shall have to work late to get the dress finished by Tuesday."

Emily Cully stands, holding her hand to the small of her back, where a niggling and persistent ache has started in the last few days. She decides not to mention it to Jack, who is carefully pinning the paper pattern to the material.

"You have done very well," she says gaily. "Should you decide to quit the Detective Police, I'm sure I could find you a job as a pattern-cutter."

Jack Cully sits back on his heels and grins.

"That will be the day Em, when men make dresses for ladies!"

They laugh, and she passes him the big cutting-out scissors, then goes quickly into the tiny back kitchen where a pot of stew is bubbling, before she is tempted to tell him about the ache.

No point in worrying unnecessarily. And she has so many commissions to fulfil. Business is booming. Married life is bliss. Sufficient unto the day. So Emily Cully stirs the stew and thinks instead about her husband and how much she loves him, and about the nice meal they will enjoy together later.

***

There is precious little love being shared at the

Undercroft dining table, although there is plenty of food. Husband and wife sit at opposite ends of the elegant oval rosewood table, given as a wedding present by her doting parents so long ago that it almost seems like a different era.

They are served. In silence. They eat. In silence. Or rather, she picks at her food, he moves it around on his plate peering at it suspiciously as he does so. It's Sunday, and his club is shut – as are the city watering holes that he likes to frequent.

This is the only reason Undercroft has joined his wife for an unpleasant family meal. Not for long. A few bites into the main course, the master of the house throws down his knife and fork with a loud clatter that makes Georgiana start, then swallow nervously.

"What is this muck we're eating?"

"It is curry. Cook got the recipe from Colonel Morton's Indian cook. It is what they eat in India."

Undercroft glares at his plate.

"Faugh! Filthy foreign food. Are you trying to poison me?"

There. It is said. The words hang in the air like birds of prey looking for a corpse to land on. Georgiana's mouth tightens into a hard line.

"If I was trying to poison you," she says, her voice clipped and harsh, "I would hardly be eating the same meal as you are."

Undercroft stares at her sullenly.

"What happened to you, eh? You used to be quite an attractive woman in your own way."

You happened to me, she thinks. Though, of course, she does not say it.

"If you do not like the food, I can always ask Cook to make you something else. An omelette, perhaps?"

Undercroft pushes back his chair. For a moment, the room spins around him and he feels his gorge rise. He grips on to the edge of the table to steady himself. Lately, he has been experiencing some worrying symptoms: his hands and feet feel numb, his limbs ache.

He has also lost his appetite. He puts it down to the stress of his current situation, where every mouthful of food eaten in his own home, *his own home* – might presage his painful demise.

"I'm going to my study to read. Tell the servants I don't want to be disturbed."

His wife watches him leave the room. She hears the key turn in the lock of the study door. Soon he will be flicking through his extensive collection of dirty books, looking at his pictures of women *en deshabille.*

She knows exactly what he keeps in his study. She knows where he keeps the spare key. She has been into his study while he was at work, or away with one of his whores.

She has seen the paintings and lithographs. Naked women in *classical poses.* Women with thinly-draped bodies lying on couches. Women with large breasts and ample open thighs.

She has also looked at the books that he keeps in a cabinet by his desk. Lurid tales of women who like having the sort of things done to them that have always utterly revolted her.

She also knows who introduced Frederick to the delights of this noxious stuff. And to the sluts he still patronises. For whom he forsook her bed so long ago. Her one consolation has been that Regina Osborne is in exactly the same position. And that she suffers doubly, as her son George also follows in his father's louche footsteps.

Undesired and unwanted, she finishes her meal and gives instructions to the servants. Suddenly unable to bear the proximity of her husband and the contents of his study a minute longer, she gets her coat and her bonnet and hurries out into the raw chill of the sooty Sunday afternoon.

Georgiana pulls her veil down over her face so that nobody recognises her. She walks towards the Heath, past the small box-pewed church of St John's Downshire Hill, where she used to go every Sunday morning and evening without fail in the early days of her marriage.

She no longer attends. God has not been kind to her, so she is repaying His unkindness by absenting herself from His house. She doubts that He cares either way.

She reaches the green fringes of the Heath. As it is a Sunday afternoon, there are lots of families out for a walk. Small children run by bowling hoops. At the crest of the hill, kites bob and duck in the nipping wind. Servant-girls, easily distinguished by their cheap finery, stroll arm in arm with their young men.

Everybody is part of a family or a couple. Everybody is happy and smiling. Only she is on her own. Alone. Unhappy. Georgiana Undercroft huddles her coat closer around herself and strides resolutely on, thinking bitter and vengeful thoughts.

***

A Monday morning in London. Sooty drizzle fills the air. Iron-shod wheels rattle over cobbles. Horses clop, drivers yell, costers shout. The sounds are thrown back by the narrow streets, so loud that it is impossible to hold a conversation.

The river Thames, that liquid coin that runs through the heart of the city, is alive with wherries and skiffs that bob and duck in the wake of larger vessels. There are hay boats, their lateen sails discoloured, coal barges and great lighters laden with bricks and ashes.

Swift, grimy steamboats chug upriver from Chelsea and Pimlico, their whistles screaming, their decks crammed with living freight, passing by oozy wharves and grim-chimneyed factories, by tumbledown waterfront pubs and vast warehouses.

Chimneys belch forth black smoke. There is the smell of gas, dung, dead dogs, decaying vegetables, ancient fish and dubious mutton pies all mixed with the smell of thousands of unwashed, unkempt human bodies slipping and sliding, scuffling and pushing their way along the slimy thoroughfare.

Look more closely. A man in his shirtsleeves wearing a floury apron, his sleeves rolled to the elbows, has just opened the door of his shop in Chalk Farm Road. His name is Alfred Turnock and he is a master baker. The sign above the door, written in very curly green and gold lettering, reads: *A & E Turnock, Bakers and Confectioners.*

There are glass shelves lined with paper doilies. At the moment, they are empty – except for two very elaborate white tiered wedding cakes, which are actually made out of plaster of Paris.

The wooden shelves behind the counter are also empty, though judging by the warm bread smells wafting out into the streets, they will not be for long. Alfred Turnock, who hails from Scotland, the great nursery of bakers, folds his hands under his apron, blinks and takes a deep lungful of foul air. He has been working all night, having risen from his bed at 3am because of the public demand for hot rolls at breakfast.

The bake-house is situated under the shop, and as a consequence is very dark. A low-ceilinged room, it is barely high enough for a man of five feet four inches to stand upright. There is no daylight, and the ventilation comes from a hatchway. There is a privy at the top of the stairs. Turnock's two journeymen bakers live on the premises in a small hot room adjoining the bake-house. They too have risen early and have been working ever since.

Now the journeymen bakers appear in the shop carrying trays of round loaves and rolls, all steaming hot. They start filling the shelves, and as if by magic cooks and kitchen staff from the adjoining streets materialise out of the sooty gloom to collect their orders.

Slightly less magically, Detective Inspector Stride and a constable also appear. Turnock folds his arms and regards them suspiciously – the default stance of most people faced by constabulary at practically any time of day.

"Nice smell," Stride says, sniffing the air appreciatively. "Mr Turnock, I presume? I am Detective Inspector Stride, from the Metropolitan Police based at Scotland Yard. I am here to ask you a few questions about some crimes we are investigating."

Turnock regards him balefully.

"Nothing criminal about my bread and cakes, Inspector. Nor my bakers."

"Indeed, I'm sure there isn't," Stride says smoothly. "However, the fact remains that two people have recently died as a result of eating poisoned cakes, and we are visiting all bakeries in the area to ask whether there have been any complaints from customers about cakes they've bought from you in the past few weeks."

Turnock shakes his head.

"No complaints at all. Poison cakes? I can't see why anybody would want to poison cakes."

Stride has a copper's view of humanity. Never say that people wouldn't do something, no matter how strange it was.

"It may not be the cakes – we are also considering the possibility that a batch of flour may have been contaminated."

"All the flour we use comes from reputable mills."

Stride digs in his pocket and shows the baker the list of cakes.

"Do you sell any of these?"

"We do." Turnock says. "What of it?"

Stride pauses and regards him thoughtfully.

"I don't suppose you recall anybody coming in recently on two separate occasions to buy boxes of cakes? Or to order cakes to be posted to two local families?"

Turnock shrugs.

"You'd have to ask one of the girls who serve in the shop. I don't deal directly with the paying customers. But we don't send cakes through the post, we deliver ourselves. See the sign in the window: *Hand delivery available.* And now, if you'll excuse me, I see my delivery boys have arrived and I have orders to get ready."

He turns and goes back into his shop, leaving Stride and his list and his constable on the pavement. The constable stares hungrily at the shop window, now being filled with newly-baked loaves and rolls. It has been a long time since he breakfasted, and his landlady is not over-generous with the food to begin with.

"If it's alright with you sir, I might just slip inside and buy myself a hot roll."

Stride regards the constant appetite of the younger members of the constabulary as a source of wonder. He is sure he didn't stop to eat as much as his beat constables do.

"Go ahead," he says. "And while you're at it, you can hang around until the counter staff get in and engage some of them in conversation. See if they have heard any complaints about the cakes. Or can remember anybody coming in to buy two boxes of cakes in the past few weeks."

Stride knows he is grasping at straws, but right now, straws are all that he has.

A very pretty servant girl saunters slowly past, her basket carried at a jaunty angle. She eyes up the young constable, giving him a look that brings a blush to his face.

"As you wish, sir," he says happily, and hurries after her.

***

Meanwhile Belinda Kite sits at her bedroom window daydreaming. The house is quiet. Grizelda is sorting through her clothes in preparation for the trip north, and Josiah is writing post-prandial letters. Belinda stares into her mirror, looking and longing, her daydream a series of emotions and sensations.

Since the dinner party, she spends more and more time in this pleasure-filled imaginary world, and as a result is becoming more and more dissatisfied with the limitations and imperfections of her real life. She runs the tips of her fingers gently down the soft skin of her throat and across the slender collarbones.

In her mind, of course, it is not her own fingers but those of Mark Hawksley that gently caress her neck. But the fantasy, with all its imagined scenarios – however pleasurable – always leaves her trembling in a state of unsatisfied longing, and brings in its wake a disillusionment as reality intervenes once more.

Which it does, in the shape of Grizelda, who suddenly knocks at her door, requesting that Belinda join her in her bedroom to consider and advise on matters of finery. Reluctantly, Belinda tears herself away from Hawksley's imaginary embrace and follows Grizelda along the corridor.

Belinda has never set foot in her employer's bedroom, and is surprised to find how light and pleasant it is. And how full of clothes. On the bed are strewn jewel-bright dresses and skirts and bodices in all the colours of the rainbow.

More dresses hang from the wardrobe doors. Gloves and lace collars spill from open boxes on the chair and the dressing table. It is a veritable cornucopia of fashion.

Belinda stands in the doorway, feasting her eyes upon the richness spread before her, unable to believe that a plain unattractive young woman like Grizelda Bulstrode could possibly possess so many beautiful dresses.

"My brother likes to spoil me," Grizelda smirks, seeing Belinda's amazed expression. "Particularly after the Unfortunate Incident, when I was so low in spirits. He has bought me almost a dress a week."

"He is very generous indeed."

"Oh, he is a kind dutiful brother and has always looked after me from the time we were children. But until I came to London, I did not know about *ton* and colour," Grizelda continues. "The dressmaker here has opened my eyes to the importance of these things."

She gestures towards a turquoise blue light wool dress with a low-necked tight bodice, black velvet ribboned seaming and lace inserts.

"I cannot believe I was ever so foolish as to wear this colour. Do you not think it strange?"

Belinda Kite stares hungrily at the dress, drinking in its cerulean perfection, while secretly thinking how wonderfully it would suit her. She imagines her creamy shoulders rising out of the frothy black lace, her tiny waist accentuated by the cunning boning of the bodice.

"It is still a very pretty dress."

Grizelda shakes her head.

"It must go. And so must this ... and this," she declares firmly, picking up dress after lovely dress. "I really have far too many clothes and most of them are the wrong colour. So, while I am away, I'd like you to arrange for all these dresses to be disposed of. I shan't wear them again. I am sure Mrs Cully the dressmaker will know people who might buy them. Or perhaps they could go to some deserving charity."

Belinda Kite has never known the concept of 'too many clothes' in her life. She decides she will bypass Mrs Cully and deal with the dress disposal herself. Given that the most deserving charity she knows is The Belinda Kite Clothing Fund.

"It shall be done," she says meekly.

Grizelda opens her jewel case and lifts out the top trays.

"Now, Miss Kite, what jewels should I take with me? My brother has secured me a seat at the top table for the royal banquet."

She holds up a diamond necklace, turning it in her thin-boned hand.

"This – do you think? Or the pearls?"

The diamonds wink and glitter, and Belinda Kite's mouth waters. One day, she promises herself, she will possess diamonds even finer than these. She will wear them every day. She will probably never take them off – even to bathe.

"I think that diamonds always set off a dress well," she replies. "And you will be in the presence of the Queen."

"Then it shall be diamonds. You have French taste so you know what is stylish to wear. And I want to look my best for ..." she pauses, looks away, a dark blush suffusing her wan complexion.

Belinda pinches her lips together. After the dinner party, she has absolutely no doubt that Mark Hawksley is not in love with, nor even remotely attracted to, Grizelda Bulstrode. But she has money and a rich indulgent brother, and that counts for everything in this materialistic world.

"I hope the visit turns out as you expect." she says evenly. "When do you leave?"

Grizelda begins to separate the items ready for the maid to pack them.

"Tomorrow after luncheon. We shall return in a week's time, and just imagine, when I return, I will have seen the Queen! What a lot I shall have to tell you about."

"How wonderful. I cannot wait to hear it."

Grizelda pauses, glances at her quizzically as if the idea has only just occurred to her,

"What will you do while we are away, Miss Kite?"

"Oh … I'm sure I shall find plenty to do."

"Good. I shall leave you out some of my new novels – I'm sure you are dying to read them."

Belinda rolls her eyes.

"Oh, that is too good of you."

"You will need something to occupy your time. I cannot imagine not being able to go out and about."

Belinda bites her lip. It was only a short while ago that she was having to force a reluctant Sissy to leave the house. Now she is willingly gallivanting off on a train. Belinda Kite, however, has no intention of remaining indoors. She has seen plenty of young women on their own without a chaperone in attendance. She is going to make the most of her employers' absence to explore London, especially the retail end.

Grizelda places the final item on her 'to pack' pile.

"There, it is done. Just my new tartan dress to be delivered tomorrow morning. Come, Miss Kite, let us go down and find my brother. I am eager to hear all the details of our trip – as no doubt are you."

***

At the Golden Cross Hotel, Mark Hawksley and his two companions have supped well. Now, chairs pushed back from the table and with glasses of fine brandy before them, they puff their cigars and contemplate their good fortune – most of which lies in a cash box under Hawksley's bed.

"How is Queenie tonight?" Hawksley inquires.

"She is fine. She has dined and gone to bed. I have told her she has a long train journey tomorrow and must prepare herself for it," Ginster says.

"She is a marvel," Pyle grins. "All this time and she has not put a foot wrong."

"It helps that she is mute," Ginster says. "Her silence and her face are her greatest attributes. And our good fortune also."

"Quite. Can you imagine if she ever opened her mouth? What foul washerwoman slang would issue forth? The game would be up for sure."

Hawksley smiles thinly.

"But that will not happen. And she is being well-paid for her silence. She was earning nothing in the workhouse laundry where you found her."

"What will you do when you've finished with her?" Pyle asks.

"She will be released from her arduous Royal duties with an ample sum, do not worry," Hawksley says. "Enough to live on – if she is frugal. And of course, as she cannot read or write, she will not be able to tell her story."

He raises his brandy glass.

"Gentlemen, let us drink to a foolproof enterprise."

Later, when his companions have departed with

three train tickets and their instructions, Hawksley steps out onto the pavement at the front of the hotel for a few breaths of air before he retires.

Dusk has fallen. He watches a lamplighter prop his ladder against a lamp. The man ascends the ladder, reaching into the glass head with a taper. There is the blossoming of yellow light, followed by a descent back down to the dark street.

Hawksley finishes his cigar, throws the end into the street and looks up into the patchy sky. There is a new moon tonight. He turns the coins in his pocket for good luck before going back into the hotel and up to bed.

***

Jack Cully is making his way to work in the smoggy foggy dawn of a cold October day.

He has left Emily putting the last finishing touches into the green tartan dress. She has been up most of the night sewing it.

Cully is always astonished at the speed at which his wife works. The tiny steel needle seems to flash in and out of the fabric like lightning. He loves the way she bends down to bite off the thread, her hair parting at the back to reveal the soft nape of her neck.

Jack Cully is a man in love. Shortly he will be a man in despair, but for now let us leave him thinking fond thoughts, and progress ahead of him to Scotland Yard and to Detective Inspector Stride's office, where a selection of the morning papers has been delivered and perused.

Beyond Stride's door the office is now full of outrage and obloquy, the Anxious Bench is full of anger and apoplexy, the corridors are full of carping and complaining, and Stride has barricaded himself in his office for his own safety.

By the time Jack Cully, who has stopped at a coffee stall to refresh himself, arrives at Scotland Yard, the scene that meets his eyes could best be summarised as uproar.

"What's happened?" Cully mouths at the desk sergeant, who is being besieged on all sides by irate individuals with voices to match.

"Another of those red paint attacks overnight. Surprised you didn't see the headlines on a newsagent board on your way in."

I probably did, Cully thinks. But I was too busy thinking about Emily and how tired she looked this morning.

Cully elbows his way through the assembled indignant and bangs on Stride's door.

"It's Jack Cully. Let me in!"

Stride opens the door a crack. Cully slips in, pushing back a couple of burly men who are trying to enter with him. Silently, Stride hands him the copy of *The Inquirer*. Cully stares at the banner headlines:

PALACE OUTRAGE! PAINT ATTACK on QUEEN & COUNTRY!

ANARCHY is TAKING OVER while POLICE do NOTHING!!

"Some railings opposite the palace have been painted red," Stride tells him gloomily. "And a notice has been affixed. Every other front page says the same thing – with variants. It seems we didn't take this paint business seriously enough."

Jack Cully, who has just spent two mind-numbing days going round a variety of small crackpot religious sects, thinks the whole business was taken pretty seriously. At least by him and Sergeant Evans. And he has the pamphlets to prove it.

"What did they write?" he asks.

"Woe unto you, Rulers of this World for You will all Perish."

"It's hardly high treason. Is it?"

"Writing words from the Bible on someone's wall is certainly not treason. Stupid maybe. Vandalism, certainly. Trouble is, it's the wrong wall and the wrong time to do it. The Queen's retired to Windsor and she's not being seen in public for nearly a year. So naturally people are getting jittery. There are already rumours that she has gone mad, or that she has died or even left the country. And now this happens. Fuel to the fire. You saw the mob out there. Half of them agree with what's been written. Half of them are baying for blood."

Stride glares at the newspapers.

"And of course, they are all looking for someone to blame. Damn these journalists – liars and thieves would be a better title. Now we are going to have to put out extra night patrols just to catch a couple of religious fanatics with a misguided mission and a pot of paint. I sometimes wonder who is driving the forces of law and order – us or the bloody hacks."

"Shall I organise a rota?"

"Do. And you might inform our good citizenry out there that the matter *is* being dealt with, and that they should *not* believe everything they read in the gutter press."

Cully turns and walks to the door, pausing on the threshold.

"I had a thought about the poisoned cakes."

Stride looks up.

"Ah. I'd almost run out of ideas on that case. Go on."

"We have assumed that the cakes have been locally

bought, as they were so fresh. But apart from one shop, where they vaguely remember a woman in a veil and a black bonnet with a white lining who could have chosen two boxes of cakes on two recent occasions, we haven't got any further. So, I was wondering whether we should switch our search and look for who might have purchased the arsenic."

"Well done, Jack," Stride says. "They would have to sign a register. And they'd have to give a reason for the purchase – not that anybody's going to say they're buying arsenic to poison someone. If we can find someone who recently bought arsenic and then see if that same person also bought the cakes, we will be getting somewhere."

Stride's face brightens.

"I'll get a message sent round to Marylebone. Some of their day constables can start making inquiries." He gestures towards the growing hubbub just beyond the door. "Politics, Jack. Almost as toxic as arsenic."

"I'll see if I can calm things down out there," Cully says reassuringly.

"Good, you do that." Stride growls, retreating behind his desk.

An investigation into what was a case of minor vandalism has now suddenly broadened and got more complicated. Stride didn't like broadened and he hated complicated.

***

A short while later Emily Cully and a large wicker basket catch an omnibus heading into central London. She secures an inside seat and, after paying her fare, gets off opposite the imposing British Museum building. But she has not come to see the exhibits, nor does she have a ticket to the Reading Room.

Instead she heads for the quieter streets of Bloomsbury, and a white stuccoed terraced house in Cartwright Gardens. Here all is hustle and bustle. Trunks and hatboxes are piled up on the pavement. They are being guarded by two servants who are in turn being guarded by Josiah Bulstrode. He greets Emily with relief.

"Ah, there you are, Mrs .... And not before time. My sister has been fretting all morning about her new dress. Another five minutes and we would be away!"

"I am so sorry," Emily says. "It took me slightly longer than I anticipated to finish the skirt linings."

"Never mind, you are here now," Josiah says, stepping up to the open front door. He calls, "Sissy, your dress has finally arrived."

Grizelda Bulstrode darts out of the house, her hair escaping from its pins. She fixes her eyes upon the basket.

"Oh – at last! But I haven't had time to try it on."

"And nor can you – see, here is Mr Hawksley's cab just turning the corner. We must be gone if we are to make the station in time."

"I am sure the dress will fit," Emily says reassuringly. "I made it to the same measurements as the other."

"Yes ... but ... I ... oh," Sissy's words trail away as Mark Hawksley, handsome and dashing in a layered travelling cape and new top hat, steps down from the cab and sweeps them an elegant bow.

"I trust you are all ready, my dear friends?"

"We certainly are," Bulstrode says, snapping his fingers at the waiting servants. "Now, Jemima, look sharp and stow those hat boxes inside. John – the trunks to go on the back."

As the servants hurry to carry out Bulstrode's orders, Hawksley glances inquiringly over Sissy's shoulder.

"Is Miss Kite not joining us?"

"Oh no," Josiah tells him. "We have no need of her. Sissy has friends enough back home to accompany her wherever she wishes to go. Miss Kite will remain here. Someone has to mind the house and make sure the servants don't run off with the silver, eh?"

Hawksley's face betrays nothing. He helps Sissy into the carriage, then stands back as Josiah scrambles aboard and takes his place. Just before he joins them, he turns and glances briefly back at the house. Belinda Kite stands in the bow window.

For a moment, their eyes meet. Hawksley nods, touches his hat and smiles, but she just stares back at him and does not return his smile. Then the coachman gathers the reins together and the carriage starts forward. Josiah leans out of the half window.

"Hurry up now, Mr Hawksley, or we shall miss our train. We must not keep the Queen waiting!"

"No, indeed," Mark Hawksley murmurs. His mouth curves into a secret smile. "It is never a good thing to keep any lady waiting."

He swings himself agilely on board. The carriage bowls along the street, and disappears in the direction of King's Cross station.

As soon as it has gone, Belinda Kite emerges from the house with a piece of folded paper.

"Here," she says, handing the paper to Emily Cully. "This is the rest of the payment for the dress."

She does not mention the other dresses that Sissy has left piled on the bed. Why should she? She has no intention of handing them over to Emily. By the time the Bulstrodes return, the dresses will have been disposed of, as Sissy instructed. All but a couple. And the money for their disposal will be in Belinda Kite's pocket book.

But that is for another day. Now, Belinda Kite puts

on one of Sissy's nice bonnets, wraps herself in her prettiest shawl, and sets off to explore London. She heads towards the sights and delights of the shops, only pausing on the way to fortify herself with a cream cake from a confectioner's shop.

She walks up the steep hill leading from the vibrant commercial district of Holborn to the exciting tempting West End department stores. She passes houses covered with signboards, and shops with plate glass windows.

Itinerant street-sellers throng the pavements, omnibuses rush to and fro in the centre of the road. Carriage wheels, horses, and the voices of busy crowds all fill the air with a bewildering noise.

A pretty woman walking on her own always elicits admiration, and Belinda has not gone far before her bright eyes and saucy face begin to attract male attention. As she pauses before a print-shop to admire the beautiful engravings, a handsome young man with gold chain and moustaches also takes his station beside her.

Belinda stands absorbed and captivated by the visual images, her mind full of vague desires and romantic thoughts, until she becomes aware of a hand slowly inserting itself into her skirt pocket where her purse is kept.

Without a second's hesitation, she whirls round, eyes blazing, her gloved hand striking the stranger's cheek with a force that makes him stagger back. Suddenly faced by a spitting little hellcat instead of a helpless female, her would-be pickpocket turns and makes off empty-handed.

Absorbing the useful lesson that it is not wise to linger in front of shop windows, Belinda resumes her walk. She recalls the dormitory battles where she acquired her fighting skills, defending her father's name or protecting her own few possessions from the incursions of other girls. Her hard-won ability to stand up for herself had just stood her in good stead.

She reaches Oxford Street and pauses to catch her breath in front of a shop selling ribbons and laces. The bright rainbow window display entices her in and she buys a length of turquoise satin ribbon the exact match of the dress now hanging in her wardrobe.

Tucking her little parcel into her bag she walks on, her thoughts turning to her employers. Josiah is awkward and clumsy, and Sissy is not somebody whose company she would ever voluntarily seek out, but they are kind people and there is no guile or nastiness in them. Belinda Kite is very good at recognising guile and nastiness – heaven knows, she has had enough experience of both in her recent past.

But the truth must be faced: she is unlikely to remain at Cartwright Gardens for much longer. Even if Sissy comes back an engaged woman (something Belinda very much doubts), her time as Sissy's companion is drawing to a close. She has outlived her usefulness, and she senses it.

New pastures beckon. New horizons are about to open up before her. Where they will lead her is, as yet unknown, but Belinda is not worried. She has beauty, a quick wit and at least four nice dresses. She cannot fail.

***

Failure is also the topic of conversation in the dark-wood-panelled smoking-room of Boodles, a gentlemen's club in St James's Street. Having dined on saddle of mutton followed by the famous Boodles orange fool, Undercroft and Osborne are now sprawled in red leather armchairs, cigars on the go. A small rosewood table contains two brandy glasses and a jug of water on a silver tray.

Boodles is appreciated by its exclusive membership as a pleasant retreat from the world's worries. Behind mullioned windows and heavy curtains, a gentleman can relax and unwind. Out there, vulgar mankind; in here, Boodles. Most appreciated also, is the absence of womankind, especially the matrimonial variety.

Undercroft has taken to dining at Boodles whenever he can. Occasionally he invites one of his female friends to dine somewhere else equally discreet, but even these occasions are becoming fewer, because for some reason the delights of post-prandial coupling are failing to live up to expectations.

The word *up*, not to mince matters, is at the crux of it. Undercroft has always prided himself on his ability to perform between the sheets. No woman, other than the one he is married to, has ever complained, nor demonstrated anything less than gasping and groaning gratitude.

Yet on two recent occasions he has been unable even to reach the foothills, let alone mount to the heights. A humiliating and degrading experience, made worse by the understanding commiseration of his female companion.

That he, Frederick Undercroft, connoisseur of the female form, possessor of erotic prints and pornographic books galore, can no longer function as a true man, is the shameful secret he carries around inside his head, his thoughts knocking against it like a bruise.

"See that red paint buggah's been at it again," Osborne remarks, from behind a newspaper. "Bloody police force couldn't catch a cold. Don't know why we bother paying all that money. Call out the regular army. They'll soon catch the blighters. And know what to do with them. World's going to pot."

He lowers the newspaper and leans forward. "So, what's your take on our little business?"

"What little business?" Undercroft is caught off guard.

"The cakes, man. What's the matter with you? Barely ate your dinner. Face the colour of candle wax. Not said a word since we sat down."

Undercroft eyes his companion sourly. Osborne is a big fleshy man with a high colour, oiled hair and waxed moustaches. His tailored suit strains across his ample stomach.

And yet once we were both young and gay, he thinks.

"I'm fine," he lies. "Bit seedy, but nothing to complain about."

"Could have fooled me. That detective chappie Slide or whatever he calls himself been to see you?"

"Not recently."

"Came around asking if I could think of anyone who disliked me." Osborne laughs harshly. "Felt like saying: apart from the wife, nobody I can think of."

Undercroft attempts a weak smile. His only consolation in his long and loveless marriage is that at least he didn't choose Regina Osborne to be his consort. The thought of seeing her hard slab of a face on the pillow next to him, and hearing her scolding tongue night after night, is enough to shrivel his manhood. Even further.

"Oh well. Nothing else has arrived in the post, so maybe that's an end to it, whatever it was, do you think?" he says.

"One of those mad people. Lot of them about nowadays. Lucky it was only a couple of servants, eh?"

Osborne throws the end of his cigar into the fire and sits back.

"Now, how's that little widow you were seein' a

while back? Seemed pretty smitten on you, by the sound of it."

Undercroft's mind throws up a picture of Marianne Corvid, her eyes too bright and snatching, her smile too quick and eager, her body too pliant and willing. He should never have let things get as far as they did. Mixing business with pleasure was always a recipe for disaster.

At least she'd stopped writing those desperate pleading letters to his chambers. And he hadn't seen her hanging around outside for some time, nor had she tried to accost him in the street, so it appeared that she'd finally got the message.

"Oh, she's gone and bagged herself a rich widower," he says, waving his hand airily.

"Women, eh. Don't know the meanin' of loyalty. Like cats. Over the garden wall as soon as you turn your back."

Undercroft cannot imagine Regina or Georgiana as cats. Harpies, yes, but not cats.

Osborne levers himself with difficulty from the deep recesses of the armchair and belches loudly.

"Well, time to go. Business calls. Oh – meant to tip you the nod, been put onto a nice little thing by that boy of mine – the Dominion Diamond Mining Company. You heard of it?"

Undercroft shakes his head.

"Young man from South Africa reopening his father's old mine. George met him in some club or other when he was in town recently. Nice chap. They got on like a house on fire. The mine's stuffed with the sparklers, apparently. We've both bought shares. Going to make us a lot of money. You want the details?"

Undercroft's head is beginning to throb with a persistent pulse, as if someone is forcing a pile-driver across his temple. He feels sick and dizzy.

"I'll think about it."

Osborne stares down at him. "You do that. And get some fresh air, for God's sake. You look like death warmed up."

He waddles towards the smoking-room door, grunting amiably at a few other members as he passes them by. Undercroft closes his eyes. The room continues to spin. The throbbing continues to throb.

Frederick Undercroft, lawyer, will be found many hours later by the staff who will discreetly wake him, and escort him to the door. He will have no recollection of anything prior to his departure.

***

It is three days since the Bulstrodes left London, and here is Belinda Kite relishing a breakfast of toast, coffee, scrambled eggs and her own company. She has never had the luxury of a dining-room to herself, nor the opportunity to eat as much as she wants.

She is wearing a very becoming ivory silk wrapper, which she discovered at the bottom of Sissy's chest of drawers. She has made the assumption that, since it was still in its tissue paper, the original owner did not intend to use it, so she has liberated it in a better cause.

Sunshine streams through the muslin curtains, promising a fine late Autumn day. Belinda signals to the maid for more coffee. Breakfasting *en deshabille* is also a novelty. She smiles to herself, imagining that this is her house, these are her servants, that she is employer not employed.

Soon, she tells herself, she will be dressed by her lady's maid in one of her many lovely handmade dresses before sallying forth for a little light shopping. Then she will meet a handsome (but unspecified) gentleman for luncheon at a nice restaurant.

Her daydream is interrupted by the parlour maid, who enters with a letter.

"This just came for you, miss."

Belinda recognises the large sloping handwriting of Josiah Bulstrode, and guesses that the contents will enlighten her as to their return. She picks up the butter-knife and slits open the envelope.

*Dear Miss Kite (*she reads*),*

I take up my pen to tell you that we are have having a wonderful time here. It has been good to meet up with old friends once again and we have been welcomed back. Everybody has asked about our London trip and I have told them all about the daughter of a French Marquis who has been a tower of strength to my poor sister.

Last night Sissy and I attended a grand banquet at the Town Hall. So many people were there – not as stylishly turned out as London folk, but none the worse for that.

Mr Hawksley gave a fine speech, after which everyone clapped. Dinner was turtle soup, fish, roast lamb and syllabub. How you would have smiled to see Sissy in her new tartan dress. She was the belle of the ball – though of course it was not a ball, only a grand dinner. Everybody remarked how fine she looked and how she had come on since her trip to London. She sat next to Mr Hawksley and it was plain that he as well as several other gentlemen admired her pretty face and sweet disposition very much.

Now I must tell you about the most exciting part of the evening. During the dessert course, a curtain was drawn back and there seated on a gold chair was Her Majesty Queen Victoria. She was dressed in black, and she wore a widow's cap, but her face was very comely and she nodded to the company.

I cannot tell you the effect of seeing Our Dear Queen seated in the town hall, just like an ordinary person – only of course she is not exactly ordinary. People stood and cheered. The gentlemen swept off their hats and we all sang Rule Britannia.

Queen Victoria waved graciously and then the curtain was drawn back. I am not ashamed to say that my heart swelled with pride and I shed a tear or two, indeed I did. I was not the only one. Such an honour and worth every guinea – not that one can measure honour in pounds, shillings and pence.

Sissy and I have decided to stay on for a couple more days. Mr Hawksley has expressed a desire to see some of our beautiful northern countryside, so we will not be back in London until the middle of next week.

We trust you are keeping in good health and with that wish,

We sign ourselves,

Josiah and Grizelda Bulstrode

Belinda sets down the letter and finishes her breakfast. Six lovely days stretch ahead of her, to be filled with whatever she wants to do and wherever she wants to go. She crumples her napkin, tosses it onto the table and rises to her feet. No point wasting a single minute. The sun is shining and the great city awaits.

***

As Belinda Kite sets out to explore the pleasures of London, Detective Inspector Stride and Detective Sergeant Cully push open the door of a busy chemist's shop in Hampstead.

Facing them and running the length of the shop is a low wooden cabinet with tiers of drawers labelled in a language that could be double-Dutch for all they understand it.

China jars containing unguents and oils sit atop the cabinet. The counter has a large ledger, a quill and inkwell and brass scales and weights. There are also a couple of big glass-stoppered bottles containing bright red and blue liquids.

Behind the counter stands a locked glass cabinet containing bottles of poison and other dangerous drugs. Beside it stands the chemist himself, a small balding man with a drooping moustache and a small unhappy face.

He wears a *pince-nez*, and a worried frown – the latter evinced by the entrance of two official-looking strangers who have clearly not come about a headache or a sick family member.

"Good morning, gentlemen," he says cautiously, shifting nervously from one foot to another.

Stride introduces himself and Cully, then explains the reason for their visit.

"We should like to see your poison book, if you would be so kind."

The chemist pushes the ledger across the counter.

"You are welcome to take a look, gentlemen. I obey the law. To the letter. You will find nothing amiss between these pages."

Stride scans the neatly-written entries, turning back the pages to see whether there are any for the purchase of arsenic just prior to the two murders.

"Can you tell me about this entry?" he asks, rotating the book so that it faces the chemist.

"Ah, that would be Mrs Marks. A perfectly respectable lady who lives in Flask Walk. She owns a teashop."

"You know her?"

"Indeed. My wife and I have patronised her establishment on several occasions. Mrs Marks makes exceedingly good cakes."

Stride consults his notes.

"She bought some arsenic, apparently to poison rats. The date of purchase is a few days before the deliveries of the boxes of poisoned cakes. Quite a coincidence, I'd say. Do you recall the purchase?"

"I'm afraid I don't, Inspector. I was away from the shop at the time – I am sometimes called upon to lecture to medical students on the toxicity and efficacy of drugs. At the time the purchase was made, I was in Edinburgh and the shop was being looked after by my assistant."

Stride picks up the poisons book.

"With your permission, I'd like to borrow this book for a few hours. My sergeant will return it as soon as we have finished with it. I bid you good day."

Stride spins on his heel and marches out of the shop, the poisons book tucked firmly under his arm.

"Now we're finally getting somewhere," he says when he and Cully reach the street. "I think a visit to this Mrs Marks is called for. Poison and cakes? It can't be a coincidence. Especially as she lives just a stone's throw away from one of the victims. Let's go and see what the good lady has to say. I shall be most interested to hear her explanation."

***

Meanwhile Belinda Kite makes her way down Oxford Street, slipping in and out of the crowd until she reaches the famous Pantheon bazaar. She has read about it in the newspapers. Now she is here to sample its delights for herself.

Reaching the colonnaded entrance, she is bowed inside by the whiskered doorman in his gold-laced hat and fine livery. Belinda looks round. She is in heaven.

So many pretty things: flowers, laces, shawls, parasols, papier-mâché trifles for the table, children's dresses and toys. It is like entering fairyland.

Belinda strolls round enjoying the lovely things until her eyes are tired of feasting upon such abundance. And just when exhaustion is setting in, here is the conservatory waiting to welcome her, with tea and arrowroot cakes and a cascading fountain with gold and silver fish and exotic plants and colourful flowers.

She sits on a comfortable chair right at the centre, directly under the glass-roofed ceiling, watching elegantly-dressed young women flitting to and fro, marvelling at the brightly-coloured parrots and cockatoos that sit on perches around the clear fountain.

It is a relief to be on her own, not having to make stilted conversation with Sissy, nor watching enviously while her employer flits from stall to stall, buying fripperies and fineries that Belinda cannot afford.

As far as the well-dressed young ones know, she could be one of them, rich, pampered, with a carriage waiting outside to transport her back to one of the beautiful big white houses that fringe the Park.

But, sadly, all good things must come to an end. Finishing her cakes, she pays at the counter and quits the bazaar, picking up a cab outside. In a short while, she is back at Cartwright Gardens, inserting her key into the lock once more, and fairyland is fading to a delicious memory.

Belinda steps over the threshold and is just preparing to untie her bonnet when she sees another letter on the silver dish on the hall table. It is addressed to her, but this time in a hand she does not recognise. She tears it open and reads:

Dear Miss Kite,
Finding myself unexpectedly back in London for a

couple of days, I take the liberty of writing to ask whether you would care to join me for tea and cakes this afternoon at 4 o'clock?

I am sure you are extremely eager to hear all about the visit of the Queen and I shall be delighted to enlighten you. I will send a cab to collect you at 3.30.

I look forward to meeting you once again.

Yours sincerely,

Mark Hawksley

For a moment, Belinda just stares at the letter, as if unable to take in its contents. Then she checks the time and hurries to the top of the kitchen stairs. She requires hot water, clean towels, and a servant to brush and press the turquoise dress. There is no time to waste.

***

The Lily Lounge is awash with the usual lunchtime patrons when Stride and Cully pitch up. Ladies wearing fashionable bonnets and surrounded by parcels are tucking in to their food or discussing the menu. An older man and his younger female companion sit at a discreet corner table, trying to look as if they are a married couple.

Stride is approached by one of the pretty waitresses, to whom he relays the information that he is from Scotland Yard and he would like to see Mrs Marks, if it is at all possible, thank you very much for your co-operation.

She disappears behind the counter. They wait, trying to keep out of the way of the serving staff who hurry back and forth, carrying trays of sandwiches, cut pork pies and pots of tea. Cully tries not to focus on the delicious food whizzing by under his nose. It has been a long time since he breakfasted.

Eventually the girl reappears with the information that Mrs Marks is initiating the new girl into the way to carve ham, but will be with them shortly. She shows them to a vacant table and invites them to peruse the menu.

"Nice selection of sandwiches," Cully remarks.

"We're not here to sample the fare, we are here to see ... Ah, I think this is her."

Stride breaks off as a tall woman with dark eyes, luxuriant black hair and an hourglass figure approaches their table.

"Gentlemen?" she murmurs.

Stride stands and introduces himself and Cully, who also gets up briefly before resuming his seat.

"You are Mrs Marks?"

She nods.

"Mrs Marks, I am here on a matter of police business – perhaps it would be better if we retired to somewhere more discreet?"

The woman's dark eyes regard him quizzically.

"I cannot think of anything I have done that could be related to 'police business', Detective Inspector, but pray continue. I have nothing to hide."

"Very well, madam. Can you confirm that it is your signature against this entry?"

Stride produces the Poison Register and turns to the relevant page.

Lilith Marks peers at the handwritten entries.

"Yes, it is. Why do you need to know?"

"All in good time, Madam. Do you also sell cakes?"

"If you look around you, you can see that I do."

"These cakes?" Stride asks, producing the list of cakes sent to the two families.

Lilith glances at it.

"We sell gingerbread and cheesecake, but not the other ones. Why?"

"We shall arrive at that shortly. Now, can you tell me exactly why you bought such a large quantity of arsenic?"

"We had a plague of rats," Lilith says. "They were coming up from the drains in the cold weather and looking for somewhere warm to nest. The kitchen became infested with them. If you like, I can show you where I had to nail boards over the holes they'd made in the skirting. Or you can talk to the kitchen staff – they spent most of their time screaming and jumping onto the table. It was a nightmare."

A thoughtful expression crosses her handsome face.

"This is not the first time I have been questioned about my use of arsenic," she says. "Two older women came into my tea-room a little while ago and accused me of trying to poison their husbands with cakes filled with arsenic. Is this visit linked to them? Ah, I see by your faces that it is."

Lilith draws herself up to her full height, a bright spot of colour in each cheek.

"Officers, I have never EVER attempted to poison anybody. I never would. And I am not going stand here and be accused of something I did not do!"

She speaks quietly, but with great dignity, folding her arms and staring directly into Stride's face. He meets her gaze, holds it, then lowers his eyes.

"I believe you," he says. "I apologise. It is clear that you are not part of this business."

"Thank you."

Cully has been observing Lilith Marks closely during this exchange. Now he speaks.

"Mrs Marks, I think we have met before." He searches his memory. "Yes – you gave us some information which led to finding a stolen emerald bracelet." He turns to Stride. "The Jewish goldsmith – do you remember?"

"I seem to recall interviewing a lady about it."

"That was me," Lilith Marks says, her face softening. "You have a good memory, sergeant."

"You were very helpful at the time," Cully tells her.

"Indeed, you were. I remember it now," Stride says, and signalling to Cully to stand up. "But I can see you are busy, and we have no further questions, so we'd better be on our way."

A plate of freshly-cut ham sandwiches passes in front of Cully. His eyes follow its progress longingly.

"Unless of course you'd like to stay for luncheon?" Lilith Marks suggests, regarding him with amusement. "On the house, of course. To show there are no hard feelings."

Cully immediately sits down again and unfolds his napkin. After a second's hesitation, Stride joins him.

Lilith signals to one of the waitresses.

"Alice, can you look after these two gentlemen? Get them whatever they want. Now if you'll excuse me, I left my new girl with a rather large ham and a very sharp knife. I need to make sure nothing is amiss."

She nods a brief farewell then walks away from the table. Both men's eyes follow her graceful swaying figure as she crosses the tea-room floor.

"Are you thinking what I'm thinking?" Stride remarks after the girl has taken their order.

Cully doubts it. He is thinking about what he's about to be served and hoping it will come with some mustard on the side.

"First principle of detection, Jack. Always ask the question: why. Why did two women – and I'm guessing that they are Mrs Undercroft and Mrs Osborne – turn up here in this tea-room? Why did they accuse our clearly honest tea-room owner of trying to poison their husbands? What do they know, or suspect that we do not? As I have said in the past, there is more to this than meets the eye."

"I agree," Cully says. "We should definitely investigate further. But after luncheon," he adds, as the waitress heads in their direction with two plates, both piled appetisingly high.

***

Georgiana Undercroft sits in the parlour listlessly leafing through a ladies' magazine. She has on a dark grey dress, the colour of mourning. An appropriate choice of attire. Not a day passes that she does not mourn the bright rosy-cheeked girl with the flying curls and ready smile, who has metamorphosed over the years into this pale sad-faced woman with the dragged-down mouth that she sees in her mirror upon waking.

The little shepherdess clock on the mantelpiece chimes two. Georgiana has nowhere she wishes to go, no friends she wishes to call upon, no friends who will call upon her in return. The long afternoon stretches out before her. Her eyes ache in the way she knows will soon spread back into her head.

The parlour maid knocks discreetly.

"The two detectives from Scotland Yard are here again, ma'am. Shall I show them in, or are you busy?"

A little more gold flakes off the day.

"Please show them in."

The maid shows Stride and Cully into the room. She half-rises.

"Please madam, do remain seated," Stride says. "We shouldn't keep you long. There is just something we'd like to ask you about."

"What is it, inspector?"

"In the course of our investigations into the poisoned cakes, we have just paid a visit to The Lily Lounge Tea-rooms and Restaurant in Flask Walk. Do you know the place?"

A beat.

"I know of it, yes."

"Have you ever patronised the place yourself?"

"I rarely eat out."

Stride regards her thoughtfully.

"We spoke to a Mrs Marks, the owner of The Lily Lounge. She informed us that two women, closely matching your and Mrs Osborne's descriptions, came into the tea room recently and accused her, Mrs Marks that is, of being instrumental in the attempted poisoning of their husbands. Can you throw any light on this?"

Her face shuts down.

"Have you spoken to Regina Osborne?"

"Not yet. Given the proximity of your house to the tea-rooms, we decided to ask you first."

She studies her hands. Stride and Cully wait.

"It was Regina's idea that we went there."

"Why?"

Again she drops her gaze to her hands, now twisting in her lap.

"She thought …" she pauses, frowns, then goes on, "that Mrs Marks, as she calls herself, might know something about the matter."

"Why should Mrs Osborne think that?"

Her hands are now almost tearing each other into pieces.

"In the past, that woman was … known to both our husbands."

"Known? What do you mean exactly by 'known'?"

She looks up, her face red with embarrassment.

"Must I spell it out to you, detective inspector?"

Perplexed, Stride stares at her but before he can say anything more, Cully, who remembers his own first encounter with Lilith Marks and his first impressions of her, steps forward and whispers a few words in his ear.

"Ah. Thank you. I understand."

Her eyes are like cold pebbles. Her lips are pinched tightly together.

"Do you? I doubt it very much. Sufficient to say the *woman* denied everything, and then we left."

"Are you aware, Mrs Undercroft, that you may have committed an offence by publicly accusing an innocent woman of a crime she did not commit?" Stride says. "As police officers acting in an official capacity, and with two unsolved murders on our hands, we have naturally asked Mrs Marks to produce a written statement. If she chooses to complain about your behaviour, we may have to charge you and your companion."

Now she stands. Clenches her hands into fists. An unbecoming flush of dark red colour rises to each flaccid cheek.

"I accused her of *nothing*! I merely accompanied Regina upon what was a wild goose chase. I have committed *no crime*, and now I should like you both to leave my house as I have *nothing* further to say about this. Not now, not ever. Nothing at all."

She lifts her chin, staring straight into his face, daring him to defy her order. Stride closes his notebook, bows.

"As you wish, Mrs Undercroft."

"I suggest you apply yourselves to Regina Osborne. I am sure she will be able to enlighten you further."

"Perhaps we shall."

After the door closes on Stride and Cully, Georgiana Undercroft sinks back into her chair. For a couple of seconds, she just stares straight ahead, her jaw rigid, waiting for the sound of the front door closing. As soon as she hears it, she stands, goes to the fireplace and slightly tilts one of the two big Chinese vases. She feels underneath it, drawing out a couple of letters.

Georgiana returns to her seat, the letters on her lap. She lifts the flap of the topmost one, extracts its contents and begins to read. It is an action she performs every time she wants to torture herself. She knows the contents of each letter by heart.

Daylight bleeds from the sky. She reads on, her head throbbing, feeling herself growing enormously small, as if imprisoned in a catafalque of her own construction, her heart pierced by a hundred spikes.

***

Belinda Kite sits in the bow window. She is freshly bathed, her russet hair becomingly curled. She wears the turquoise dress, its colour enhancing her emerald eyes and accentuating her creamy white skin, its boned bodice outlining her shapely figure. Over it she has thrown a cape of black cashmere trimmed with black silk – another of Sissy's discards.

She watches the street for signs of Hawksley's cab, and attempts not to count the minutes that tick by oh-so-slowly on the small mantelpiece clock behind her. Eventually, just as she is beginning to fear that he has forgotten her, a hansom draws up in front of the house and Hawksley steps down.

Belinda holds her hands together in her lap and sits back, trying to pretend that she has not been peering eagerly out of the window like a small child. She hears the bell ring twice, and the maid go to the door. Then the parlour door is opened and he enters. She graciously extends her hand. He bends low and kisses it.

"Miss Kite, I am truly delighted that you could spare me some time in your very busy social calendar."

He keeps hold of her gloved hand, his dark eyes

dancing with amusement.

She snatches her hand away and tosses her head.

"Of course. I wish to hear about the banquet and the Queen."

"That is your only reason?" he teases gently.

"Oh – and my employers the Bulstrodes, of course. I wish to hear all about them."

"And so you shall. But come, the cab awaits."

She follows him out to the cab and gets in, placing herself as far from him she can. If he notices, he does not remark on it, merely giving the driver instructions.

They travel in silence for a while, then Hawksley says, "I have a programme advertising the banquet. Perhaps you might like to see it?"

He unfolds a piece of paper and passes it to her.

She reads:

A Grand Banquet
To be held at the Municipal Town Hall, Leeds
In the presence of
The Mayor &
The City Aldermen
Local Business men and Factory Owners
After the Banquet
There Will Be A Presentation by
Mr Mark Hawksley, Owner of the Dominion Diamond Mine Company.
There will also be a Special Appearance by An Honoured Person of Great Note.

"It does not actually say the Queen will be present," she remarks.

"Of course it does not. There have been several attempts upon her life already – the palace security could not permit the general public to know the true identity of the 'Honoured Person' who is mentioned as a special guest. Who knows what mad people might try to force their way in?"

Belinda's eyes are wide with horror.

"People have tried to *kill* the Queen? I did not know that."

He places a finger to his lips.

"It is not widely known. And you must never mention it, Miss Kite – I'm sure you can be trusted."

She nods mutely.

They travel on in silence. Then she remarks, "I was given to understand by Grizelda and Josiah that you were all going to do some sightseeing in the north."

A wry smile crinkles the corners of his mouth.

"When you have seen one blasted heath and one desolate moor, you have seen them all. Besides, I would rather feast my eyes on something far more pleasant."

His glance brings a blush to her cheek. She drops her gaze to her lap and keeps it there until the cab draws up at the Golden Cross Hotel.

Hawksley hands her down.

"Tea is laid in my suite of private rooms. I thought it more suitable than taking you to a public restaurant. We don't know who might be listening to our conversation. We wouldn't want anybody of ill intent hearing about Her Majesty."

He takes her arm lightly, leads her across the carpeted foyer and up two flights of stairs. Unlocking a door, he shows her into a nice little sitting-room papered with bright flower-patterned wallpaper.

There are two comfortable armchairs and a sofa covered in maroon velvet. A fire crackles in the grate, and on a little table at the centre is a plate of thinly-cut bread and butter, rolled neatly, and a selection of delicious-looking cakes.

Belinda Kite's mouth waters.

Hawksley pours and serves the tea, handing her one of the bone china cups. Then he passes her a plate and the bread and butter.

"I hope you are hungry, Miss Kite. May I now, as we are on our own, call you Belinda?"

She nods. She is always hungry. For food, for experience, for sensation. For life itself. She makes short work of the bread and butter, and moves swiftly on to the cakes. While she eats, he describes the banquet, practically word for word as Josiah Bulstrode has already done in his letter.

She watches him, listening to his voice but not hearing the words. It is her first time alone with a man – other than Bulstrode, and he hardly counts, being her employer and not very attractive.

She notices the way his dark eyes look into her face, warm and caressing, his gaze occasionally moving down to her bare shoulders and white neck.

When the cakes are nothing more than crumbs and memories, Hawksley goes to the sideboard, where a bottle protrudes from a silver bucket.

"I thought a glass of champagne might refresh us," he says.

The cork emerges with a loud pop. She utters a little scream of surprise. He smiles at her, pouring the frothy pale liquid into two long-stemmed glasses. He hands her one. Bubbles bead the rim.

Belinda sips. It is sweet and delicious. She can feel the cool champagne in her throat, and the heat of her skin as the fire warms it. It is to do with being watched, this sudden self-consciousness. Being watched and wanted. The intoxication is subtle, as is the growing awareness of her own desire.

Hawksley gets up and comes over, raising her to her feet and bending his face to hers. His mouth finds her lips. Her first proper kiss. Tender, unhurried. A declaration of intent. A taste of fruits to come.

She leans against him. He lifts her hand and kisses the racing pulse at her wrist, kisses her neck, puts his mouth to the little hollow below her throat. He gently cups her breasts. She moans, already wet with desire for him.

He moves his hands to her shoulders, then down her back, unhooking her dress with practised ease. She steps out of the clothes that made her appear desirable, protected, and stands naked, her body an explicit invitation. He lifts her effortlessly, wrapping her legs around his waist, and lowers her onto the sofa.

Time stretches. The clock seems to rest in its relentless journey.

He is a thoughtful lover who wants only her pleasure. His hands stroke her breasts, her inner thighs, unhurried and tender. His fingers circle subtly and teasingly between her legs. Only when he senses that she is absolutely ready, does he part her thighs and enter her.

The fire crackles in the grate. The velvet is warm under her back.

When she eventually comes, it is a miracle, an unexpected gift. Their lovemaking over, she lies in his arms, amazed and exhausted. They sail on through what is left of the afternoon. Hawksley initiates her into the delights of lovemaking in all its varieties, his long caresses releasing her into more delight than she ever imagined from her illicit night reading.

Eventually she falls asleep in his arms. When she wakes, it is with a start. She is lying across his body, her face buried in his chest.

"What is it?" he asks, looking down.

"I was dreaming of monsters. What does that mean?"

He cups her face between his hands.

"Monsters are warnings."

"Of what?"

"Of whatever you are afraid of."

She looks up into his eyes and he reaches for her again. Finally, long after the last gas-lamps have been lit, he helps her into her clothes and accompanies her back down to the street where he whistles up a cab for her.

Belinda Kite is carried away through the bewitchment of the night-time streets, through the dream world of pain and pleasure, where the heavy hazy mist which hangs over every object makes the gas lamps brighter and the brilliantly-lit shops more splendid by contrast.

On the return journey, which flashes by in daze, her cab passes amblers and idlers, strollers and *flâneurs,* rich and poor, wending their way to club or garret, and a heavily-bearded elderly man and a boy carrying a tin of red paint.

***

For an explanation of this last phenomenon, we revert to a few hours earlier, and a small sub-meeting of The Gathering of The Select & Apocalyptic Brethren, led, as always, by Senior Prophet About.

The meeting has been called to discuss the progress and plot the future development in the campaign to Bring God's Holy Wrath Upon the Great Whore of Babylon.

It has come to the Senior Prophet's attention that though many are called (or, in this case, shouted at), few have chosen to follow the path, so it might be better to save his energy for those who are willing to sally forth, brush in hand, pot in other hand, and God's Holy Word in mind.

Thus, two or three (and the dog) are gathered together in the usual venue.

About gives the latecomers time to assemble. When they fail to materialise, he stands up. It is always easier to dominate any group by standing. By default, they have to look up.

"Brothers," he begins sonorously. "It is God's Holy Work we are here to do. So, let us offer up ourselves in silent prayer and meditation and I shall seek His Guidance."

He closes his eyes and begins to rock on his feet. The group watches him for a few minutes, then begins unconsciously to imitate him, swaying from side to side in their seats. Just as they are getting into a nice rhythm, About unexpectedly opens his eyes wide.

"The Lord has spoken to me!" he announces.

The acolytes instantly cease gyrating and sit absolutely still, eyes fixed raptly upon his face.

"Behold this is what The Lord says: *I have seen your Good Works, my Brothers of Christ, and I am Well Pleased. Now go forth and attack the Idols and Statues that Men have built to honour themselves.*

"They must be shown the Error of their ways. For Lo! I am God and there is No Other. And I will cover each of you with a Cloak of Invisibility so that you can go about My Work unseen."

Silence greets his words. Then one of the followers ventures cautiously:

"When He says 'invisible', does that mean nobody will see us?"

About acknowledges the interpretation with an incline of his head.

"Like, we will be *invisible?*"

"That is what the Lord says."

"Ah," the follower nods thoughtfully. "I thought that was what it meant."

"What about Ralph?" a second follower inquires, indicating the Jack Russell. "Will he be covered with a cloak of invisibility too? Only I wouldn't want to lose him on a dark night coz I couldn't see where he was."

About mentally rolls his eyes. Sometimes he wonders why the Lord is testing him by giving him this mission, and these missionaries. If it was just up to him and the Infant Prophet (currently at home, seeking divine inspiration over a plate of whelks), all things spiritual would run a lot more smoothly.

"I am sure you will be able to see Ralph quite clearly," he says.

"Ah. So it's not the same cloak of invisibility for dogs as for people then?"

About fixes the interlocutor with a stern gaze.

"My brother, surely ye seek not to question The Lord's commands?"

"Umm … I wasn't *questioning*. Not as such. More like finding out the exact details, if you understand me."

About draws himself up to his full height, spreads his arms and does the *filling-the-space-with-his-presence* manoeuvre that always reduces his audience to subdued acquiescence.

"Brothers, ye have heard Our Lord's words. Let us sally forth, armed with the weapons He has provided. The Night wears on. There is much to accomplish."

With that he closes his mouth firmly and folds his arms, daring them to venture any further down the slippery road of interpretation.

***

Marianne Corvid is dreaming of white hair. It is growing down through her head into the muscles of her heart. She can feel it, silky and smooth, cold as clarity.

It crystallises into something hard and monstrous. Even in her dream she knows that she will always be aware of its presence inside her.

The dream changes. Now she is walking along a street. The houses lean in at grotesque angles; they seem to crowd together, blocking out the light. She sees a man in the distance walking towards her. Her heart pulses, then withers.

As he comes nearer, she recognises him, though his face is hidden from her. He grows taller and taller, looming over her like a man-mountain. Marianne calls out – and wakes to find herself crying silently, her face contorted with sorrow.

Her life draws her back like gravity, filling her with vague dread, as if she is falling through the routine of days towards something unforeseen and terrible. She has a feeling of being trapped, of wanting to walk out of her life into another.

She sits upright in bed, slowly reacquainting herself with the familiar atmosphere of the room, the valency of light. The lovely moony night slides through her casement window, dappling the room.

There have always been women like her, all wanting the same thing. It is what connects them, this thick rope of desire. She feels the connection, even as she recognises the futility. It is a kind of drug, this longing, a kind of fetish.

She has seen it in the eyes of other women, bright, eager. In their hands clinging tightly to the arm of some man, as if they are drowning. She has even seen it in the sad sullen stares of the whores in the doorways.

Marianne Corvid takes stock of her situation. She listens to the silence, hears what it is saying to her:

It is time to stop dreaming dreams, and pull all the pieces together. One of those pieces is you.

An icy cold morning. Cold enough to freeze the extremities off a copper statue. But this is no ordinary statue: it is the famous sculpture of King Charles the First on horseback that has, since 1812, dignified the entry to Westminster with its presence.

At the foot of the statue are gathered the inevitable crowd of bystanders who specialise in standing in an updraft waiting for something to happen. Now they stare bemusedly at the red-painted indignity, upon whose surface the words **THOU SHALT NOT WORSHIP GRAVEN IMAGES** shout their slightly uneven and trickly message.

Near the foot of the statue lies a brush, and next to it an upended pot of red paint, dribbling carmine onto the cobbles. Stride and Cully, who have just arrived on the scene, survey the statue with perplexity.

"How in God's name did they get up there unnoticed?" Stride muses. "There are cabs and carts passing by all night. Let alone people."

Cully narrows his eyes.

"I think they must have used a ladder to mount the pedestal. From there I suppose they could have hauled it up, propped it against the horse and—"

"Yes, I get the picture," Stride says.

"They have been disturbed – they made off leaving the paint pot and brush behind."

Stride glances round and swears under his breath as a familiar figure barrels through the crowd, coming to a halt beneath the statue.

"I heard it on the grapevine and I have to say, I didn't believe it when I did. So I came straight down to see for myself," Dandy declares.

Behind him, *The Inquirer's* illustrator flips open his sketchbook and begins drawing furiously.

"How has this been allowed to happen *once again*, Stride?"

"Detective Inspector Stride."

Dandy pulls out a notebook, removes a pencil from the brim of his hat and repeats the question.

"I have nothing to say to the press," Stride says woodenly.

Dandy writes this down, enunciating every word loudly and clearly so that the crowd, now gathered around in a semicircle, can hear.

"Maybe not, Stride. Maybe not. But what do you have to say to The Man in The Street – whose money went to pay for this noble and patriotic statue of our beloved ex-monarch?"

"Yes, let's hear what the p'licman 'as to say," the inevitable man's voice from the back calls out.

Strides mouth tightens.

"We have doubled the night patrols."

"Seems they weren't patrolling down here last night though, were they? Stopped off for a smoke and a chat in some convenient doorway like what they usually does," the critic interjects. "Never find a p'liceman when you want one, that's what I say."

"It's true that," a woman in a shawl agrees. "We had a robbery in our shop last week. Not a p'liceman in sight. Had to send the boy over to Drury Lane to find one."

Dandy writes furiously, his florid features one big beam of pleasure.

"So," he asks innocently, looking hard at nothing in particular, "do any of you good and upstanding citizens feel that the Detective Division, as represented by these two officers standing here before you now, is not fit for the purpose for which it was created?"

"I certainly do," the man says.

"I agree with him," a second man says.

"Thank you, good gentlemen. And your names are?"

Without a second's hesitation, the two men supply Dandy with their names, ages, addresses and would probably have gone on to add the names of other family members and their pets if Stride hadn't jostled the reporter out of the way.

"Oi, that's harassment, that is!" Dandy exclaims, bending down to pick up his pencil.

"And you are impeding myself and my fellow officer in the pursuit of our duty," Stride growls. "And if you don't cease from impeding forthwith and get on your way, I shall have no hesitation in arresting you and escorting you to Scotland Yard to answer charges."

Dandy smirks.

"You think you're so bloody high and mighty, Stride? You couldn't stop a couple of people covering a statue with red paint. Truth is, you can't stop them painting whatever they want, wherever they choose, and whenever they like. You know it, I know it, and they all know it too."

He turns to face the crowd.

"Ladies and Gentlemen, I'm sure you'll all agree that the forces of law and order have become the farces of the same. So, we at *The Inquirer*, the ONLY newspaper that speaks for The Man in the Street, are prepared to offer a generous reward to anyone who can give us the names of the miscreants who have desecrated our fair City with their painted outrages."

"You can't do that," Stride snaps.

"I think you'll find that I can, Stride. Freedom of the Press and all that. Anyway, I just have. So there."

Dandy spins on his heel.

"We're off now. Let's see who catches them first, shall we? 'Scum of the earth' – isn't that what you lot call us? Maybe not for much longer."

He gestures to the illustrator and they both hurry

away in the direction of Holborn. Stride watches them leave, his face red with fury.

"There must be something we can arrest that swine for!"

"Impersonating a civilised member of the human race comes to mind," Cully says drily.

Stride rolls his eyes.

"I wish. Right, Jack, whistle up some constables and let's get the statue clean and back to what it ought to be. And then let's prepare for the worst ... The press are going to hound us to kingdom come and back again over this. You mark my words."

***

Georgiana Undercroft enters the dining-room and seats herself opposite her husband. The table is laid for breakfast. Starched white linen napkins are set by both plates.

Eggs and bacon wait under a silver-domed dish. Toast sits in its rack, surrounded by new butter and a dish of marmalade. Clean breakfast china sparkles in the early morning sunshine that streams through the window.

The maid pours coffee into two porcelain cups.

Georgiana Undercroft unfurls her napkin and places it on her lap. The same mechanical gesture that she has performed every day of her married life. The napkins were a wedding present, as was the china and the silver toast rack.

Thus, every morning as she goes through the familiar routines, she is reminded of the day that united her with the man she has come to hate with a passion so great that she could not imagine she would be ever capable of feeling for another human being.

"I trust you slept well, Frederick," she says, her

voice flat and toneless.

He gives her a glance from under heavy eyelids. Last night was spent in the soft fleshy arms of Hectorina Rose, whose comforting curves are a complete contrast to Georgiana's skin-and-bone body.

He didn't leave her bed until the small hours, then, unable to find a cab, he walked home through the night city, just another lost soul. As he turned the key in his own front door, the street lamps were going out and milk carts were beginning their rounds.

The green hills of Hampstead were starting to come alive in all their beauty. The house was silent, torpid with sleep. Giddily, he had mounted the stairs to his bedroom, throwing himself down on the bed without taking off his clothes.

"I slept as I always do," he replies.

Matrimonial pleasantries thus exchanged, each partner concentrates upon the matter in hand: the consumption of breakfast. She cuts her bacon and eggs into tiny squares, pushing the bits around her plate. He butters his toast so ferociously that it splinters into charred fragments.

"Why does that damn cook have to burn the toast every morning?" he snarls. "Cannot a man enjoy a half-decent breakfast in his own home?"

He rises, his face a rictus of disgust.

"Enough of this rubbish. I'm off. I'll get something on the way into town."

She does not look up.

"When will you be back?"

"How do I know? I have a full day's work ahead of me. Maybe I shall call in at the club and dine there."

"I see. So, shall I tell Cook to prepare dinner for one tonight?"

"Tell her whatever you damn well want. It is of no matter either way as far as I am concerned."

He tosses his napkin onto the table and strides out of the room. As she hears the front door bang shut, a feeling of relief settles over her. She sips her coffee, relishing its taste.

Life is so much easier without her husband's malign presence, confusing things by his coldness, making her bite her tongue for fear that she let slip something that she will regret later. Or something that he will make her regret later.

Georgiana Undercroft finishes her breakfast alone, then goes upstairs to her bedroom to choose a suitable dress to wear. She is going out for the first time for ages. An old friend from her golden girlhood has unexpectedly got back in touch, suggested that they meet in town for shopping and a spot of luncheon.

She is fed up of modelling the betrayed and helpless woman suffering in silence. She rifles through her wardrobe looking for something more colourful and upbeat, suggestive of a woman who can still maintain a successful public persona. Her life, her marriage, are both one big sham. What does another lie matter now?

***

In another bedroom in another part of London, Belinda Kite lies on her back imagining herself back in the warm hotel sitting-room. Once again, she feels the delicious weight of Hawksley's body on hers, hears his sighs rising to a crescendo.

It is not just the lovemaking that occupies her thoughts, but the realisation that her body has a power that she never knew it possessed before last night. In a world where her life has been blown about by any wind of chance, such knowledge comes as a revelation.

She is not sure what she will do with her new-found power. For now, just the mere fact of its existence is sufficient to lift her heart, raise her flagging spirits and cause her to spring out of bed with a smile, newly invigorated, to face the day ahead.

Humming happily to herself she breakfasts well, dresses herself, then sets about the business of the morning, which is to dispose of some more items from Grizelda Bulstrode's extensive and largely unworn wardrobe. She will sell them off for the best price she can get and then pocket the money. With a lover comes ongoing expenses.

She intends to spend the money that she makes this time round on a new dress for herself. Not a handmade dress (that is still beyond her wildest dreams), but a machine-made one. She has seen some in a shop in the West End. They are not cheap, but with a bit of haggling and a lot of charm, she reckons she can raise the money she needs.

In the evening, she is meeting Hawksley in town for supper. A full day of work lies ahead of her. Followed by a full night of pleasure. Belinda Kite bundles up half a dozen brand new dresses and sets off in search of a cab.

***

Later that morning Emily Cully picks her way down the dingy side alley that leads to the sewing-room in the basement of one of the big department stores in Regent Street.

As she circumnavigates the filthy puddles of standing water, she breathes a silent prayer of gratitude for her deliverance from the sweatshop slavery of the sewing-room. She recalls Mrs Crevice, the sharp-eyed, scissor-lipped overseer, whose only mission in life seemed to be to make her young dressmakers' lives as hellish as possible.

Entering the busy confines of the sewing-room now, she is immediately struck by the difference. The light is brighter. There is a pleasant hum of conversation. Even the mite sweeping up the scraps of material and bits of thread and lace looks clean, happy and reasonably well-fed.

Emily is greeted warmly by her best friend Caro. The two young women used to work together as shop dressmakers until Emily married and Caro took over the sewing-room as overseer. Under her kindly (if somewhat rough and ready) regime, the girls are at least allowed regular breaks from the eye-straining, backbreaking work.

"You here again, Em?" Caro grins. "Business must be good."

"I have another order for a ball gown. I wanted to look at your new silks."

"Come this way and I'll show you what's in stock."

Caro leads the way up the familiar dusty stairs to the busy ground floor of the store. She pushes open the baize curtain that separates the shoppers from the slavers.

Emily is confronted by floor-to-ceiling wooden shelves stacked with bolts of cloth. Lemon, puce, violet, forest green and pale ivory silks and satins jostle for space.

She feasts her eyes on the material. She loves making dresses, and this is always the best part of the job: choosing the right colour for the client. Caro goes behind the counter, ignoring the raised eyebrows of the young male floor-walker who clearly does not approve of overalled women appearing on his floor.

"Oi! You can take that fucken look off yer face, Thomas Hinde," Caro remarks, tossing her head. "I remember you when you was a snotty kid, yer backside hanging out of yer breeches. C'mon, Em – have a close look and take your pick."

Emily points to a couple of rolls. Caro lifts them down and spreads them on the wooden counter. They study the silks carefully, looking for any flaws. When none are found, and Emily has chosen her material, Caro orders the shop assistant to cut off the required amount and parcel it up.

"Now let's go and look at matching thread and trimmings," she says.

They are just making their way to the next counter, when a very striking young lady and a fitting-room woman emerge from the showroom and pass them by. The fitter carries a beautiful ready-made leaf-green tiered velvet dress, with puffings and gathered sleeves. The smiling customer follows her to the till, her eyes fixed on the lovely gown.

Emily Cully pauses and frowns. She looks at the pretty young woman, observing her slim straight back and her russet-coloured curls tumbling down from a very fashionable bonnet. She recognises her as the companion of the Tartan Dress (a true professional, Emily tends to think of her clients in terms of their clothes rather than their names).

Caro catches her gaze.

"Nice dress, that one. Sewed it myself on one of them new machines. Got to have the right complexion to carry it off though."

Oh, she has, Emily thinks, mentally visualising the young woman wearing the tight-bodiced green dress. It will suit her down to the ground.

"Not cheap neither. Top of the range," Caro continues. "We're doing more of these ready-made dresses all the time. Not everybody can afford to have handmade or wants second-hand. Nor wants to wait for a dress to be finished either."

Emily watches from a distance as the young woman

produces a couple of notes from her purse and hands them grandly to the cashier. She wonders how a poorly-paid ladies' companion can afford to purchase an expensive off-the-peg item. It is a mystery. But then, much about this particular young woman falls into that category.

"You look like you know her, Em," Caro remarks.

"I might possibly have seen her before."

"Well, there she goes. Good luck to her, whoever she is. I hope she enjoys wearing the dress. Velvet's a bugger to sew, isn't it? Creeps everywhere. And those French seams nearly wore my eyes out. C'mon, Em, let's see what we can find to trim your silk. I'll work out a good price for you, and *then* we're going to have a cup of strong sweet tea and a good catch up. You're looking a bit peaky, my gal. Thought as much soon as you stepped into the sewing-room. Anything the matter? That husband of yours not keeping you short on the housekeeping?"

"I'm fine," Emily says with a gentle sigh. "But a cup of tea would go down nicely, dear Caro. I'll not lie to you, it'll be a long walk home."

***

Belinda Kite lies in her lover's arms. This time they are not upon the velvet sofa, but in Hawksley's feather bed. He is drowsy, on the verge of sleep, sated by their lovemaking. She on the other hand, is wide awake. She feels his body relaxing, his arms growing heavy.

"It must be wonderful to own a diamond mine," she murmurs. "Can I see one of your diamonds before I leave you? I should so like to do that."

Hawksley looks at her with an expression of sleepy amusement.

"What diamonds, sweetheart?"

"The ones from the diamond mine. I have never seen a diamond close to, nor actually held one. I should to very much like to, if it is no trouble."

He laughs.

"I'm afraid I have no diamonds to show you, lovely girl."

"But what about the big diamond you showed us at the meeting?"

His expression changes. Just a fraction.

"That is locked away safely. You don't think I carry diamonds around in my pocket, do you?"

She shakes her head.

"And the other diamonds?

"They are still waiting to be dug out of the earth."

"When will that happen?"

"When I have got enough money. Digging for diamonds is not like digging up potatoes. You have to hire men to dig, and equipment to aid them."

She frowns.

"When will that be?"

"Soon, my pet. Very soon."

"But there are diamonds," she persists.

He props himself up on one elbow and regards her, his face almost tender.

"You really like them?"

"All my life I have always wanted a beautiful sparkling diamond necklace," she sighs, her eyes gleaming in the waning candlelight.

He smiles down at her eager face.

"Well, I cannot promise you a necklace, lovely Belinda Kite, but you shall have some diamonds, if that is what your heart desires. Give me a day or two to arrange my affairs, then I shall take you to Hatton Garden, to the finest jeweller in all of London, and buy you a pair of diamond earrings that would grace the ears of the most beautiful lady in the land. How does that sound?"

She likes the sound of that very much indeed. Her eyes sparkle at the prospect.

Hawksley's arms tighten around her slender waist and he gently puts his lips against her poppy-red mouth.

"Ah, what a face you have – let me kiss it. Come, my girl with the Autumn hair, we have much better things to do than discuss diamonds."

His hands caress her, his lips place soft seductive kisses along the line of her throat. Belinda relaxes, letting him have his way with her body. But even while he is making love to her, she is already imagining the diamond earrings, and seeing them sparkle as she holds them in the palm of her hand.

***

London by night. A church clock strikes one, the spreading circles of vibration opening out into eternal space. Walk the streets after dark and you take flight from the familiar everyday existence of the daytime city, and cross the threshold of a strange new world, where the ghosts of the past commingle with the outcasts of the present.

The late public houses have turned their lamps out, the last shouting drunkards have been ejected by the potman into the street. Now there are only stray people and stray vehicles.

Walk on. A cab rattles by, followed by two others, the sound breaking the silence like a glass dropped onto a flagged floor. There are few lights in the windows now. Only the pattering rain accompanies you as you walk the interminable tangle of streets.

You reach the river, which at this time of night has a dead and terrifying look. The houses on either bank rear up, black and forbidding, windows shuttered, as if wrapped in black shrouds. Pause on the bridge and look down. This is the last sight seen by those poor souls who choose to make their bed in the shadowy depths below.

Walk on. Here is a prison, heaving its massive sides into the night sky. Touch its stony walls as you pass, and imagine all the prisoners inside, locked in their cells, turning fitfully in tormented sleep as they wait for a dawn that brings no cheer, no hope.

From this dismal place, you walk until you reach one of the great city churches, whose dark arches and pillars are guarded by an elderly watchman. He walks among the graves with a dark lantern, making sure none have been disturbed. Here the air is heavy and full of ghosts.

Stand awhile and consider all the millions and millions of dead buried throughout time, and imagine how if they all came back to life and filled the streets once more, there would not be space enough to place a hatpin between them, and the vast armies of the dead would overflow the great city, filling the fields and hills and byways that stretch away into the distance, almost to infinity and beyond.

Finally, in the early hours of the morning, you reach a great railway terminus. Now there is light and company aplenty, for the early morning mail is coming in. The lamps are ablaze, and post office carts and cabs are drawn up ready. Porters rush around with trolleys, and then, with a screech and a hiss and a cloud of white smoke, the night train comes in.

The guard in his red coat opens the van doors and the nets of letters and parcels are disgorged and taken away to be sorted. A few sleepy passengers step down and are hustled away in cabs. And then the lights go out and the porters scurry away to their place of concealment, to await the next train.

Look. The night is fading. Dawn is rising over the hills of Highgate and the houses of Hammersmith. The first straggling workers are already in the streets; the first street-corner breakfast sellers are lighting their braziers. It is time to quit the desert regions of the night and make your solitary way back home to your own hearth.

***

November is a cruel month. Bare trees, frost that seizes the ground and won't let go. Belinda Kite sits in the breakfast room, wearing her new warm woollen wrapper, a cup of hot coffee at her elbow. The parlour maid enters, carrying a silver tray.

"A letter has come for you, miss."

She grabs it, her heart beating wildly. It has been two days since she last lay in Hawksley's arms and he promised to take her to Hatton Garden to buy some diamond earrings.

For two days, she has suffered the pains of waiting and longing, her mind ticking over with him, so loud it is as if she hears it. Without bothering to turn the letter over and check the superscript, she seizes the butter-knife and rips the letter open.

Dear Miss Kite (she reads),

All good things must come to an end and so Sissy and I are bidding farewell to our friends in the north and coming back to London. By the time you receive this letter we will be on the train, to arrive Tuesday afternoon.

We shall return without Mr Hawksley, however, as he has been suddenly and unexpectedly called away on business. I am delighted to report that prior to his unexpected departure he and Sissy have been getting on like a house on fire, as the saying goes.

While he was with us, they spent much time in each other's company and I think it fair to say that he is well on the way to being truly smitten with my sister. As she is with him. We hope to meet up with him again when we are all back in London.

Please make sure the house is well aired for our return, and the fires lit in our bedrooms. I should like cook to prepare a hearty beef stew with dumplings for our first supper. We look forward to renewing our acquaintance with you and hope you have not felt too lonely in our absence.

Yours sincerely,
Josiah and Grizelda Bulstrode

Belinda Kite's spirits plummet. Somehow, in the transforming events of the past week, she has lost sight of her true reason for being in London. Now she feels the prison bars of the paid companion getting ready to enclose her once again.

No more venturing out to the shops on her own. No more leisurely tea and cakes in some nice little tea room. Definitely no more delicious lovemaking with Mark Hawksley. And no diamond earrings.

It is enough to make a lesser woman burst into tears and beat her fists on the table in frustration. But Belinda Kite is made of stronger stuff. Finishing her coffee, she goes straight out into the hallway and lifts down her shawl.

Then, cramming on her bonnet, she sets off briskly in search of the finest jeweller in all of London. Maybe she will never own a pair of diamond earrings, but she can still look at them. And dream.

***

Sally's Chop House is a dark low-ceilinged place off Fleet Street. The customers sit on rough-hewn wooden benches and eat off chipped plates set on rough-hewn wooden tables.

The sawdust on the floor is patterned with boot prints, gravy and the odd chop bone. It is the sort of place that *Bradshaw's Guide Through London And Its Environs* (purchasable at any railway station) might probably describe as: *Best avoided.*

It is, however, Detective Inspector Stride's favourite watering hole. Here he is, sitting in one of the back booths, a plate of mutton chops and a baked potato in front of him.

Sally, the eponymous owner dressed in his traditional food-stained apron, hovers in the background. There is a copy of *The Inquirer* on the table. Stride is reading it while he eats. Every now and then he stabs at it with his fork and splutters, lost in the maze of his own thoughts.

Sally bends forward from what would have been a waist if he wasn't spherically built, and peers down.

Red-Paint Outrage!! Reward Offered!
Detective Police Have 'Nothing to Say'!

"Everything to your satisfaction, Mr Stride?" he inquires.

Stride glowers.

"No, Sally, it certainly is not! Look at this! If newspapers are going to go around offering money left right and centre, I can see a time coming when people will start doing things just to get paid by the newspapers for doing them. Then where will we be?"

This is a logic path of some complexity, down which Sally is reluctant to tread.

"'Nother glass of ale, perhaps?"

Stride drains his glass.

"No, thank you. Need to keep a clear head. Report to write this afternoon. Not that it's going to make a gnat's tit of difference one way or the other."

He pushes himself to a stand.

"Tell me, Sally, if you wanted to get rid of somebody by poisoning them, how would you go about it?"

Sally glances around nervously. His expression says that of all the chop houses in all the city Stride could have walked into, he had to walk into his. Several regular customers, who know who Stride is and what he does for a living, are leaning into the conversation with hugely interested faces.

"Umm … Can't help you there. Coz I'd never do a thing like that, Mr Stride, would I? Never."

Stride recollects where he is.

"No, Sally. Of course you wouldn't. Sorry. I was just thinking aloud. Downside of the job."

He pays and leaves. Sally feels his shoulders untense. The only thing that stops him banning Stride altogether is that he always pays for his meal and doesn't attempt to steal the cutlery. Plus, of course, he isn't sure what his legal position might be if he tried to.

***

Meanwhile, over in the green and pleasant district of Hampstead, Lilith Marks, proprietor of The Lily Lounge, has decided to stretch her legs and relieve her aching back, which has been bending over a mixing bowl all morning.

She removes her cook's apron, and donning a fetching blue woollen coat and a discreetly-trimmed navy bonnet with veil, she sets off to take the air. She has not gone further than the end of Flask Walk when she spies a couple she recognises.

Or rather, she recognises the woman. She is one of the snooty pair who barged into The Lily Lounge and accused her of trying to poison their husbands. Now here she is, walking on the opposite pavement with a man Lily presumes to be that very husband – the presumption being based on the stiff, rigidly-set expressions on both their faces and the distance between them.

He wears a smart tailored suit and a dismal expression. She flutters along in rags and tags of finery; one of those women who, Lilith thinks, can never look well-dressed whatever they wear.

Lilith lowers her veil and crosses the road. She follows the couple. They enter Elmer Pettinger's chemist shop. She peers through the window, and sees them approach the counter and engage the chemist in conversation.

The man rolls up his sleeve and exhibits his arm. Even from where she is standing, Lilith can see the red sores. They look very painful. The chemist studies them, purses his lips, then reaches for one of the big china jars of ointment.

More conversation ensues, presumably about when and how to apply the ointment. Then the chemist writes the purchase in the sales ledger, the man pays him and they both turn to go.

Lilith scuttles into a side alleyway. She doesn't recognise the man at all from her past. She didn't think she would, although she guesses he would be mortified that she had forgotten him. Men were such vain, foolish creatures. They did not realise that in the dark, all cats are grey. She smiles at the thought.

The couple head off towards Chalk Farm. Lilith waits until they are out of sight, then enters the chemist's shop. She purchases some hand salve for her kitchen girls who are always complaining of sore hands from washing up. As the chemist writes it down, she cons the previous purchase, together with the name and address of the customer.

Lilith's ability to read upside down is something she perfected in her former life. It was always useful to be able to read what was written on a charge sheet.

The cream that Mr Undercroft of Downshire Hill has been prescribed is one for lesions of the skin caused by "an internal irritant." The chemist's own words.

Lilith has seen blisters similar to those on Mr Undercroft's skin before. A woman in her former line of work contracted a fatal disease from a client, and Lilith watched her slow and painful decline into tertiary syphilis, madness, and finally death.

Back in the busy high street, Lilith walks on. She wonders whether this might be the true reason for his illness. Under her business-like exterior, Lilith has a soft heart. She cannot imagine what sort of an individual might possess the determination and ruthlessness to carry out the deliberate extinguishing of another person's life.

**

At the same time that Lilith is making her way back to the Lily Lounge, a station cab is making its way towards Cartwright Gardens, where it stops, and decants Josiah Bulstrode, Grizelda Bulstrode and their luggage onto the pavement outside Number 11.

They are looking well and refreshed, all the better for having spent so long breathing air that has not been polluted by the smoke of a million chimneys.

"Well, Sissy, here we are again," Josiah says, rapping loudly on the front door to summon a servant to help carry the bags inside.

"Indeed, Josiah," Sissy says, licking her lips nervously. "But I had forgotten how dark and gloomy everything was in London. And how bad the air smells."

"We shall soon brighten things up, I have no doubt. Wait until Miss Keet hears all about the party we were talking about on the train." He pauses. "But, where is she? And where are the servants?"

Further knocking finally brings the small scullery maid to the door. Her eyes widen when she sees the Bulstrodes standing on the step.

"Oh, sir, miss – you are back!" she stutters.

Josiah hefts the cases into the hallway himself. He goes into the parlour.

"Why is there no fire lit to welcome us?"

The scullery maid dithers in the doorway.

"We was not expecting you, sir, miss."

"But I wrote to Miss Keet – where is Miss Keet?"

"She is not at home. She went out after breakfast and has not returned."

Josiah's face falls.

"This will not do. No, indeed it will not. No fire? And no beef stew with dumplings?"

The scullery maid wrings her hands.

"Cook has taken a half day, sir. And the parlour maid too. Miss Belinda has not dined at home recently, so Cook said she wasn't going to waste her time."

Grizelda plucks at his sleeve.

"There must be … nay, there will be an explanation, Josiah. We just need to wait for her to come home."

"Home?" Josiah kicks at one of the cases. "No warm fire to welcome us, no dinner cooking? Fine homecoming this is turning out to be, Sissy."

Even as he speaks, there is the sound of running footsteps up the path and Belinda Kite hurries into the hallway, her bonnet askew.

"Oh, I am so very sorry," she gasps. "I had forgotten the time. I meant to be home hours ago."

Josiah regards her sternly.

"Now, Miss Keet, did I not write to you to inform you of our return?"

Belinda nods earnestly.

"Oh, you did. And I received the letter. But then I had a message from an old school friend of mine who has been taken to hospital. So I rushed round to visit her, and in the shock of seeing her lying in that hospital bed, I clean forgot. Oh, I am so very sorry," she cries again, wringing her hands and rolling her eyes.

"Well, now, I knew there had to be an explanation. Wasn't I saying that just a few moments ago, Sissy? Our Miss Keet would never leave us in the lurch."

"What is the matter with your friend?" Grizelda asks interestedly.

"She was knocked down in the street by a runaway horse," Belinda says, wiping away an imaginary stray tear.

Josiah shakes his head.

"I have often remarked on the speed of some of those drivers. They go far too fast. Poor young woman. I'm sure you were able to offer her some succour in her hour of need."

"Oh, I was," Belinda assures him. "But it has meant that I have neglected you and your sister."

"We shall rub along as best we can," Josiah says. "Mary here can light a fire in the parlour, and as for supper, why I'm sure there are eating houses aplenty that we can visit."

"Oh, you are *too* kind," Belinda says, smiling sweetly.

"Let me carry these traps upstairs, and we'll soon be as right as ninepence."

Belinda follows the Bulstrodes, congratulating herself on the "friend in hospital" who was a stroke of genius, invented as she came back from Hatton Garden in a cab.

The thought that she might never be alone with Mark Hawksley again prompted the fiction of the fallen friend. She also needs an excuse to leave the house unaccompanied.

Josiah pauses on the first-floor landing.

"Sissy nursed our beloved parents in their final days," he says thoughtfully. "I'm sure she'd be only too happy to come with you to the hospital when you next visit. And if your friend has nowhere to go to when she is discharged – why, she'd be welcome to stay here."

"That is so kind. But I would not dream of imposing upon you."

"Of course she must, Josiah."

Belinda's smile stays where it is, but suddenly the rest of her face no longer wants to be associated with it. One minute life is simple, then suddenly it stretches away full of complications.

***

Complications also abound at Scotland Yard, where Detective Inspector Stride has spent all afternoon looking for any intelligence in the intelligence reports. It seems almost impossible to believe that with the amount of night patrols now out in the streets, not a single sighting of the Phantom Red Painters of London Town has been recorded.

Meanwhile opprobrium of the press continues unabated. Letters from indignant members of the public fill the pages on a daily basis. In the case of *The Inquirer*, Stride is cynical enough to believe that

Richard Dandy, chief reporter and first-class pain in the backside, has probably written most of them himself.

And the outrages also continue. Overnight, the *Red Paint Revolutionaries* (as they have been nicknamed by the press) have managed to cover several of the green-painted railings of Russell Square with red paint, and have attached a notice proclaiming:

He will send the RICH hungary away.

The square houses some of the richest people in London, including bankers, city financiers and several aristocratic families, many of whom have sent their servants to deliver hand-written notes of protest at the vandalism. Not to mention the lamentable fact that the police manning the Watch Boxes appear to have seen nothing.

Stride eyes the pile of letters sourly. They are all written on expensive notepaper, some bearing crests. The rich have a nice turn of vitriol when it suits them, he thinks, though some of the analogies to the events of 1789 in Paris are a little far-fetched. This is London, after all, and nobody has erected a guillotine in the street. Yet.

There is something vaguely disquieting, however, about the way the perpetrators seem able to go about their business undetected. Stride feels as if he is chasing ghosts. He rereads the reports, underlines a few sentences in the hope that a level of meaning as yet undetected might rise to the surface, then sits back and stares gloomily out of the soot-encrusted window.

Which is how Jack Cully finds him when he comes to announce that as it is Sergeant Evans' birthday, and he is a long way from home and family, a group of fellow-officers have clubbed together to buy the young man a cake, currently being shared out in the back office.

"I can bring you a slice if you're too busy to join us," Cully says.

"No, of course I'll come straight away," Stride says, getting up. "I was only chasing ghosts. Nothing that won't wait."

Cully gives him a quizzical look.

Stride gestures dismissively.

"That's the thing about ghosts, Jack: they'll always be there at the end of the day."

***

Two days later, breakfast at Cartwright Gardens is proceeding apace, at least for one of the participants. Josiah is making a hearty meal of the viands on offer. Sissy is doing her usual picking and crumbling act, and Belinda Kite is discovering that food and frustration do not mix.

Despite telling herself that she must not think about it, Belinda cannot stop recalling the time she lay in Mark Hawksley's arms and he promised to buy her some diamond earrings.

Neither he nor his promise have materialised. To add to her misery, she has had to endure both Bulstrodes talking about him as if he were Sissy's beau, without betraying a flicker of emotion.

As she eyes her cold cup of coffee grimly, the parlourmaid enters.

"A note for Miss Belinda has just arrived," she says.

Belinda almost snatches the little piece of paper out of her hands.

"If I may, I should like to read this in my room," she says, rising.

She hurries from the dining room, her eager fingers ripping open the envelope as she runs lightly upstairs.

Dearest and loveliest Belinda (she reads on the landing),

Please accept my deepest apologies. Business matters have kept me from London and from your side for too long. It is now my intention to make good my promise to buy you those diamond earrings – and how fine they will look in your pretty little ears.

If it is acceptable, shall I send a cab round for you at 11.30? We can then have luncheon at a nice little place I know.

Yours,
Mark

Belinda Kite stuffs the note into her dressing table drawer and makes her way back downstairs, composing her features before re-entering the dining room. The Bulstrodes glance at her.

"Not bad news about your friend, I hope?" Josiah says.

"Oh, no," she says. "The note was from somebody whose acquaintance I made while you were away. They have asked me whether I am able to accompany them later this morning to advise about buying a present for a friend of theirs."

The thing about a good lie that it always needs to contain a modicum of truth.

"I expect they want to take advantage of your French taste." Josiah nods.

"It is very flattering to be asked." She smiles. "But of course, if I am needed here, I shall refuse."

"No, you must go," Sissy says. "Mustn't she, brother?"

"She must. I shall shortly leave on business, and you have letters to write to our friends back home. So you see, we can spare you, Miss Keet."

"Oh, you are too kind," Belinda says, lowering her eyes meekly. "I shall return sometime in the afternoon – my friend mentions a light luncheon after our shopping."

***

Edmund Randell, of Randell & Knight, Jewellers, is standing behind his counter watching the world go by. Or rather, he is watching a couple who have just stopped in front of his curved glass window to admire the display of rings, brooches, jewelled combs, chains and other small items of personal adornment.

They make a handsome pair. The man is a little older than his female companion. He is tall and dark-haired, with the sort of rugged good looks that would draw the female eye in any circumstances. The young lady clinging to his arm has a pretty peaches-and-cream complexion, with sparkling green eyes, and auburn hair that frames her face in two sets of becoming ringlets.

Edmund Randell tries to guess their relationship, and decides they must be a newly-engaged couple. It is a game he likes to play – and he prides himself that he is rarely wrong. He can tell from the moment a customer comes into the shop what it is their heart desires. And how much they are prepared to spend to get it.

And now here they are entering his shop, the man standing aside to allow the pretty young thing to go first. She hurries to the counter, her face alight with expectation, her small red mouth curving at the corners into a smile.

The man follows her, then catching Randell's eye, says, "We should like to see some diamond earrings."

Randell produces a number of small oval leather boxes from the glass showcase and opens them. Diamonds wink and glitter on their pale velvet beds.

The young lady's eyes glisten almost as brightly. She considers each box, weighing up the contents, then stretches out a gloved hand, and points.

"These. I like these ones the best."

The man smiles down at her indulgently.

"Are you sure?"

"Oh yes," she says. "They are the biggest."

"They are indeed. And they will suit you admirably."

He picks up the box and places it in her hand.

"Why don't you go over to the mirror and try them?"

She does, and while she is busily admiring herself in the cloudy shop glass, tilting her head from side to side to better see the effect, her companion produces a wallet stuffed with notes and pays for the gems. The jeweller writes out details of the purchase in a ledger. The name the customer gives, out of earshot of the young lady, is not Mark Hawksley.

The couple leave the shop, the young woman almost dancing with delight. Randell stows the money away in the cash box under the counter. The diamonds are not the finest quality; he cannot afford stones like that (nor can most of his customers, who patronise him because they know what they are getting), but the jewels are showy and eye-catching, and she is clearly delighted with the purchase.

A good morning's trade. A beautiful young lady and her clearly besotted suitor. He wishes them a long and happy life together.

A short while later Mark Hawksley and Belinda Kite (wearing her new diamond earrings) enter a small discreet hotel off Cavendish Square and make their way to the second floor, where Hawksley has recently engaged a suite of rooms.

Hawksley closes and locks the door. He helps Belinda off with her shawl, then unties her bonnet and takes the pins out of her hair, shaking her curls free.

"So, are you pleased now, Belinda?" he asks.

"Oh, I am," she says, rolling her eyes.

He slides her dress from her shoulders, his eyes devouring her greedily, hard with desire.

"And are you happy that you have your precious diamonds?" he murmurs, caressing her bare shoulders.

"Oh, I *am*," she says.

Hawksley lifts her effortlessly off the ground.

"Then why don't you show me how happy you are," he says, as he carries her towards the open door of the bedroom.

***

It has been some time since Jack Cully has been on duty in an official capacity after dark, but here he is now, out and about on the mean (and tonight very foggy) streets of London. The only scenery comes from above the forest of twisty chimneys, where a few bright stars are managing to pierce the fog.

Desperate times call for desperate measures, and the ongoing rash of red painted outrages has resulted in a plea for men to volunteer for night duty. Cully has left his wife Emily sewing by candlelight. His last sight of her was the white nape of her neck as she bent over her work. He carries the image of it in his head as he proceeds steadily along the streets.

He stops to check on a couple of constables, who inform him that they have seen nothing paint-related pass them by so far tonight. He strolls on. He has just reached the Commercial Road, an old stamping ground of his from when he was a constable, when his sleeve is suddenly plucked by an importunate hand attached to a thin youth in a coat, muffler and cap.

The youth leans closer and whispers hoarsely, "Mister Cully? You needs to come along o' me."

Many might be suspicious of such a greeting and on such a dark night, but Jack Cully has patrolled these streets for so many years that very little surprises him. He nods, and starts following the youth.

For a while he loses his bearings in the narrow maze of side streets and back alleys. Then he hears the splash of water, sees the outlines of tall masts looming above the house tops, and recognises where the youth has brought him.

They are close to the docks. Sinister grey fog rolls up through the street from the distant waterfront, where Cully pictures it dripping from rigging and coiling snakily around ropes and creaking timbers. The fog has a rich fruity quality to it, with top notes of rotting vegetation and a bouquet of raw sewage and rancid fat.

The youth ducks down an alley. Cully follows, crossing a narrow street and entering another alley so narrow that the upper storeys of the houses seem to touch. There is no artificial light here; no cressets of flickering gas lamps, only watchful darkness and a sense that unspeakable things might be being enacted in the shadows.

The alley widens into a small square of brick-banded houses clustering round a small cobbled courtyard, inch-thick with things Cully doesn't want to think about. At the far end of the courtyard, smoky gaslight illuminates a painted signboard above a door. There is a picture of a woman in a crown painted on the board, an indication that the building attached to it via the other end of a short rusty pole is a local hostelry.

Beneath the painted signboard is a dark wooden door, on each side of which small grimy windows are set in peeling frames. To the casual visitor who has accidentally lost his way, it looks exactly like a disreputable tavern.

In actual fact, the Queen's Head is a reputable

disreputable tavern. Its regulars have a certain rough-hewn respectability: they do not produce weaponry unless the need arises, and they have been known to assist the casual visitor back out of the maze of passageways without relieving him of his personal possessions along the way.

As Cully stands in front of the peeling door, waves of memory wash over him. He had forgotten all about this place. Now the sight of it looming out of the darkness takes him back to his early days as a beat constable. He is surprised that it is still standing. Literally. Bits of it were falling off even then.

The Queen's Head used to be a very late-night and definitely very illegal drinking haunt, where for a discreet knock and a back strategically turned, a man could obtain a glass of cloudy beer and a warm-up in front of a fire on a cold winter's night.

The youth lifts the latch and pushes open the door. Inside the tavern, flies crawl down the walls, dark and slow, as if they are waiting for someone to finish them off. There is only one person present: a small bald-headed man in shirtsleeves, a check waistcoat and greasy brown corduroy trousers.

The man sits in the corner, watching the door expectantly. He has a very large white cat on his lap, which he is stroking with one hand. The hand is missing two fingers. He glances up as Cully enters, and gestures towards a chair set strategically opposite where he is sitting.

"Evenin', Mr Cully. Nice of you to drop by."

His smile is bright and cold, like the smile on the face of the moon.

"Nevis, drink for Mr Cully. Drop o' brandy – something to warm the cockles of his heart."

Cully starts, then stares very hard at the youth.

"Nevis Thewl? No – that's never young Nevis!"

"He's all grown up, innee, Mr Cully? Not like when you knew him back in the good old days."

Nevis Thewl, Cully thinks, sitting down and accepting a glass of brandy from the youth's hand. His mind spirals back ten years to when six-year-old Nevis Thewl was the leader of a local gang of pre-pubescent entrepreneurs whose forte was robbery with innocence.

It was while escaping from one such robbery that their paths crossed – or rather, young Constable Cully rescued junior Nevis Thewl as he was about to dart across a road where a herd of cows was running amok.

The heartfelt gratitude of Nevis' parents upon the safe return of their errant offspring couldn't be expressed in words, but was subsequently visited upon Cully in free beer and the odd tip-off. He guesses this latter is the reason for the renewal of their acquaintanceship now.

The bald-headed man's mouth is like a hole with a hem.

"Long time since we seen you in this neck of the woods, Mr Cully. We understand you are a married man."

Cully nods. He is not surprised. News, good or bad, travels fast. Especially around the less salubrious parts of the city.

"That's pleasing to hear. A man shouldn't have to darn his own socks or cook his own dinner."

The white cat jumps down and pads over to Cully, where it begins a thorough investigation of his trouser cuffs. Satisfied that they contain no rodent elements, it scrambles onto his lap, turns around a couple of times, and settles down.

The cat's owner watches it intently.

"Do you like cats, Mr Cully? I always feel they're a good judge of character."

Cully sneezes. In his experience, cats knew instantly who was allergic, and gravitated to them.

"I brought you here because I have two words to say to you, Mr Cully," says Thewl *Père*. "And them two words is: Red Paint."

"Ah."

"We gather as how the police is baffled by it."

"And you know something?"

Thewl taps the side of his bulbous nose with what might be, but isn't because it is missing, his index finger.

"I hear as how that Bob Murdoch who has the chandler's shop down by the docks is suddenly doing a roarin' trade in paint. And he ain't sellin' it to shipwrights. Might be worth askin' why, and who to."

Cully digests this information.

"How did you find out?"

Thewl's face darkens ominously.

"You remember Nevis' twin sister Annathema?"

Cully recalls a small wispy-haired girl with a grubby pinafore, bare feet and a pathetic expression. He often encountered her standing on street corners with a basket of violets. Sometimes the violets were replaced by watercress, or matches, depending on the time of year. He looks round the room expectantly.

"Oh, she ain't here, Mr Cully. Gone into service. Doing alright for herself. Not alright enough for bloody Bob Murdoch's son though. Courted her all though the summer, then dropped her. Fair broke her lovin' little hart. So you see, I don't owe them Murdochs any favours. Ho no!"

"I understand," Cully nods.

"You go round there toot sweet and ask him. Ask him who's buying all that paint."

"But don't mention your name?"

Thewl laughs. The sound is like a metal spoon being

put through a cheese grater.

"Got it in one, Mr Cully."

He chirrups to the cat, which uncoils itself from Cully's lap and jumps lightly down. Cully wipes his smarting eyes on the back of his sleeve.

"Better get going," he says, rising to his feet. "Thanks for the tip. And for the brandy."

"Don't make it so long next time," the small man says. "Always a drink for you at the bar. For old time's sake. Bring your lady wife next time, why don't you? Mrs Thewl likes a good gossip, and 'eaven knows there ain't many ladies around here for her to gossip with. Nevis, show Mr Cully the way back."

Outside, the fog is so thick you could cut it and serve it in slices. Cully follows Nevis Thewl back through the maze of tiny passageways and crooked streets until they reach the main thoroughfare.

Then Nevis tips his cap and is gone, blending seamlessly into the foggy darkness and leaving Cully to make his way back to Scotland Yard. Before he departs, he prepares a short report on the night's events and places it on Stride's desk.

Back home at last, Cully removes his boots at the door and tiptoes in stockinged feet to the back bedroom where Emily sleeps, her face turned to the wall. Quietly as he can, he takes off his outer clothes, then slips under the blanket and curls himself around his wife's back.

Emily gives a little sigh, but does not wake. Cully closes his eyes and relaxes into the warmth of her body. Before his heavy eyelids close, he experiences a brief moment of utter contentment. His life is perfect. He cannot think of a single way it could be improved.

***

A smoggy day in London town. It has Stride low and has him down. Here he is walking into work, keeping company with the usual inhabitants of the dawn streets: the homeless, the hungry, the people of the mists and mud, those whose lives are as rickety and insecure as their houses.

These are not the people who live in fine mansions, who go to balls and dinner parties and to the opera in coaches, but the other ones. These are the people Stride knows best, for he deals with them every day, and was once one of their number.

These are the people who make everything work: the toilers and labourers, the sweepers and servers. These are the ones who cart away the night-soil; the faces in the crowd, the invisible ones whose insignificant lives are of no consequence in the grand scheme of things.

Once Stride walked the streets of London every day of his working life as a beat constable. Back then he knew where he was by the feel of the streets beneath his boots. Now, he cannot remember the last time he went on patrol, the last time he stood in a doorway watching the moon, with the rain tipping down from an overhead gutter, the last time he chased some criminal through the backstreet alleyways and courts.

Now he rarely moves faster than a walk. He has an office and a desk and paperwork. Always paperwork. And politics. Sometimes Stride feels a pang of regret for the old days. It was simpler back then. Then, he was a hunter. Now, he moves folders around and writes reports.

He enters Scotland Yard, and grunts at the desk sergeant as he makes his way to his office. Somewhere in a back room the night duty constables will be writing up their reports, which will be placed on his desk in due course. As will the morning papers. He does not know which of the two he is less looking forward to.

Today is not going to be a good day. Later he has to meet the lawyer Frederick Undercroft and regretfully inform him that after exhausting every avenue of inquiry, which has involved his men showing the cake box to every bakery in the area, and visiting every chemist enquiring after the purchase of poisons, he has come to the conclusion that the identity of the person who sent the parcel of poisoned cakes may never be known.

Stride hates failure even more than he hates paperwork. Or the press. But the truth has to be faced and communicated. He has thought long and hard about this case, staring at the ceiling in the watches of the night and trying to get his mind around its various tortuous possibilities. And this is the conclusion he has reached. There are also other conclusions he could have reached. But he has no proof.

Stride closes his eyes and for a moment wishes himself somewhere else. Then he picks up the top folder from the pile that never seems to go away, however hard he works at ignoring it. He is somewhat surprised to recognise the neat copperplate hand of Jack Cully. Intrigued, he opens the folder and begins to read.

When he has finished reading, Stride closes the folder and stares thoughtfully at the opposite wall for a bit. Coincidentally, Mrs Stride has been complaining about the state of the hallway, which she insists needs repainting. He can't see the need himself, but then, he leaves home early and returns late. And his decorating skills err on the side of extreme reluctance.

Maybe now would be a good opportunity to investigate the potential cost of said repaint job and look at some colours. If only to stop her nagging the life out of him, and to give the impression that he is going to get around to it. One day.

***

Murdoch's Chandlery is a small old-fashioned shop tucked away in a small old-fashioned street running parallel to the Commercial Road. It can barely be described as a shop – it resembles more the front room of a house that has somehow been overrun with accumulated and very random stuff.

Goods spill out onto the pavement: a basket of firelighters props up some twiggy brooms that lean witchily against the smoke-blackened outer wall. Fire irons in various sizes and combinations lay wait for the unwary passerby, ready to trip them up.

Here are coal shovels, dusters, caustic soda, cones of sugar, household soap, door stops, mangles, washing tubs and rolling pins, all higgledy-piggledy. Presiding over all this is a small elderly woman with a downturned mouth and piercing black eyes in a flat doughy face. Her hands are encased in black lace fingerless gloves, and she eyes Stride and Sergeant Evans suspiciously as they step over the threshold.

"Good morning, madam," Stride greets her pleasantly. "We are interested in the purchase of some paint."

"Ow, are yer now?" the woman says, raising one eyebrow. "And why should two gents such as yerselves come all the way here to buy paint when there must be a hunnerd or so other shops you could have gorn to?"

Stride recognises her instantly as one of those women who belong to the *you-can't-pull-the-wool-over-my-eyes-don't-think-you-can-for-one-minute* school of elderly females. He is married to a member of the cadet branch.

"We were recommended to come here. Is Mr Murdoch on the premises?"

"No, he ain't. Stepped out on a bit of business."

"That's a pity." Stride strokes his chin with a thumb and forefinger.

"Is it?" The woman snaps her mouth shut and stares at him.

While they have been exchanging polite hostilities, Sergeant Evans has been looking round the shop. He now approaches the counter carrying a black coal shovel.

"This is just what my Megan – my sweetheart – has been looking for," he says triumphantly. "The one she uses is all old and bent out of shape."

The woman glances up at him, her features instantly softening.

"Well, young man, I can tell you have got an eye for quality," she says. "And where does your sweetheart work?"

"She's an under-housemaid in a fine house in the Welsh valleys," Evans says in his lilting accent. "That's where I come from too."

"Aww, you pore young man," she croons. "Ain't yer a long way from home?"

"I am indeed, madam," Evans says, laying the shovel down on the counter.

When Sergeant Evans had joined the Metropolitan Police straight from the Neath Police, his accent marked him out immediately as a 'foreigner'. That he survived was largely down to two things: his physical appearance, and the fact that he was incredibly likeable.

Sergeant Evans got on well with people, even those he was arresting. And in a city noted for its rudeness, he was always unfailingly polite. Watching him in action was like watching some miraculous talent unfolding magically in front of your eyes.

Stride takes a step backwards, and waits for the

magic to begin.

The old lady smiles soppily at the young sergeant and reaches for a roll of brown paper, some string and scissors.

"We never sold anything to abroad before. I shall have to tell my son when he comes back. Wales. Who'd have thought it?"

While she fusses with the brown paper, Sergeant Evans casually introduces the subject of paint: general uses of. While she cuts off the requisite lengths, he moves the topic on to paint: supplies thereof. As she loops and ties the parcel with string, he narrows it down to specific colours of paint: recent purchases of.

By the time she has dripped sealing wax on the knots, it is clear that this is, indeed, the source of the red paint used in the recent attacks on buildings and monuments in the city.

They leave the shop, the shovel tucked under Sergeant Evans' arm.

"Ooh, my Megan is going to be so pleased when she opens this," Evans says happily.

Stride stares into his big honest face.

He really means it, he thinks. *He does. He hasn't a clue how the world works, how women work, how anything works, but it doesn't matter because people just look at him and they like him. And somehow, that's what works.*

They retrace their steps, passing several newsvendors' boards all proclaiming variants on the headlines of:

Red-Hand Gang Strike Again!
London on the Verge of Total Anarchy!
Police Force Unable to Cope!

"Would you like me to arrange for someone to watch

the shop?" Evans asks.

"Yes, why don't you do that, lad," Stride says wearily. "After all, what have we got to lose?"

***

The end of the working day, and the working man makes his weary way back to home and hearth, where domestic bliss in the form of his helpmeet and household angel await his return.

Such, however, are not the experiences of Frederick Undercroft, lawyer, and Georgiana Undercroft, lawyer's wife. The fleeting domestic bliss they once experienced has fleeted away, leaving only sullenness and mutual resentment.

Here they are, seated on opposite sides of the sitting-room, awaiting the arrival of Detective Inspector Stride. He is still in his lawyer's garb, she wears something dark and shapeless that hides her figure and does not flatter her pale and lined face.

Undercroft regards her sourly, recalling that he could have spent his evening in the arms of the buxom Hectorina Rose, who always wears a smile in his company, enjoys his anecdotes, and laughs uproariously at his little puns and witticisms.

He is an amusing chap. He is considered excellent company by his fellow-man. He is well-read. He is admired by many in his profession, loved by many outside his profession. Only here, in the arid bosom of the woman he mistakenly chose to be his wife, is he unappreciated.

Silence drips into the icy chasm between them.

"Are you going to inquire about my day?" he says.

She does not glance up from the small lace handkerchief that she is rolling and unrolling between her fingers.

"Why? Do you want me to?"

He does not reply. His thoughts are like a shower of red-hot glowing needles in his head; the pain is almost unbearable.

"Perhaps you would care to ask me about my day instead?" she says, after a few unpleasant seconds have slunk silently by.

He does not pursue the subject further.

She returns to picking the lace edging of her handkerchief.

They wait in uncompanionable silence until the front door bell rings, and Detective Inspector Stride and Detective Sergeant Cully are shown into the room.

Stride has often complained to Cully about difficult people – a category which, according to his definition, includes almost everyone. Although he did his best to minimise contact with them, as he told Cully on numerous occasions, one could never avoid them altogether.

For Stride, difficult people were like eels; you tried to keep hold of them but they wriggled free from your grasp. Another similarity in his mind was that eels came out at night. Not that difficult people only inhabited the hours of darkness, he hastened to assure Cully. Their darkness was of a different order.

It was a darkness they carried inside. They seemed totally oblivious to the problems they caused to other people by their actions, nor to the effect they produced on those around them.

Now, as Cully stands with his back to the Undercrofts' fireplace, listening to Stride outlining the various investigations of their case and the conclusion he has reached, these musings about difficult people come unbidden to his mind.

Frederick Undercroft, lawyer, has never told them about his extramarital relationships. His wife has not told them that she confronted one of the women involved. Eels. Slippery, and difficult to hold on to.

As Stride speaks, Cully studies their faces closely. Neither betrays a smidgeon of emotion, either to the news being broken to them, nor to each other. When Stride finishes speaking, Undercroft waits a couple of seconds, then raises his head and looks Stride directly in the face.

"So, am I correct in thinking," he asks coldly, "that upon the balance of probability, you have now decided to cease the investigation of this matter?"

"We have no further leads. You are unable to supply us with any more helpful details. Apart from the unfortunate footman at the Osborne household, and your own servant, nobody else has suffered any ill effects. It is just possible, therefore, that it may have been a case of mistaken identity to begin with."

"Two cases of mistaken identity," Undercroft corrects him sharply.

"Indeed so."

"You have spoken to the Osbornes? What do they say?"

"A couple of detectives have relayed the news to them. They feel that, as no further parcels of cakes have arrived, and in the light of no untoward symptoms occurring from anything they or their servants have eaten subsequently, that our surmise may be the correct one."

Stride has clearly rehearsed this statement, Cully thinks. It contains words he has never heard him use in everyday conversation.

"Have you suffered any further ill effects, sir?" he asks.

Undercroft's mouth tightens. Cully notices a little pulse come and go in his temple.

"My health is not currently good. Whether that is

because of the distress caused by the events leading up to the death of our maid, or some other external factor, I cannot say."

"But neither of you has been taken ill from anything eaten in this house?"

"I have not," Mrs Undercroft says in a low voice, her eyes on her lap.

"I rarely eat at home," Undercroft says.

Stride shrugs his shoulders.

"I am prepared to leave the case open, if that is what you want. Should either of you," he pauses, letting his eyes travel slowly from one face to the other, "wish to discuss anything further, you have my card. Good day to you both."

Stride's face betrays no emotion as the servant shows the two detectives out. Only when they are back on Downshire Hill does he give vent to his feelings.

"Two innocent young people have died, horrifically and in terrible agony, Jack. And these Undercrofts sit there in their nice suburban drawing room as if butter wouldn't melt in their mouths, and they couldn't give a tuppenny damn. And I know, I just *know,* that if they wanted to, they could tell me what has been going on behind the scenes, because sure as eggs are eggs, something has. I felt it from the moment I crossed their threshold. But short of arresting them both for being cold unfeeling brutes, there is nothing we can do except hope that justice of some sort catches up with them eventually."

He stares back at the house, where the blinds have already been drawn, shutting out the world.

"Come on, Jack, there has to be a public house around here somewhere. I need something to wash away the foul taste of middle-class respectability."

***

It was once believed that sleep came in two parts. A first part that begins when one goes to bed, and then a second instalment just before one wakes up in the morning. In between the two is an interval of an hour or so, a 'watch'.

Emily Cully sits by the dying embers of the fire. She listens to the sounds of the night-time world: church bells chiming the quarter-hour, the rattle of wheels on cobbles as a wagon passes by. She hears a drunk raising his voice in a wordless tuneless lament for something. Two women start a high-pitched argument, which quickly subsides when a constable intervenes. Someone walks past in noisy shoes, sobbing.

Everybody in the world is lonely at some time of their lives, Emily thinks. She stirs the embers with the poker and recalls the miserable small tenement room she used to rent, and Violet, her best friend, who died at the hands of a brutal murderer before she had even begun to live.

Today she was so overwhelmed with fatigue that she almost lay down on the filthy pavement and fell asleep. She thinks about the pain in her lower back, and how her body seems to be made out of rocks and china.

Emily knows she will have to tell Jack about it soon. She thinks about what he will say when she tells him. She sits, very still and very quiet, in a silence embroidered by the beating of her heart and the noise of her neighbours returning to their beds. This is her watch.

**

Marianne Corvid is also awake. She is perusing a small book of poems by her favourite poet, Lord George Byron. She bends forward, straining her eyes in

192

the flickering candlelight, and reads:

"When we two parted
In silence and tears,
Half broken-hearted
To sever for years."

Marianne Corvid is a great fan of the Romantic poets, especially Byron. In his emotionally fervid sentiments, she finds the consolation she does not find in the world around her.

Reading Byron by candlelight in the dead of night is her illicit pleasure. One of her illicit pleasures. The other one is to stand in the shadow of a doorway and watch who enters the chambers of her former lover and seducer – she likes to think of him in these terms. They are suitably Byronic.

This afternoon she had seen a young woman enter the chambers. She was dressed in widow's weeds, her face hidden under a thick veil. Marianne had stared hard at her pliant figure, feeling the itch of pain, the familiar wasp-stab of jealousy. The reminder of desire, ordinary and dangerous.

This is how it begins. The sympathetic smile, the air of fatherly concern which in time led to … and now …

She turns a page:

"So, we'll go no more a-roving
So late into the night,
Though the heart be still as loving,
And the moon be still as bright."

She'd waited in the shadows until the door opened and the woman had reappeared. She'd watched her walk away, biting back the temptation to run after her, to ask if he had arranged to see her again upon some minor legal pretext, to warn her not to allow herself to think of him in any other way than as a lawyer.

Later that day Marianne had visited her husband's grave, as if trying to atone for what she had felt, what she had done. *'Forgive me my trespasses, as I forgive those who trespass against me.'* But she did not forgive, so how could God possibly forgive her? Not for her, then:

> *"A mind at peace with all below*
> *A heart whose love is innocent!"*

She closes the book, tucking it under her pillow. Words are precious as wishes. She lies back. Rain smatters against the windowpane. Her hands are ice-cold. She places them between her thighs to warm them up.

She must not go wandering through the labyrinth of the past any more. But even as she tells herself this, she knows it is a lie. She will return. There is one more visit that she has to make. And then she will be done with the whole rotten affair forever.

***

Affairs, and their progression or regression, are also the hot topic of conversation at the Bulstrode tea-table. Much to Belinda Kite's astonishment, it appears that the master of the house has returned from the north with a possible romantic attachment.

Not towards her, thank goodness, though he continues to treat her with a creaky sort of flirtatiousness based on her 'French' origins. Belinda first becomes aware of Josiah's amorous addition when a letter arrives the day after his return.

Since beginning her secret trysts with dashing

though slightly unreliable Mark Hawksley, letters have become very important to Belinda. Thus, she has taken to finding an excuse to be near the front door whenever a postal delivery is expected.

Thus, it is Belinda who retrieves the letter addressed to Joseph in very large curly writing, which, when delivered makes him puff and go rather red in the face.

"Is it from ...?" Sissy asks, raising her eyebrows archly.

Josiah clears his throat, goes even redder and fans the letter back and forth in front of his face, while Belinda stirs her tea, crooks her little finger and watches with mild amusement.

"My brother is not used to receiving letters from ladies," Sissy tells her.

"Now then, Sissy! I'm sure Miss Evangelina Lumpton merely writes to ask after our health and whether we returned to London safely."

He folds the letter and places it in his pocket.

"Miss Keet, your plate is empty. Some more fruit cake?"

Belinda dimples her thanks.

"I am surprised that you have not heard from our friend Mr Hawksley though, Sissy," Josiah continues, his mouth full of food. "And him so attentive to you. I was sure you had caught yourself a nice beau at last."

Belinda almost chokes on her slice of cake.

"He did say he had business matters to attend to and might be absent for some time," Sissy says hesitantly.

"I expect it is the diamond mine," her brother nods. "I shall write to him though, to advertise him of our return. I am sure he will not be long in leaving his card once he knows we are back in London."

Later, alone in her room, Belinda Kite opens the little jewellery box. The diamonds lie on their velvet bed. She thinks of Hawksley's face as she pirouetted in front of his mirror, naked except for a sparkling jewel in each ear, and she wonders whether this is what she has been looking for ever since she came up to London.

She shuts her eyes, sees the curve of his jaw, feels his arms holding her, his mouth warm on her cheek. She sees his dark eyes winding her in to their curve. There is a black hole at the middle of each. It is their still centre.

She remembers looking into his eyes, and feeling giddy, as if she might fall into them. She recalls his strength, and her heart goes falling away inside her, because she is young, and she has never felt love before, and nobody has ever bought her presents and desired her.

She goes to the casement and looks out over rooftops and trees to a clear black sky studded with diamond stars. This is how it feels, she thinks. There is nothing she would change now, nor tomorrow, nor the tomorrow after that.

***

Sadly, Georgiana Undercroft could not be said to share Belinda Kite's philosophical outlook. Not for her the optimistic belief *that tout va mieux dans le meilleur des mondes.*

But then, Georgiana Undercroft is no longer young, and that period of life when all seems sunshine and roses has long passed. Here she is now, venturing forth into the foggy morn of a lacklustre day.

Georgiana has agreed to meet Regina Osborne. Reluctantly. Given the choice, she would much prefer to cut that lady completely, but her husband and Regina's husband have dined at their club, and the subject of the little *froideur* between the two ladies has been discussed.

Annoyingly, it is Georgiana who has been blamed by both men for the cessation of the friendship, so she has been forced into writing a short polite note suggesting the two ladies meet at a suitably neutral venue in town, for of course she will never allow Regina to darken her threshold again. She does not include this last sentiment in the note.

A cab drops Georgiana Undercroft outside one of the big department stores. She has arrived early, so she stands looking at the sumptuous window display of silks and velvets and other inviting delicacies, all artfully displayed in rich and glittering profusion, while all around her the streams of people pour on and on, jostling with one another and hurrying forward without appearing to notice the riches that surround them on all sides.

Eventually she hears her name being called. She turns to face the woman who was once, many years ago, her best friend and confidante, but whom she now meets as almost a stranger.

There is an awkward silence, during which both ladies assess each other for levels of hostility. Then Regina gestures towards the shop window and says, "I see they have brought out some new bonnets."

And Georgiana replies, "I find I have very little need for any more bonnets."

And Regina states, "No, one can become a slave to the latest fashions."

And Georgiana suggests, "One can become a slave to anything, if one chooses."

And Regina asserts, "I'm sure I don't know what you mean."

And Georgiana retorts, "Oh, I think you understand me very well."

And Regina's mouth tightens.

And Georgiana tosses her head.

And after another silence, which actually speaks enough volumes to fill Mudie's Circulating Library, both ladies walk off in totally opposite directions.

***

The offices of Undercroft & Cumming are located in a gloomy little street close to Smithfield. The air has a mournful chill to it, as if it has absorbed over the years all the disappointment of those arriving to peruse the Wills of their nearest relatives.

It is early afternoon, and a woman in black waits in the outer office.

The clerk, who is new, has told her that Mr Undercroft is lunching at his club and he does not know when (or indeed if) he will return. The woman has indicated that she will wait. And so she does, sitting very still, almost unnaturally so, in one of the cliental chairs fetched from the inner office.

After a while the clerk forgets that she is there, and so when Undercroft re-enters from the street and asks if there is anything demanding his immediate attention, the clerk shakes his head.

At which point, the woman rises.

"*I* demand your attention," she says.

Undercroft turns to face her. His expression instantly hardens into something impenetrable.

"I think we have no further business to enact, Mrs Corvid," he says coldly. "I believe I have carried out your late husband's wishes exactly as he instructed."

"But what about MY wishes?" the woman bursts out passionately.

The clerk raises his head from his copying desk. There is the tiny sound of a pen being carefully set down.

Undercroft glances at him, then says abruptly, "Very

well, Mrs Corvid. I can spare you five minutes in my office. That is all."

He leads the way, closing the door firmly behind them. The clerk listens hopefully for a minute, then dips his pen into the inkwell and continues writing.

On the other side of the door, Undercroft and Marianne Corvid face each other across his rosewood desk. Undercroft folds his arms and regards her woodenly.

"I thought I had given instructions that you were not to enter my office."

"But I am not one of your clerks, to be ordered around," she counters.

"Sadly, you are not. For if you were, you would know your place."

"And what is my *'place'* as you call it, Frederick?" she exclaims, two spots of bright colour lighting up her pallid cheek.

"Your place is certainly not here, disturbing my chambers with your emotional outbursts," he declares pompously. "Know once and for all, Marianne, that I will not tolerate your strange behaviour any longer. Whatever we once were, we are no longer. Besides, I am a married man."

"You were a married man when you came to my bed," she retorts. "It did not seem to matter to you then."

"That was a mistake. I have told you, over and over again, that I regret my behaviour. You were a very vulnerable woman, lately bereaved. I took advantage of your unfortunate state, and in a moment of weakness I allowed myself to behave in a way that I now deeply regret. I have explained all this to you. Why must you continue to pursue me in this unpleasant manner?"

"What kind of a man are you, Frederick? You did not answer my last letter. You have answered none of my recent letters."

"I have received no communications from you, Marianne, I assure you."

There is a pause, during which Marianne Corvid leans forward in her chair and scrutinises his countenance intently for a few seconds. Then she sits back with a sigh.

"No, I see from your face you have not read them, even though I sent them to your house. Then let me disclose to you the contents of my most recent letter: I told you that I needed to see you. And I needed to see you to tell you that I have recently lost a child."

For a moment Frederick Undercroft does not seem to grasp what she has just told him. He frowns, tapping the end of a pencil upon the desk.

"I am sorry – I do not understand you, Marianne. What child? Where did you lose it?"

"My child. Our child. The child conceived from our brief time together."

Now he understands. A look of utter horror crosses his sallow features.

"I don't believe you!"

"It doesn't matter whether you believe me or don't believe me, it is nevertheless true. I was carrying your child. But I lost it. At the time, I was unable to summon medical assistance, for obvious reasons. The child was born so early that it stood no chance of surviving. That is what I wanted you to know. That is why I have come."

Frederick Undercroft opens his mouth, then closes it again.

Marianne Corvid folds her black-gloved hands in her lap.

"I should now like to go abroad, to somewhere warm where I can recover my health and my strength. I have been unwell since I lost the child, and it is so cold here in England. I dread the winter. I believe another winter in London will kill me."

"Then go. I am not stopping you."

"I have insufficient funds to make such a journey," she says.

She waits. He says nothing. His face betrays nothing.

"I thought you might provide me with a little money, given my unfortunate situation. And its cause."

He rises.

"Mrs Corvid, as you have failed to supply me with any actual proof that the child – if indeed there ever was a child in the first place, which I doubt – was mine, I am afraid that I am both unable and unwilling to help you in any future plans. Now, if there is nothing more, I think we are done here. I have clients waiting. My clerk will show you out. Good day."

She utters a low cry of despair. He stares fixedly down at the pile of folders on his desk, refusing to look her in the face.

"This is your final word, Frederick? You will not grant me the one last favour that I will ever beg of you?"

"I refuse to be compromised by the behaviour of a woman for whom I no longer have any regard or respect. I refuse to fall for your tricks. I see straight through them. You are trying to entrap me – it will not work. If you have suffered misfortune, then it has been of your own choice and volition. I repeat, I have clients waiting. Please go now. We have nothing further to say to each other."

She rises, staggers, almost collapses. Then taking a deep breath, she pulls herself together, squares her slight shoulders, lifts her chin, and regards him with burning eyes.

"Shame on you, Frederick Undercroft! You have wronged me and you have ruined me. And one day, I pray with all my heart and soul, you will pay for what you have done."

Then she is gone.

He stares at the space she has just quitted. A sense of immense relief overwhelms him. The idea that he could have fathered a child out of wedlock … The implications for his career, or his social standing in the legal community, hardly bear contemplating. But he has not. And so he will not contemplate it.

He rings the bell to summon the clerk.

"If that woman ever comes here again, you are to bar the door to her. Do you understand?"

The clerk understands only too well. He saw Marianne Corvid leaving the office, her face contorted by grief, her jaw clenched, her hands balled into fists. She bore all the appearance of a madwoman.

"Good. Now bring me Colonel Anstruther's folder, if you please. His family will be arriving shortly to hear his Last Will and Testament."

***

Meanwhile, in a dark alley where the sun never shines (or if it does, only with extreme caution), two groups of ragged street urchins face each other. Under layers of facial grime, their expressions are taut, their eyes narrowed and watchful.

Knuckles are whitened, boots are being scraped down walls – by those that have the luxury of a pair of boots, that is. The Commercial Road Killers and the Dockside Devils are about to engage each other in the time-honoured way of all street gangs everywhere.

At either end of the alley, piles of rags, stones and a dead dog mark the place where some goalposts might have been. An inflated pig's bladder is carried into the alley by a boy whose swaggering walk indicates his elevated status in the gang hierarchy. This elevated status is also confirmed by his cap, and the fact that he possesses a marginally cleaner face, and boots with actual laces.

The game begins. What it lacks in finesse and gamesmanship it makes up for in sheer animal brutality and noise.

From time to time the ball is accidentally kicked out of the alley and into the main thoroughfare. When that happens, a shouting cursing group of boys rush after it and attempt to get it back, diving between the legs of passers-by and knocking them over.

Just as the game reaches its height, a small figure enters the alleyway. It is the Infant Prophet. He is dressed in white, his long fair hair tucked under a white cap. He carries a quartern loaf wrapped in waxed paper.

His arrival causes an immediate halt to the game. The boys stand and stare open-mouthed as he picks his way carefully along the filthy mud-encrusted alley. He seems oblivious to their presence, the expression on his face and the movement of his lips suggesting that he is communing with some Higher Presence. As he reaches the midpoint of the alley, a couple of the bigger boys step forward, arms folded, and bar the way.

"Oi, Whitey, where you goin'?" one of them demands.

The Infant Prophet regards them thoughtfully, but says nothing.

"I *sed*, where you goin'?" his interrogator, who goes by the name of Scummer, repeats, kicking muddy water at this fascinating new prey.

He stretches out a filthy hand, grabs the white cap from the Infant Prophet's head and throws it into the air. It lands in a puddle.

Catcalls and jeers break out as the Infant Prophet's long blond curls cascade down his back.

"Ferkin' hell, wot is it?"

"He's a gurl, innee?"

"Aww … lickle gurl … Let's see wot he looks like under them pretty clothes, then."

A chorus of "*Off … off … off!*" breaks out. Scummer holds the Infant Prophet down, while another boy known as Nosser begins to unbutton his tunic. The Infant Prophet grips his bread tightly to his chest, lifts his mud-spattered face to the heavens and begins to wail.

At which point Sergeant Evans, who just happens to be passing by, having checked on the men watching Murdoch's Chandlery, is attracted by the howls and catcalls.

He sticks his head into the alleyway, makes a lightning assessment of the situation, and advances on the two boys closest to the Infant Prophet. Evans grabs them by their ragged collars and hoists them effortlessly aloft until their faces are level with his and their legs are dangling off the ground.

"Now then, Oliver and William – what's going on here?"

The two boys exchange horrified glances. Nobody knows their real names. *Nobody.* Kids they grew up with don't know their real names. The gangs they bunk down with under the tarpaulins in Covent Garden don't know their real names. It is highly probable that their own mothers, who abandoned them at birth, have forgotten their real names. But somehow, Sergeant Evans has found out. Even though he has only been on their patch for a brief while.

"Nuffink, mister. We woz just having a bit of fun."

"Doesn't look like fun to me. I suggest you all cut along and play somewhere else, or I'm going to get cross and take your ball away. And you wouldn't like that, would you?"

The boys mutter under their breath. Then they pick up their ragged possessions and edge away, trying to convey that wherever they are going, they were intending to go there all the time.

Sergeant Evans retrieves the Infant Prophet's cap and wrings it out.

"I'm afraid your mother will have to wash this," he says, shaking his head sadly.

The Infant Prophet sniffs, and stuffs the sodden cap into his coat pocket.

"Now then, my little boy, where do you live?" Evans asks.

The Infant Prophet winces, but tells him.

"Oh, that's just a step from here, isn't it? I'll see you safe to your front door. Wouldn't want any more harm to come to you, would we?"

Looking strangely incongruous, the pair traverse the alley, cross a couple of streets and come to a halt outside a rather dilapidated cottage fronting a less than fragrant drainage ditch.

Evans knocks on the door, which is opened by a pleasant-faced older woman wearing a sacking apron and a lace cap with old-fashioned lappets. Her expression changes as she catches sight of the Infant Prophet, who is trying to hide behind Sergeant Evans.

"Oh. my goodness! Look at the state of you! What has happened now?"

"A slight altercation with a group of boys," Evans says, helping the sodden Infant Prophet over his doorstep by applying a large hand to the small of his back.

"No bones broken, and nothing a good scrub down won't cure."

The woman rolls her eyes.

"As if I didn't have enough on my plate," she mutters. "I dunno what your father will say about this, I really don't. Fighting in the street – and you a Brand Plucked from the Burning!"

Sergeant Evans opens his mouth to explain, but the woman cuts him off.

"Thank you for bringing him back, mister," she says, and slams the door.

Sergeant Evans shrugs, turns and makes his way back to the main road. As he walks back to Scotland Yard, he thinks about what he spied, albeit briefly, over the woman's shoulder just before she closed the door.

There was a pot of paint in the hallway. A large pot, with a big brush balanced on the lid and a dribble of red paint running down the side.

***

Frederick Undercroft leaves his office promptly at five o'clock. He emerges cautiously, glancing round to see if *she* is lurking in some doorway ready to accost him once more with her mad fantasies.

Reaching Chalk Farm unmolested, he pauses to buy a copy of the evening paper from a newsvendor before striding up Haverstock Hill in the direction of Hampstead. He finds the evening paper useful as a screen between him and the misery-faced woman he is tied to.

Undercroft would have preferred to spend the evening in more convivial company at his club, or between the ample thighs of Hectorina Rose, but the visit from Marianne Corvid has unsettled him to such a degree that he feels unfit for anything but the lacklustre companionship of Georgiana.

Besides, there is a pressing matter he has to deal with.

He unlocks the front door, the action bringing the maid hurrying out of the parlour. He hands her his top hat and coat.

"Where is your mistress?"

"In the dining-room, sir. We were not expecting you home this evening."

He pauses on the threshold.

"You pick up the letters, don't you, Anna?"

"Most times, sir. Sometimes the mistress does it."

"Do you recall any private letters arriving recently, addressed to me?"

She frowns.

"I think I recall a couple of letters, sir."

"And what did you do with them?"

"Same as I always do. I took them in to the mistress," the maid says. "Have I done something wrong, sir?"

He forces a smile between gritted teeth.

"Certainly not. Now get along with your work."

Undercroft enters the dining-room. Georgiana is seated at one end of the oval dining table, a bowl of soup in front of her and a novel at her elbow. She glances up, raising her eyebrows in surprise.

"I was not expecting you, Frederick. Shall I ring the bell for some more soup?"

He sits down heavily, feeling a tightness in his chest. The long walk and the evening smog must have caused it, he thinks. And the unpleasant visit from Marianne. He pours himself a glass of water.

"Have you seen any letters arriving here, addressed to me personally?" he asks.

"Letters from whom?"

"A client of mine. An ex-client, I should say."

She fixes her pale eyes upon his face.

"Why should an ex-client be writing to you here? Surely your chambers would be the appropriate place to send any such letters?"

He stares at her, trying to read behind the bland

expression, the cold-eyed stare.

She must have intercepted Marianne's letters, he thinks. Though the post is inconsistently reliable, he reminds himself. The maid could be mistaken.

"This particular person has become a little unhinged since the death of her husband. She has developed strange fancies. It is possible that she may have written in a strange and alarming way."

"Really?" Georgiana props her chin on her hands. "What might she have written?"

He is being drawn into a trap – he sees it clearly.

"I am not at liberty to divulge client information," he says, adopting his most pompous legal tone of voice. "I merely asked whether you had seen any letters."

She continues spooning up her soup.

"You do not answer?" he says.

"What answer do you wish me to make? You clearly believe me culpable of hiding your private correspondence. Nothing I say will make any difference to that opinion, so I chose not to respond to your accusation. Now, if you will excuse me, I should like to finish my supper and continue with my book."

He glares at her bent head. He would like to strike her, to take out on her all the frustration of the past few months. He reminds himself that he is the master of the house, the head of his chambers. It behoves him to behave with decorum. Nothing must ever get out into the public sphere where it could damage his reputation and ruin him forever.

"Did you meet with Regina Osborne today?"

This time she does not even raise her eyes from the novel.

"We met, briefly."

"Good. Good. I would not like us to fall out with them. Old friends are the best after all."

She rises from her seat.

"Is it your intention to stay here this evening?"

"I have not decided. I may do once I have eaten something."

"I see. Then I shall tell Cook to serve you some soup. If you require my presence I shall be in my room."

A swish of grey silk and she is gone, leaving the faint scent of lavender water behind her. He wrinkles his nose. He hates lavender, always has done. He decides he will go out after all.

Maybe a visit to the Argyll Rooms? He hasn't been in a while. A couple of his friends go there regularly. There are always pretty girls, wearing low-cut dresses that show the full roundness of their breasts. And there will be dancing, and champagne.

He can drink and dance and maybe find himself an amiable woman to spend the night with. A woman with a voice soft as the cooing of turtle doves, and a body to match. He is a man, after all, with a man's needs. And he has had a very trying day.

***

The Argyll Rooms, or the Gyll as it is known to regular patrons, is one of the most popular places of entertainment in London. It is situated in Great Windmill Street, next to a church and only a stone's throw from the hub of the West End that is Piccadilly Circus.

Step over the threshold into the brilliantly-gaslit rooms whose walls are covered with large gilt mirrors in which you can see yourselves stretching away into infinity. A glass of champagne (only twelve shillings a bottle) in your hand, you can watch the dancing and flirting from the edge of the dance floor, or from one of the plush seats in the gallery, with its secluded alcoves.

The orchestra, who entertains from behind an elaborate screen of gold trellis-work, is about to play a polka. Pay your shilling and you can join the dance. Not got a partner? The master of ceremonies, dressed in white tie and tails, will select a suitable person for you and effect an introduction. For the Gyll is a well-run night spot, and certain conventions are enforced.

Look more closely. One of the men is known to you. Elegantly turned out in evening dress, Mark Hawksley has just been introduced to a very pretty blonde, dressed in blue to match her eyes. Her fair hair hangs in ringlets and her little slippered feet beat time to the music.

She has come up to London to 'better herself', and is here for excitement and in the hope of attracting some presentable and wealthy man who will stand her a dance and a supper, and then maybe take her back to his rooms afterwards. Ultimately, she has her eye on a nice little villa in Maida Vale or St John's Wood.

They make an elegant couple as they spin round the floor, his hand in the small of her back, his eyes occasionally flicking down to her soft white bosom. When the dance ends, he conducts her to a table, where a glass of sherry-cobbler and two straws are waiting.

But Hawksley's pretty partner is going to be disappointed in her elegant beau, for he is here to ingratiate himself with the older more prosperous city men (married, of course) who are here at the Gyll to pick up girls for a night's pleasure.

The pretty blonde will eventually pair off with one of the dashing young army officers who have come up from camp for a night out. He will be as free with his money as with his embraces, and a good time will be enjoyed by both, ending in a frantic dash to Nine Elms Station, where the kindly guard will let them travel back to Aldershot in the guard's van. And what they get up to in there is nobody's business but their own.

**

Business of an entirely different nature is being conducted not a stone's throw away in Soho, where The Gathering of The Select & Apocalyptic Brethren is taking place in its usual venue above the music publisher's shop.

Senior Prophet About is doing business with The Almighty, while being watched by a slightly anxious flock. They have been summoned to an extra-ordinary meeting as there are Concerns. The Concerns pertain to the sudden and unexpected refusal by Bob Murdoch to supply more red paint.

After a brief silence, during which the flock holds its corporate breath, About opens his eyes and scans the room slowly, letting his gaze travel from face to face. "Where is Brother Robert?"

There is a general shifting of position and a group clearing of throats. Everyone knows that two smartly-dressed men had recently visited Bob's shop while he was elsewhere, had asked his old mum a lot of paint-related questions, but had bought no paint.

After Bob had returned and been told, it was agreed that the men weren't *boney fido* decorators, but were there to snoop in an official capacity of some sort. Their visit indicated that somebody had fingered Bob Murdoch, and that the finger in question was not attached to the Hand of God.

"Err ... his dog's not well."

"Heard it was the wife."

"Nah – it's his youngest lad: he's got that throat thing that's going around. My Flo had it, proper poorly she was."

The flock, having thus supplied a pick-your-own mix

of excuses, settles back in their seats with the air of having done their duty. About casts his eyes to the heavens, via the smoke-blackened ceiling, and intones:

"Who amongst us has any paint left?"

"Got half a pot," someone ventures.

"Think I might have a lick somewhere," adds another.

The Chief Prophet sighs.

"And how are we supposed to proceed with The Lord's mighty Work of Retribution on half a pot of paint and 'a lick'?"

"Fish!" a voice from the back row sings out loudly.

All heads swivel round to view the singer, who is grinning happily with the air of a man who has solved the riddle of the universe. Seeing he has their full attention, he continues, "It's like in the Bible, innit? When there was that crowd and all they had was one loaf of bread and a couple of fish, but Jesus prayed over them and there was enough to feed five thousand. We could pray over the paint and it could turn into … a lot more paint … maybe it might even …" His voice tails off as he catches the corner of About's hard stare.

"Thank you, Brother Inkerman, for your valuable contribution," About says drily. "I'm sure that The Lord, if He chose, and in His Infinite Wisdom, could indeed supply us with enough paint to cover the entire city. However, as I also possess a nearly full pot, we should have sufficient for our immediate needs. Let us now bow our heads and pray for Brother Robert – yes, let us pray long and hard for him. And then let us sally forth into the highways and byways of this Iniquitous Cesspit of Evil."

The flock closes its eyes and mentally focuses upon Brother Robert, who is even now (secretly and under cover of darkness) pouring the last of his stock of red paint into the River Thames, on the basis that if he had to choose between God and Mammon, it is a no-brainer. And when he confirms the name of the bastard who shopped him to the authorities, they will be picking up their teeth from the pavement.

Won't they just, Harlow Thewl. Oh yes.

***

It is brisk step from Scotland Yard to that part of London known to the initiated as "Down by the Docks", an area that the various tourist guides to the City might designate as 'brimming with local colour'.

Down by the Docks is where they eat the largest oysters in the world and scatter the largest oyster shells in the world. Here you will find tally-shops, slop-shops, coffee-shops, and greengrocers' shops that sell vegetables that seem to have a saline and scaly look, as if they have been scraped off the bottom of ships.

Down by the Docks you can buy telescopes, sou'-wester hats, pewter watches, nautical instruments and Union Jack pocket handkerchiefs. You can feast on sausages and polonies and saveloys made of who-knows-what besides seasoning. Down by the Docks is a roaring, fiddle-scraping, shrieking, shouting, arguing place. A place that is like no other place in the whole of the city.

It is a clear crisp morning, and a small crowd has gathered to watch a man up a ladder very carefully painting THE WAGON & HORSES A PUBLIC HOUSE on an inn sign. He has almost finished. At some point, he is going to realise that he has left out the L. The crowd is looking forward to the entertainment.

Detective Sergeant Cully and Sergeant Evans approach the crowd and attach themselves casually to the back, on the basis that whereas a single man will have his wits about him, a crowd generally shares a single wit amongst many. You can learn things from crowds.

"Nice day," Cully remarks to nobody in particular.

"Gonna rain later on," a man in a bowler and shabby suit responds lugubriously, his walrus moustache drooping.

"Ow, thank you, Horace. I've just put a load of washing out in the back yard," a well-upholstered woman replies, folding her meaty arms under her apron.

"Must be hard keeping things nice and clean – my missus is always complaining about the soot and smuts," Cully says to the same nobody in particular.

"She's right to complain," the washing one nods. "Seems it gets sootier and smuttier every year."

"My Megan says all the washing and mangling plays havoc with her hands," Evans says.

There is a pause while the woman looks him up and down. Her eyes soften. Her mouth curves into a smile.

"Well, you could always help her out. Big man like you can always make yourself useful around the house."

"Oh, I shall once we're married. But right now, she lives in Wales."

A couple of other women transfer their attention from the painter to the sergeant and eye him with predatory interest.

"Your sweetheart ever gets tired of waiting for you, darlin', I'm always available," one says.

Her friend nudges her in the ribs.

"Oooh, Lizzie Duke – don't let your old man hear you carrying on!"

"Well, can you blame me? Fine figure of a man – wouldn't kick him out of bed, would you?"

"You want any *washing* done, lovey? I got a hot tub all ready and waiting," a third woman says, winking suggestively.

Sergeant Evans blushes furiously. The fan club giggles.

"Actually, ladies," he says when his face has returned to its normal colour, "there is something you could do for me, if you'd be so kind."

"Oh, *kindness* don't come into it," Lizzie says, to more raucous laughter.

"The other day I rescued a little lad from some bullies – he was dressed all in white. Never seen anything like it. Do you know his name?"

The women click their teeth and exchange meaningful glances.

"You mean The Infant Prophet."

"Possibly. What's his name?"

"That. Leastwise, if he has another name, I ain't never 'eard it. You?" The woman appeals to her mates. Who all shake their heads.

"His dad used to be called Millbank Tendring," Lizzie says. "Only then he got religion. Now he calls himself Prophet About – about as useful as a wet week of Mondays. Rents a place up west where they all meet."

"They?" Cully queries.

"The people what belong to his church. If you can call it a church. Praying and carrying on, while his poor wife is at home slaving over the washing and ironing to keep that boy's clothes white. *White!* I ask you!"

Cully indicates silently to Evans by tugging on his sleeve that if he agrees, a strategic withdrawal at this point might be a good plan. Sergeant Evans bestows his wide guileless smile upon the fan club.

"Ladies, it has been a pleasure talking to you this fine morning. May we bid you all good day."

"Anytime you wanta drop by for a *talk,* don't hesitate, big boy," Lizzie replies with a smirk. "I love a good *talk*."

Cully and Evans step away from the crowd.

"Are we going to arrest this man?" Evan asks quietly.

"No, we aren't," Cully says. "Not yet. We're going to bide our time until we actually catch him in the act. Otherwise, what's the point? Better to get the man who did it than the man who looked as if he was going to do it. Especially when people start saying: 'Prove it'."

"So, what happens now?"

"We'll head back to the Yard and work out a plan."

They move off.

A few minutes later the sign painter climbs down the ladder and looks up to admire his handiwork. He utters a heartfelt groan. The crowd nods in satisfaction.

***

The course of true love rarely runs smoothly, and, at the moment, for two young women, it is barely moving at all. Mind you, it might help if the gentleman who is the focus of their heartfelt affections was a little more generous with his presence.

For Mark Hawksley, secret lover of one and object of interest for the other, is currently proving somewhat elusive. A letter sent to his hotel by Josiah has been returned, marked: *No longer staying here.*

Three days have passed since this startling development, but now, just as even good-natured Josiah Bulstrode is beginning to look worried – for, after all, he has invested a lot of money in the Dominion Diamond Mine Company – behold, a letter is delivered.

Josiah opens it, watched by two pairs of interested eyes. He reads aloud:

My dear Josiah,

A hundred apologies for not getting in touch. As you can see, I have moved residence and am now renting some rooms in Highgate. I should like to invite you and your sister (not forgetting Miss Kite) to take tea with me at 4 o'clock this afternoon.

It will give me the chance to repay you, in a very small way, for your generosity during my trip to your home town. I also have news of an exciting nature to share with you.

I look forward to our meeting.

Yours,

Mark Hawksley

"There now, Sissy," Josiah says, folding the letter and placing it in his coat pocket. "I knew he'd be in touch. Didn't I say as much? Exciting news, eh? I wonder what that can be about?"

Belinda Kite, who is pretending to be very absorbed in the dregs of her coffee cup, also wonders. She speculates that it will be nothing to do with her. Nor, despite her flustered and excited demeanour, to do with Grizelda either.

As soon as Josiah leaves the house, Grizelda seizes Belinda by the arm.

"Let us go up to my room, Miss Kite – I should like your advice on matters of dress. It is important that I make the right impression on Mr Hawksley this afternoon. He has not seen me for some time. He has exciting news! Oh, I am *wild* to know what it is, aren't you?"

Reminding herself that this is, after all, what she is paid to do, Belinda follows her *wild* employer up to the well-appointed bedroom with its chintzy curtains, thick Turkey carpets and dark walnut furniture. Grizelda flings open the wardrobe door.

"So, what shall I wear?"

Belinda gasps. Dress after dress hang in serried rows of pastel profusion. It is as if they have been duplicating themselves since the Bulstrodes returned. Grizelda catches the edge of her glance.

"I am afraid I have been rather extravagant while we were away. I discovered this lovely department store in Leeds. Such well-made dresses – though of course I always remembered what you and Mrs Cully recommended: no bright colours."

Belinda stands in front of the wardrobe, mentally reflecting on the poverty of her own. The dresses she brought with her to London have been smartened and made over in the quiet of the night. She has the dresses that belonged to Grizelda, of course, and the new green dress bought using the money from the sale of Grizelda's other dresses. But she cannot wear any of these at the moment, without having to indulge in some rather awkward explanations.

A naughty thought enters her brain that it probably doesn't matter what she wears, as handsome Mark Hawksley clearly prefers her *toute nue.* She dismisses the naughty thought and focuses on the matter in hand.

One day, she promises herself, as she starts to sift through her employer's silks and satins, she will have a handmade dress, and it will be stunningly beautiful and it will fit her perfectly. Belinda has never owned a dress that fitted her perfectly in her whole life.

Eventually, after a lot of trying on and twirling in front of the mirror, Grizelda settles for a pale apricot satin, with black lace inserts and a black wool short jacket, which is handed to the maid to brush out the creases.

The whole of the morning and beyond has now passed. Belinda Kite is starving; it has been a long time since she ate breakfast, but Grizelda declares herself too excited to partake of any luncheon, so of course Belinda cannot have any either. And then Grizelda says that a small walk in the fresh air is what she needs now to calm her nerves before she gets ready.

So coats and bonnets are donned, and the two young women set out to take a turn around Bloomsbury and its environs, where Grizelda marvels at the booksellers and fan makers and print shops and framers, while Belinda tries not to think about her rumbling stomach. They return in time to await Josiah's promised carriage.

Eventually, at 4 o'clock precisely, the cab drops them outside a terraced house in a quiet side street. A canopied walkway screens visitors from prying eyes, and there are Venetian blinds at all the windows. Grizelda hurries ahead of Belinda and raps on the door.

The door is opened by a man whom Belinda recognises from her first encounter with Hawksley at the Golden Cross Hotel. He greets them, takes their outdoor garments and shows them into a snug sitting-room on the ground floor, where Hawksley and Josiah are seated on opposite sides of a roaring fire.

Hawksley rises. He is wearing a green striped silk waistcoat, a green silk cravat at his throat, and a green handkerchief in his breast pocket. The effect is striking. He bends low over Griselda's gloved hand.

"Miss Bulstrode, what a pleasure to welcome you to my humble abode."

"Oh, Mr Hawksley, how nice everything is," she flutters.

His eyes meet Belinda's. He gives a small incline of his head in acknowledgement of her presence.

"I was just telling our good friend Mark all about the new business contacts I have found for him," Josiah says.

"Oh brother, do you never talk about anything else

but business?" Grizelda scolds.

She seats herself on the sofa and indicates that Belinda should join her.

"Money makes the world turn, isn't that right?" Bulstrode appeals to Hawksley, who nods his agreement.

"Indeed, friend Josiah. But now that our delightful companions have finally arrived, let us put business aside and turn to pleasure. I hear the rattle of teacups," he says, going to the door and letting in William Ginster, who is acting as butler for the occasion, and who carries a tray loaded with good things to eat.

Belinda Kite's mouth waters as she surveys the plates of tiny crustless sandwiches, the pile of scones, the pats of butter, the jug of cream and the iced sponge cake. She is absolutely ravenous.

Ginster hands each guest a delicate bone-china plate, then serves the scones and sandwiches. Totally ignoring the social convention that states a lady should rarely be seen eating anything in public, Belinda Kite fills her plate, then lets the conversation pass her by as she enjoys her food.

When she rejoins it, it is to hear Grizelda (who has barely eaten a thing) saying, "You have not yet told us your exciting news, Mr Hawksley! I am sure I am agog to find out."

Hawksley flicks an invisible crumb from his waistcoat.

"I have already told your brother, Miss Bulstrode. It concerns the development of a second shaft on my dead father's property. Initial mine-digging has uncovered a new seam, possibly loaded with priceless gems."

Griselda's mouth forms one big O of wonderment.

"I was astonished when I received the news, as you can imagine, Miss Bulstrode. But without the necessary funds, as I was telling your brother before your arrival, it may have to remain unexplored."

"Oh brother – surely we must support Mr Hawksley in this exciting new discovery?"

"I have already promised him my support, Sissy," Josiah replies. "And I have agreed to write on his behalf to my friends and business associates back home. It will mean another trip north, though. Letters of business are always best followed up in person. Particularly when they concern matters of a financial nature."

"Oh, I don't mind a few more days away," Grizelda gushes. "If it will help Mr Hawksley's cause."

"Then it is decided," Josiah says.

"You are kindness itself, Miss Bulstrode. I do not know how to thank you and your generous brother for your esteemed support of my little enterprise." Hawksley smiles and bows in her direction. "I think when the diamonds are lifted from their rocky bed, you shall have first pick."

Grizelda goes bright pink and chokes on a cake crumb.

Josiah gets to his feet.

"Then I say: let us strike while the iron is hot. Ladies, if you are ready? I shall write those letters as soon as we return to Cartwright Gardens. Come, Sissy, we have work to do."

He offers Sissy his arm and leads her out of the room and into the hallway.

Belinda follows them, but Mark Hawksley reaches the door first. He turns to face her, blocking her way with his body.

"You have a good appetite, Belinda. I like to see a young woman enjoying her … food," he murmurs, imbuing the word *food* with a significance that is not lost upon her.

She feels her mouth going dry. She looks down, hoping he cannot hear the beat of her heart.

"The temporary absence of your employers will leave you alone and unprotected once again, will it not?" he continues. "It will be my duty … nay, it will be my pleasure, to look after you."

He moves closer, his hand stroking her arm, then moving up to her shoulder.

"Should you like that, lovely Belinda Kite?"

She swallows.

"Miss Keet, where are you? You are keeping us waiting!" Josiah calls from the hallway.

Hawksley draws her close, lifting her face to his. He brushes her mouth with his warm lips.

"I cannot wait for us to be alone together again," he whispers.

In the carriage going back to Cartwright Gardens, Josiah is full of plans, Sissy is full of admiration, and Belinda Kite is full of desires and daydreams. And cake.

***

A few days later, Frederick Undercroft, lawyer, convivial fellow, and supporter of the specialist independent book trade, sits behind his desk in his lawyer's office surrounded by law books with gilt-lettered spines and marbled endpapers.

He has a morning appointment with a man he met at the Gyll on his last visit. He remembers precious little about that evening; indeed, he cannot even recall whether he spent it in his own bed or in the bed of some woman he met at the nightclub.

He certainly does not remember the man, but here is his name in his diary. Here is his card on his desk, and here, if he is not mistaken, is the gentleman himself arriving in the outer office now.

The clerk knocks discreetly, opens the door and announces, rather stiffly:

"A Mr Mark Hawksley to see you."

Hawksley enters. Freshly-shaved, his top hat brushed and shiny, he wears a city suit that fits him like a glove. And gloves that fit him like a second skin. A discreet aroma of expensive cologne enters with him. Undercroft notes all this. The man is exactly what he himself used to be before he started feeling seedy.

Now, Undercroft's clothes hang off him, and his top hat is frequently unbrushed as Georgiana does not bother to remind the new girl to attend to it. He is neglected and rundown, like some old nag fit only for the knacker's yard. He shakes the client's hand and gestures towards the cliental chair.

Hawksley sits, adjusting the sharply-ironed creases in his suit trousers (another thing the maid fails to attend to, Undercroft thinks).

"I am delighted to make your acquaintance again, Mr Undercroft." He smiles. "I prefer not to mix business with pleasure, so after our conversation at the Gyll, I decided to arrange an appointment at your place of work."

"You want me to draw up your Will?"

Hawksley smiles and shakes his head.

"Indeed no. I have a few years ahead of me before I need concern myself with matters like that. I am here to offer you the chance to invest in my business: I own a diamond mine – you recall we talked about it when we met at the Gyll. I believe your friend Mr Osborne has also mentioned my name? He tells me that he has. He and his son have both invested in it."

Ah. Undercroft's mind drifts back to the last time he dined at Boodles.

"Yes. He has mentioned it."

"How fortuitous that we should then run into each other," Hawksley continues smoothly.

He draws from his pocket a leaflet which he places on the desk, facing the lawyer.

"Here are the details of the Dominion Diamond Mine Company. As you can see, returns on your investment are likely to double in the first year, and rise steeply thereafter. The first seam is already being dug out, and the yield of gems is likely to exceed the estimation of the mining experts I have consulted."

Undercroft leans forward. He tries to look nonchalant, as if gentlemen offering him shares in diamond mines is an everyday occurrence. But at the back of his mind he is totting up his diminishing client list and his demanding mistress list.

"At this stage," Hawksley continues, "I am only offering this opportunity to a few select individuals. Your name was put forward by Mr Osborne, who indicated to me privately that you might be interested in investing. And of course, you yourself expressed such an interest in my project and desired to know more when we met the other evening."

He did? Undercroft strains to recall exactly what he said.

Hawksley extracts a gold watch from his waistcoat pocket.

"I am shortly to depart for South Africa to oversee the work, so time is of the essence. But of course, I am quite content to let you study the leaflet at your leisure and consult with your friends before making any decision."

Frederick Undercroft steeples his fingers together.

"The returns on any investment are guaranteed, you say?"

"Oh, I can guarantee you will not lose. And of course, all investors will have the chance to buy any of the diamonds before they go on the open market. A diamond necklace or a ring made from gems you yourself helped to dig up, as it were – how could any woman alive resist such a present?"

Undercroft opens a drawer.

"Will a banker's draft do? I do not have sufficient cash about me."

"Perfectly," Hawksley nods. "And I shall send your share certificate to you by close of business this afternoon."

Undercroft writes out the draft and hands it over.

Hawksley glances briefly at the amount without letting his face betray any emotion. Then he pockets the draft and stands up.

"I am pleased we have finally met," he says. "I have heard so much about lawyer Undercroft from my friends and fellow business associates. Your reputation precedes you, sir."

The two men shake hands once more.

Hawksley bows and departs. He is delighted with the success of the visit. So delighted in fact, that he fails to notice the extraordinary behaviour of the lawyer's clerk, who stares fixedly at his face as he shows him out, and then shakes his fist through the window as he walks away.

Some time later Hawksley stands outside a Regent Street department store. He taps his feet, glances up and down the busy thoroughfare, checks the time. He is waiting for Belinda Kite, whom he is 'looking after' during her employers' absence. She is fashionably late.

Eventually Belinda emerges from the store, where she has been browsing the latest ladies' fashions in Godey's magazine and looking at the new arrivals from Paris. She has fallen terribly in love with the dearest little bonnet and some satin slippers.

Actually, she has fallen in love with an awful lot of things, but she has realistically pared it down to a bonnet, shoes and a new dress. None of these things are affordable, of course, but a girl can dream. Belinda Kite has got very used to living on dreams.

Now she approaches Hawksley, noting how well his coat fits his shoulders and his manly figure. He is by far the best-dressed and handsomest man on the street, she thinks, as he turns at her approach and bows low in greeting. She has waited for him all her life, without knowing it.

And she is going to luncheon with him.

Hawksley takes her to a nice little restaurant off the Strand, the sort that has separate boxes, at the back and low discreet lighting, and a *Maître d'* who might recognise one from previous visits with other women, but would never betray this by the slightest facial movement or inadvertent remark.

Over a delicious luncheon, Belinda chatters happily about the lovely things she has seen, especially the dresses, while Hawksley smiles indulgently. She is delightful, young, and innocent of the ways of the world. So unlike the women he normally frequents.

Her peaches-and-cream skin, green eyes and titian hair are striking. Her small waist accentuates her high, round breasts He noticed several of the other male diners eyeing her with interest as they both passed by their tables. He likes to see other men envy him his companion.

Hawksley has done a good morning's business. He can afford to be generous. Besides, there is the prospect of sweets to come later on. He lets her run on, then at the end of the meal he opens his pocketbook.

"So, my little extravagant spendthrift, I gather you have your eye on a new dress. How much are you planning to take me for?" he says, play-frowning.

Belinda Kite stares at the pocketbook, trying not to let her amazement show. The sight of all those banknotes almost takes her breath away. That anybody should have so much money – and that the anybody in question should be sitting opposite her and offering her some – almost renders her speechless.

Almost, but not quite. Belinda does some rapid calculations in her head. She wishes to reply honestly, but she is avid, as only the once-impoverished can be.

"It would depend," she says thoughtfully, "upon whether the dress was bought ready-made or handmade by a private dressmaker."

"Would you like a handmade dress?" he asks.

She almost stops breathing.

"I should like that above all things," she murmurs.

"Then let it be so," Hawksley says, handing over the pocketbook. "Take what you want, my beautiful Belinda. And as soon your dress is made, let me know and I shall escort you to the theatre and then to one of the finest restaurants in town. Should you like that?"

She feels tears pricking her eyes. Her heart swells. When you have had doors slammed in your face all your life, to have one left open for you is almost too much to bear.

"I shall tell you when I have it," she says, helping herself, then handing back the pocket book.

He laughs.

"For that sort of money, I should hope it will be the finest dress in London."

"Oh, it will," she assures him earnestly. "It truly will."

***

Emily Cully is used to the ebb and flow of the dressmaking business. In Spring, at the start of the

Season, when the cream of London society (rich and thick) descend on the capital to dine, party and launch their daughters onto the marriage market, the seamstresses and dressmakers work flat out to sew the beautiful gowns they wear, sometimes only once.

Now, in the dark days of Autumn, with Winter breathing over its shoulder, the demand for her services has temporarily slackened. The Christmas season has not yet begun. Therefore she is delighted to receive a letter requesting her presence to advise, measure and fit a new customer for a winter dress.

Having lit the fires, made breakfast, seen Jack off to work, cleared up the dishes and washed a few clothes, Emily sets out in the grey dawn with her pattern books and sewing equipment. She vaguely recognises the address, but it is not until the omnibus drops her off outside the British Museum that she associates it with a former client.

She reaches the house, knocks on the door and is shown into the parlour. Here, instead of the pale, lanky young lady she fitted previously, she is greeted by the young woman who had been her companion.

"Good morning, Mrs Cully," she says. "I wrote to you because I should like you to make me a winter dress."

Emily places her basket on the table.

"I hope Miss Bulstrode is well?" she asks.

The young woman tosses her auburn ringlets.

"Oh, she is quite well, thank you – I received a letter from her yesterday. She and her brother have returned to their home town for a while."

She picks up *Mrs Demorest's Muse of Fashion* and flicks through it.

"Here – this is what I had in mind. It is all the rage in Paris right now, so I believe."

Emily glances at the picture, which shows two

elegant ladies wearing dresses of rich green and purple tarlatane, very low-cut at the front, with puffed sleeves, three skirts edged in narrow black velvet, and bretelles of lace. She purses her lip.

"These are very beautiful dresses indeed, I think. But," she suggests gently, "to have such a dress handmade would be very expensive."

The young lady's smile is that of a cat that owns a creamery.

"Oh! Do not worry yourself about the *expense*, Mrs Cully – you shall be paid whatever you decide to charge. Now, I have already visited a few department stores, and Marshall's have a very nice bronze velveteen. It will be just the thing, as it is a colour that suits me, I think. With cream puffed sleeves and black velvet edging. Do not you think that would look fine?"

Emily concurs, even though she dislikes sewing velveteen because it frays so easily, and she dislikes sewing black because it makes her eyes hurt, and the evenings are getting dark so early that she is spending a lot of the housekeeping money on candles.

"Then perhaps you would like to take some measurements?" the young lady suggests, turning her back so that Emily can unbutton the rather shabby day dress she is wearing.

After Emily Cully has left, Belinda Kite skips downstairs, humming happily to herself. She has just ordered a beautiful dress for herself, and with the money left over, she will now also be able to fund the purchase of the pretty little bonnet and satin slippers.

If anybody had told her, when she was just a poor, abandoned, despised, put-upon little drudge, that her life would turn out this way, she would have laughed in their face. But it has. And here she is to prove it.

***

Emily Cully carefully times her arrival at Marshall's to coincide with the departure of the sewing-room girls. Then she and Caro make themselves a pot of tea on the tiny gas hob in the supervisor's office, and sit down to study *Mrs Demorest's Muse of Fashion.*

"That's going to take a whole world of basting and fine hand-sewing," Caro remarks, nodding at the picture of Belinda's future dress. "Luverly though, innit."

"I was wondering whether you might be able to help me with it."

Caro pours tea into her saucer and blows on it.

"Course I will, Emily, love, if I can. Wotcher want me to do?"

"I don't think I have space to lay it all out at home anymore," Emily sighs. "Jack has started bringing paperwork back, and he leaves it out on the table. Then there is the mud from his boots."

Caro rolls her eyes.

"Men, eh? Always in the way or under your feet, bless 'em. Mine brought home a couple of pig's ears the other night. Didn't bother to wrap 'em, just dumped 'em on the dresser. Why don't you come by after closing tomorrow, and you can use the big cutting-out table here? I'll give you a hand if you like."

Emily's face brightens.

"Would you? Oh, I should be so grateful."

"Trade's slack at the moment, and they're buying in more ready-mades from factories all the time. I'm even thinking of laying a couple of girls off until the Spring – yes, I see your face, and no, I don't want to have to do it, but there just ain't the work for them right now."

"Are they good needlewomen?"

"One of them is. T'other – I don't think her heart's in it. Never was from the off. I'm guessing where she will end up, and it'll be no loss to the dressmaking business."

"Perhaps I could use the first girl? One of my sewing women has moved to Bristol with her husband."

Caro nods.

"That'd be great, Em. I'd hate to see the poor girl on the streets or in the Workus. And I'm happy to help too where I can. When does your client want it?"

"As soon as possible."

Caro rolls her eyes.

"Ain't that how it always is! Like we has a magic wand to wave. *Allacazam:* here's your dress madam. And I guess you won't get paid until you deliver it."

Emily pats her pocket.

"The young woman who ordered this dress has already paid me generously."

Caro raises an eyebrow.

"Young woman? Ordering a dress like this? Surely you mean Fine Lady?"

Emily grins mischievously.

"It is that same one I pointed out to you a couple of weeks ago, upstairs in the store. She's the companion of a young woman I made two nice day dresses for a while back."

"Oho! And how can a 'companion' afford an expensive dress like what you've just shown me?"

Emily pinches her lips together. The two of them eye each other for a second, then start giggling.

"Picked up a rich fancy man?" Caro splutters.

"Must have," Emily concurs.

"Well, good luck to her. Won't last, of course. Never does. Probably got a wife and five kids tucked away somewhere. Still, ours not to inquire, eh?"

They finish their tea. Emily leaves her shopping list with her friend, who promises to work out the best price of each item. They agree that she will stop by next day at the same hour to start work.

"You get some good red meat into you tonight," Caro says, as the two hug each other fondly on parting. "You're still looking proper peaky to me."

***

Proper peaky is probably not an expression Frederick Undercroft, lawyer, lover of fine wine and accommodating women, would use. Though whatever terminology he'd come up with, the fact remains that he is currently confined to his bed in the green-papered bedroom with the lock on the door.

He is not sick enough to call out his physician – nosebleeds, trembling of the lower limbs and a disinclination to connect to the world outside his bedroom window hardly justifies paying the exorbitant fee he will be charged to be told exactly what he already knows.

No, he will be right as rain in a few days. He has convinced himself of this. Besides, he doesn't want the quack ferreting out his other little problem … which he can barely admit, even to himself. Rest, beef tea brought at regular intervals by the unattractive new girl, and he will soon be up and out again (in all senses).

Meanwhile Georgiana Undercroft is supposed to tiptoe round the house in slippers, like a mute mouse, because the slightest sound reduces her lord and master to apoplectic ragings and brings on his nosebleeds. So, she tiptoes. But every now and then she cannot resist slamming the front door on her way out. Because she knows it annoys him. And just because she can.

***

No doors are being slammed in Belinda Kite's face. Quite the opposite. It is still dark, tinted with the promise of dawn, as she dismounts from the cab carrying her back from a night of passion with her handsome lover.

Awoken to the demanding music of physical desire, Belinda Kite is greedy for all that life is now showing her. She is young and vital: she believes in the power of true love.

She also believes in wonderful things, including that amazing marriages can happen. Why not? She reads of them every day in the novels she finds in Sissy's bookcase: *Young Lord Whatshisname falls in love with Miss Nobody, whose charm and beauty captivates his heart so much that he spurns the rich heiress his family has chosen for him in favour of the poor girl who has won his undying affection.*

It is fiction, but then from an early age Belinda Kite has made up stories about herself to survive. The life she now lives as the daughter of a French Marquis is a story. Her *résumé* is all fiction. She believes totally in the power of make-believe. This is what has got her to where she is today.

She walks up the front path, telling herself that Mark Hawksley is rich. He clearly finds her enchanting. Why should she not hope for more? Much more? She steps up to the front door. Wait till he sees her in the new dress, she thinks gleefully. He won't be able to resist her.

She unlocks the door and goes in. The servants have left a candle on the hall table. She lights it, and sees, by the flickering flame, that lying next to the candle-holder there is a letter with her name on it. The envelope has a black border.

Mystified, Belinda picks it up and carries it and the candle up to her room, where she sits down on her bed, opens the letter and reads:

My dear Miss Kite,

It is with heavy heart that I take up my pen to inform you that my beloved sister Grizelda has suffered a terrible accident. Three days ago, while traversing the main high street, she was knocked down and trampled by a pair of carriage horses that had been panicked by a loud gunshot.

Her suffering, I am reliably told by the doctor who attended her, was brief, and she died at home of her injuries. She was the best sister a brother could have, always kind, and always believing well of every person she met.

Her death will be a great loss to me personally, as well as to the friends she had here and in London – in which capacity I include you, Miss Kite, as you made her short stay in the city so very pleasant.

I shall not be returning to London. I have the funeral arrangements to make, of course, and the trip was mainly to cheer my poor sister after her great disappointment. The rent on the house is paid until the end of December, and you are welcome to live there until then in lieu of wages.

Please do not hesitate to apply to me when you have found another position. I shall be happy to furnish you with a good testimonial.

I remain,
Yours sincerely,
Josiah Bulstrode

For a couple of seconds, Belinda Kite cannot quite take in what she has just read. It pulls her abruptly away from the happiness she feels, from the future life she was imagining for herself, and takes her straight back to that other time when she was always looking over her shoulder, waiting for the next setback or the next desertion.

She folds up the letter and places it on her night table. Tomorrow she will write a letter of condolence to Josiah, for whom she feels genuine sadness. She didn't warm to Sissy, but his devotion to her was never in question.

She still has a roof over her head, albeit a temporary one, she reflects, as she pinches out the candle and settles back on her pillow. And at least she won't have to go into black.

***

Belinda Kite opens her eyes. It is early morning. For a moment, she lies in her warm bed, thinking contented thoughts. Then she remembers the letter from Bulstrode, and the doubts (that are never far from her mind) return to trouble her.

If she doesn't find another situation … If Mark Hawksley fails to live up to expectations … Once again, her life is at the behest of others, over whom she has very little control.

Belinda gets up and throws back the curtains. There are frost patterns on the window. Perfect crystalline symmetries. They remind her of the diamonds she saw in the jeweller's showroom. The diamonds she has promised herself she will own one day.

She puts on her morning wrapper and makes her way downstairs. Breakfast is laid in the dining room. She helps herself to bacon, eggs and toast while she works out what she is going to say to the servants later.

After eating her breakfast, she sits down at the writing-desk and composes a suitably sorrowful letter to her former employer, and a slightly less sorrowful one to Hawksley informing him of the contents of

Josiah's letter.

It is nearly noon by the time she sets out to post both letters. It is also Sunday, and the city has a shut-down air. The shops are closed, the streets deserted. The smog cuts off emptiness from emptiness. London feels like a ruined place, all darkened brick and ashlar stone.

After posting her letters she decides, upon a whim, to keep walking.

She passes rows of small terraces with drawn blinds and smoke-blackened walls. Someone has hung a cage of finches from an upper storey: she hears their tiny piping *me-me*. A woman sings to the rhythm of her work. A swarm of ragged children hurtle round a corner, parting like a wave in the sea as they pass by on either side of her.

London is an easy place to get lost in. It has no centre. The streets lead off one another. They enclose and then enclose again, like a system of Chinese boxes, opening one into another, the perspectives endlessly changing.

Step away from the main thoroughfare, and the city changes into small unnamed footstreets, now full of shuttered small businesses: pawnbrokers, muffin-bakers, makers of incorrodible teeth, and a locked washhouse.

Belinda rounds a corner to discover an old man in a battered top hat and filthy coat turning the handle of a hurdy-gurdy for three little barefoot girls, who hop and skip solemnly in time to the music.

The air smells of alcohol and rotten oranges. Around another corner she finds herself in a dead-end alleyway full of rubbish, rotting meat, and a sad little heap of dead kittens.

Recoiling, Belinda retraces her steps and starts walking back the way she has come. This is where she might end up, if things don't work out for her. She stumbles over a loose cobblestone and almost falls.

For a split second, she feels the old despair rise up inside her, but she forces it down. She reminds herself that this is the greatest city in the world. Full of opportunities and amazing possibilities. She is Belinda Kite, and just around the next corner something marvellous is waiting for her.

***

Monday morning, and the only thing that is currently waiting for Detective Inspector Stride as he arrives at Scotland Yard is a load of aggravation. This takes the form of a small crowd gathered outside the building, and Richard Dandy, chief reporter on *The Inquirer,* who is busy handing out business cards to them.

The crowd has *"Rent-A-Mob"* written all over it. The people are the sort that can be guaranteed to materialise out of nowhere whenever something happens. It is a constant mystery to Stride how they actually know what has happened and where to assemble. But they do and here they are. Stride even recognises a few familiar faces. Dandy spots Stride and raises his voice.

"Here he is, gents and ladies. Morning, Stride – I see the police force are once again failing to protect the man in the street's property from wanton vandalism."

Sensing blood, the crowd begins backing up behind him.

"On the contrary, Mr Dandy," Stride retorts, pushing past and holding his breath to avoid the strongly-scented cologne. "My men have been working steadily and diligently behind the scenes, gathering evidence and conducting interviews, and we expect to make some arrests imminently."

Dandy pauses, mid-scribble.

"How imminently?"

"Very imminently. And now if you wouldn't mind, gentlemen – and Mrs Curvage, how nice of you to put in an appearance once again – I need to go and brief my officers."

The crowd parts, still muttering, but now with a side order of added interest.

Dandy attaches himself to Stride's wake.

"Are you going to give us a tip, then?"

Stride turns.

"My tip to you, Mr Dandy, is to use less of that foul cologne. Good day."

He hurries into the building, where Jack Cully is waiting for him to arrive.

"I heard what you said," Cully remarks. "Is it true?"

Stride makes a seesaw motion with his right hand.

"Yes and no. The men watching Millbank Tendring's house have reported a bit of coming and going. Paint pots being brought round and taken way again. It looks as if something is being planned. I'm going to put young Evans in charge tonight. Time the lad had a bit of a chance to show us what he's made of."

Cully raises his eyebrows.

"Oh, I shall be there in the background, don't worry."

"I think it's a full moon tonight," Cully observes.

"Yes," Stride says drily. "That sounds about right."

***

Emily Cully has packed her basket and is on her way to visit her latest client for a first fitting. The elaborate dress is coming along well and she is pleased with its progress. Today she is walking – saving the omnibus fare so that she can buy something to eat later. It is a cold morning, and she is grateful for the warm shawl her late parents bought her as a wedding gift.

A phaeton passes, heading south towards the river. At its window, a sudden flash of bright colour. A young woman's clothes. Emily glanced up as it passes, and smiles. She has never lost her love of bright colours, but they are not practical in her line of work.

She stops at the corner of Tottenham Court Road to buy a cup of coffee from one of the stall-holders, remembering how Jack bought her coffee and a ham sandwich the first time they met – that sad day when she learned that her friend Violet had been brutally murdered.

How kind he was to her then. How kind he still is. She hears the street gossip about husbands who come home drunk, beat their wives, demand their 'rights'. She has been lucky. Her lines have fallen in a pleasant place.

Emily crosses the street, imagining it full of all the good people who have brought her to this point in her life, letting the memories come flooding back. She had once promised herself that she would never forget, that she would always hold them in her heart.

But time goes on, and the world fills up with other things to remember, other things to do, other calls on her time – and it becomes too easy to forget the things that are important, the real things. Now she recalls their faces one by one, ending with the face of dear Violet. They have all stayed with her, although she will never see most of them again.

***

It is one of those London nights when the rain is endless and the street lights are brightened by the reflections of water. The sort of night when sensible people and prospective criminals decide to stay indoors.

Detective Inspector Stride stands in the lee of a doorway watching the empty street, across which the rain is marching like an invading army.

Water swirls round his boots and drips off his cape. In theory, he should be feeling miserable as sin. It is three in the morning. He is wet, alone and cold. Yet Stride is, albeit temporarily, a happy man.

He's spent some of the best nights of his career like this, he reflects. On a rainy night like this you could just wrap yourself up, pull your head in and become almost invisible. A little hunch of warmth, your mind just ticking over and putting the world to rights.

In the old days, when Stride was just a lowly beat constable, nobody cared about what you were up to; you were just boots on the ground. All you really had to do was keep out of trouble and be seen apprehending the odd criminal. Now, everything was bigger, more important, and came with added responsibilities.

A gust of wind catches the water pouring from a leaky gutter and dumps it down Stride's neck. Somewhere up ahead there is a sudden crash, followed by a scream.

Stride, like most of his colleagues, has learned over the years to be good at interpreting screams. To the connoisseur there's a world of difference between *I'm drunk and I've fallen over and bitten my tongue and Aarrgh, he's got a knife.*

He starts running.

***

Since her first induction into the art of lovemaking, Belinda Kite is rapidly becoming quite the expert. Hawksley teases her that under his tutelage she can now sip champagne in such a way as to make it seem like a powerful aphrodisiac.

The arrival of Josiah's letter has freed her from the drudgery of being a paid companion, and with no threat of her employer's imminent return she has seen her handsome lover most days. Sometimes she meets him in town for luncheon; sometimes a cab comes for her in the early evening and she is transported to the small quiet hotel that he has moved into, where a dainty supper and other entertainment awaits.

Now he lies in her arms, spent and satisfied. His head is pillowed on her firm young breasts. Her legs are wrapped around his thighs. She stirs and utters a little sigh. Hawksley looks up at her with an expression of sleepy amusement.

"What are you thinking about, my Belinda of the Autumn curls?"

"My new dress. The dressmaker came yesterday for a fitting. It is going to be so lovely."

"And when it is finished, I shall take you out to the finest restaurant in London and show you off to the world, as I promised."

He runs a finger down her soft arm. She shivers.

"And I was thinking about the diamonds."

"You are always thinking about them. Aren't the earrings I gave you enough?"

Enough for now.

"I was wondering about all those big diamonds lying in your diamond mines. When are they going to be dug up?"

He laughs, raises himself on one elbow, and eyes her speculatively. Then he sits up, draws her closer, and whispers in her ear.

"Can you keep a *very* big secret, Belinda Kite?"

She nods. She can. She is good at keeping secrets. After all, her whole life is a secret that she has been keeping for a long time.

So he tells her. About how he thought up the idea of a fake diamond mine. About the public meetings he arranges to sell the concept; about the way people fall over themselves to buy shares.

"People are greedy. They want to get rich quickly without any effort on their part. I have merely offered them the chance to do exactly what they want," he tells her.

She stares into his face, her eyes wide with amazement.

"But the Queen – surely she is not part of this?"

He laughs fondly.

"Oh, my dear sweet innocent little love – of course there is no Queen. Just a workhouse washerwoman whom one of my men discovered by accident. She bears a striking likeness to our beloved monarch. Remember, as you yourself pointed out, I never actually *say* that the Queen herself will be present."

"And the diamond you showed to everyone at the first meeting?"

"Glass, my dear."

Her head is spinning.

"So – is nobody going to make any money?"

"Well, I am. Indeed, I have already made a great deal of money. It is all locked securely in a cash box under the bed. Apart from what I give to my special girl to spend on clothes and such, of course."

"But what happens when you are found out?"

"*If,* my pet, not *when*. And if that ever looks like happening, I shall just change my name and quit these shores and live somewhere else. Italy, perhaps? Or Greece? It is always warm there, and there is ample wine."

She can barely take it in, her mind is whirling.

"There now," Hawksley says. "No more questions."

He yawns, pulls her closer. "Let us sleep. You have quite worn me out, my greedy little girl."

He slips into a deep contented sleep.

But Belinda Kite cannot sleep. She remains wide awake and lying on her back, her fingers latched behind her head, just staring and staring at the ceiling.

Later, back home, what stays with her is his voice. She thinks of it again in the dark, in her own room which could be anywhere, any time. Her arms close around herself like a lover.

It feels to her as if everything is suddenly unreal, as if her happiness has shifted, and a door has been opened onto a place where she is a stranger who does not know the rules. There is a tightness in her chest. She has been here before; she has never been here before.

***

Stride runs down a side street, ducks through an alley and arrives in one of the squares that are made up largely of lawyers' offices. Sergeant Evans is standing in front of some railings from which a man is suspended, upside down.

The man appears to be caught by the bottom of his jacket. There is a pot of paint at the foot of the railings, and a small Jack Russell is barking furiously and trying to bite his dangling arms.

Evans turns as Stride come up.

"Good evening, sir. A wet night, isn't it? I seem to have found this gentleman in pursuit of some night painting."

Stride regards the upside-down culprit thoughtfully.

"Well, well. You are in a bit of a predicament, sir. Good thing we came by. Looks like it's your lucky night."

A nervous expression flits across the man's face. Unless the person saying it is wearing a low-cut dress and an accommodating smile, nobody likes being told it's their lucky night. When someone tells you it's your lucky night, you just know something unlucky is about to happen.

Stride and Evans unhook the man and set him on his feet. The dog stops barking and sits down on the pavement, regarding the trio with a look of canine disdain.

The man stares incredulously at his two rescuers.

"You can SEE me? Both of you?"

"It would appear so, sir," Stride says drily.

"But you're not meant to see me."

"I'm sure we aren't. But luckily for you, we do."

"But the Prophet said that The Lord promised I shall be wrapped in a Cloak of Invisibility!"

Stride and Evans exchange a quick meaningful glance.

"Perhaps it got caught on the railings," Stride suggests.

"Or fell into the area, with the paintbrush you dropped," Evans adds.

"So, sir," Stride says, "in the event that you are NOT invisible, would you like to furnish us with an explanation for why you are out in the middle of the night with a pot of red paint and a brush?"

"And a dog," Evans adds.

The man lowers his eyes and studies the damp cobbles.

"I was doing The Lord's work," he mutters.

"Then I suggest you stop doing it and return home forthwith," Stride says crisply.

The man hesitates.

"But The Lord says—"

"Look upon it as the lesser of two evils."

"What's the other one?"

Stride's smile is the sort that lurks on sandbanks waiting for unwary swimmers.

"Me," he says, getting out his official police badge. "I might be tempted to arrest you."

The man draws himself up.

"For what?"

Stride counts on his fingers. "Let me see now: there's loitering with intent … not to mention with paint. Travelling with the purpose of committing a crime, obstruction, trespass, malicious lingering, and carrying a concealed weapon."

"Sir, I don't think—" Evans interjects.

"*I* can't see it, sergeant, can you?"

Stride returns his attention to the man, who is now looking slightly abashed.

"At the end of the day, I could just arrest you on suspicion of being suspicious," he remarks, adding, "Of course, in some circles, what you and your friends have done over the past few weeks might be interpreted as treason. Do you know what the punishment for treason is?"

The man shakes his head.

"First you'll be dragged to the place of execution on a hurdle. Then you'll be hung, drawn and quartered."

"I know all about hanging and quartering, sir," Sergeant Evans says thoughtfully. "But I'm never sure how you're drawn."

"Depends who's in charge of the pencil," Stride replies without a flicker of expression crossing his face.

The man picks up his pot of paint.

"Wait a moment," Stride says, "before you go, my sergeant here would very much like your full name and current address. Just in case he wants any painting done."

Evans gets out his notebook and looks expectantly at

the man, who mutters a few words.

"Thank you, sir," the young sergeant says politely. "I shall be checking up on it tomorrow first thing. And should you have given me a false address …" He lets the words hang in the air.

"I haven't, officer. Honest to God."

Evans shuts the notebook.

"If you'll take my advice, sir," Stride says, "you'll tell your Lord you've decided to jack in this painting lark. Ask Him to find you something else to do. Preferably something that isn't against the law of the land."

"Gardening," Evans suggests. "That's not against the law, is it? And it's mentioned in the Bible too – the Garden of Eden."

"Good suggestion, sergeant. Now, sir, on your way. And don't let any of my officers catch you or anybody else with tins of red paint after dark ever again. Or I WILL be making arrests, believe me."

The man touches his dripping cap, whistles to the dog, and hurries off.

"Religious idiots," Stride says. "I thought that would be the case. No point arresting him – chances are the whole group was in on it. We could spend between here and Christmas trying to find out who exactly painted what when. That's if any of them will talk to us in the first place. He's had a good scare, and I don't think we'll be plagued by any more slogans."

He claps the young sergeant on the back. "You've done a good job on this, Sergeant Evans, and I'm going to make sure those in authority know about it. Now, let's get out of this blasted rain before we both catch our deaths."

***

The following morning, Senior Prophet About is unexpectedly interrupted in his morning's meditations by a small deputation consisting of four of the flock accompanied by the dog.

Having hammered on his door and been admitted by a weary-looking wife, they settle awkwardly on the sofa and two chairs, shuffle their feet, and stare at the threadbare carpet. They have only ever seen About in his official capacity leading a meeting of the Select Brethren, but desperate times ...

About enters, carrying his Bible.

"My dear brothers," he says raising his eyebrows and looking slowly and intently into each face, a technique usually guaranteed to cow people into silence. "What brings you to my door at this unseasonable hour?"

The flock clear their throats and nudge each other until they run out of nudges and throat-clearing, and the man at the end of the sofa is stared into speech.

"See, it's like this," he begins. "We don't want to do any more writing. Coz the law says it ain't legal."

About opens his mouth to interject. Too late.

"And as for the Cloak of Invisibility what you promised us, it don't work. Leastwise, it didn't last night, and my missus says I'm not to go out at night any more unless it's to the Beetle and Jam Jar, and then only on the strict understanding that I'm back by ten sharp or else she'll lock me out."

There is a corporate nodding of heads, indicative that similar sentiments are being expressed *(sotto voce)* by the others.

"And that's all I want to say – except that I won't be coming to any more meetings as the wife says she has things for me to do in the house of a Thursday evening."

"Mine says that too," the second flock member adds.

The other two, who are both wifeless, say nothing, but try to convey that IF they had wives, this is exactly what their wives would also say.

"So we apologise for coming round so early," the former painter continues, getting to his feet. "And we bid you good day."

The flock rises, troops out of the back parlour, and is shown into the street by the weary-looking woman who admitted them in the first instance. She, as soon as she has closed the door on the last of them, rounds on the Senior Prophet.

"Right," she says grimly, folding her arms. "I heard all that and what I have to say is: that is the last straw. I have had ENOUGH! I can't be doing with all this God stuff no longer. It's making us the laughing stock of the neighbourhood. Every time I leave the house, people point at me and laugh behind my back. And I can't be doing with all the washing any more. It's wearing me out before my time. It's got to stop. Do you hear me? Now."

Senior Prophet About stares at her bemusedly.

"But ... God has given me a Vision. You know that. And then there's the Infant Prophet to consider."

"He's not an Infant Prophet, he's just a naughty little boy. At least that's what he oughter be. It ain't healthy for him to be cooped up in the house all day. He should be out in the fresh air playing with the other boys. I'm warning you, either you drop all this religious malarky and go back to being Millbank Tendring again, or, so help me, I shall take the boy and go and stay with my sister in Poplar."

About sways slightly as if he has been struck a blow.

"I shall seek the Lord in earnest prayer," he says meekly.

"You do that," his wife replies tartly. "And while you're at it, tell Him exactly what I told you. And make sure He listens. Or there will be Consequences. And you can tell Him that from me as well."

She gives him a fearsome glare before she strides to the back kitchen, where behind the closed door the Infant Prophet, a slice of bread and jam in one hand, is presiding over a washtub of hot water.

"Get your jacket and cap, Jo," she tells him. "We are going to the barber's. Time all those baby curls were cut off. And then we're going to buy you some new clothes. And this time, they ain't going to be white."

***

It is a cold morning, three days after Detective Inspector Stride and Sergeant Evans put a dramatic stop to the red-paint outrages that had so shocked those shockable members of London society – most of whom worked in Fleet Street.

And here is the hero of the hour, Sergeant Evans, standing outside Stride's office, whither he has been summoned. It is never a comfortable feeling to be summoned by a higher authority, and the young man is going over the past few weeks to try to work out what he has done that he ought to have left undone, or vice versa.

In his pocket is the latest missive from Megan, another source of anxiety. It is unopened, as yet. He stares at the closed office door and mentally prepares for the worst. On both fronts.

Meanwhile on the other side of the door, Stride and Cully are gleefully flicking through the morning papers. Each one carries some pun-ishing variant of *The Inquirer's:*

Caught Red-Handed! Artful Anarchists Apprehended!

"I wonder how long it took Dandy to come up with that headline," Cully says. "It's not even accurate, is it? We allowed them to go, in the end."

"I'll let Dandy off – this time," Stride says, "given that his rag has fulfilled its obligations. Or is shortly about to. Now, let's have the young man in and break the good news to him."

Cully ushers a very nervous Evans into the office.

"Good morning, Sergeant Evans," Stride says, switching his face to solemn and serious. "I expect you've seen the headlines in today's papers?"

"I heard the newsboys shouting it on my way in, sir," Evans says, turning the brim of his hat frantically between his hands.

"You've checked the address of the man you apprehended?"

"Oh yes, sir. The very next morning. I spoke to his wife. And she promised me that he wouldn't do it again. Ever. Very adamant, she was."

"Excellent," Stride says. "I don't know if you were aware, sergeant, that our good friends on *The Inquirer* were offering a reward for any information leading to the capture of the miscreants?"

Evans shakes his head.

"Well, they were. And as you not only discovered the address of the main culprit, organised the surveillance team, and then apprehended one of the group in action, as it were, I have taken the liberty of writing to the editor to inform him of the vital part you played in freeing the City of London from Anarchy and Revolution." Stride's mouth twitches. "And here is the reply I received last night."

He hands Evans a letter.

"As you can see, sergeant, the sum of twenty guineas is waiting for you in *The Inquirer's* office. I suggest you jog along now and collect it before they change their minds."

The expression on Sergeant Evans' face could light up the night sky.

"Oh sir! It is more than I deserve – I was only doing my job after all."

"And doing it extremely well," Stride says. "Now go and claim your reward."

A beaming Evans is shown out by Jack Cully, who lays a hand on his coat sleeve.

"You'll have some good news to write to your young lady now," he says.

"Oh, I WILL, Mr Cully. And maybe she might believe that I am deadly serious about our relationship."

"I hear on the grapevine that there is an inspector's job coming up with the Cardiff Police next Spring. Why don't you apply for it? I know Detective Inspector Stride would be happy to write you a glowing testimonial. So would I."

Sergeant Evans grabs Cully's hand and shakes it vigorously. There are tears in his eyes.

"I cannot thank you enough, Mr Cully. No, indeed I can't. Nor Detective Inspector Stride. You have both been so good to me since I started work here."

"One thing though – I gather they'd prefer a married man ... Would that be a problem?" Cully asks innocently.

A few seconds later Cully returns to Stride's office, massaging his right hand.

"That young man will go far," Stride remarks.

He is going to be proved right. Sergeant Evans will rise to the top of his profession, earning the loyalty and respect of all who encounter him. But he will never forget the kindness of the two men from Scotland Yard who made it all possible. And one day, that kindness is going to be repaid. With interest.

***

But all this is yet to be. Let us re-enter the prosaic present, in the form of a quiet public house not far from the City Road. Understand, however, that this is not one of your stuccoed, French-polished, illuminated West End palaces with its marble bars and gilded affluence.

Here the gaslight hangs from the ceiling, and there are long narrow wooden tables with wooden benches, sanded floors and strategically-placed spittoons. People do not come here of an evening to be amused, to stare at painted women, or to gamble their money away at whist.

Oswald Pyle and William Ginster are seated at a table in the far corner, nursing tumblers of brandy. They have a preoccupied air, as of men waiting for something or someone to happen to them.

What happens is that Mark Hawksley enters the public house, accompanied by a small dumpy woman dressed in black, with a heavy veil covering her face.

"Here she is, gentlemen," he says cheerfully. "Returned into your care once more. Give her a good dinner and then take her back to where she came from. She has served her purpose."

He gives a purse to Ginster.

"Money for your train tickets. The rest is to be given to her upon parting."

He motions to the woman to sit down.

"I shall leave you in these two gentlemen's care. You recognise them? Good. You will be safe with them. They will see you safely back home. You have done well, and you are going to be well rewarded. Just make sure you remember exactly what I told you in the hotel, or it will be the worse for you."

He nods at Ginster and Pyle.

"I shall see you both when you get back. We have much work to do – but I will tell you all about my latest plans upon your return."

Hawksley swings on his heel and strides jauntily out of the pub, whistling the latest music hall ditty under his breath as he goes.

***

Gaslight creates a dream world, blurring the uncertain boundaries between the real and imagined. A world of beauty and poetry, danger and disorder, where the heavy lazy mist that overhangs everything makes the lights look brighter and the brilliantly-lit buildings even more splendid by contrast.

Look more closely. Mark Hawksley, top-hatted and in full evening dress, is dismounting from the cab that has brought him back from a select dinner party at the home of Mr and Mrs Osborne. A dinner party where he was the guest of honour.

There were also various banker friends of Osborne at the table. By the end of the evening they were his friends too. It has been a most successful evening. He has eaten lavishly and made several promising contacts.

Hawksley steps down from the cab. He pays the driver, bidding him a cheery goodnight, and is just about to enter the foyer of his hotel when somebody calls his name.

Hawksley stops, turns, and glances round in the direction of the voice. A man steps from the shadows and strides towards him. Hawksley does not recognise him. The man removes his leather gloves and strikes him hard across the face. Hawksley recoils.

"What the hell do you think you are doing?" he exclaims angrily, rubbing his cheek.

"I am striking a blow for the young woman you wronged," the stranger declares in a hoarse voice, his eyes blazing hatred. "The young woman you promised to marry and then abandoned. I struck it on behalf of my beloved sister Evelyn."

Hawksley's face freezes.

"I do not know what you are talking about. Perchance you have mistaken me for somebody else."

"Oh, I know who you are alright! I recognised you as soon as you walked into lawyer Undercroft's office the other day – though you didn't recognise me, did you? Why should you? I was just the lawyer's clerk. Too lowly for you to pay attention to me, Godfrey Sharpe."

At the sound of that name, Hawksley's face loses its colour.

"Yes – not so confident now, are you?" the man says. "Not so swaggering and full of yourself."

Hawksley takes a step back.

"It was just like the conniving cunning cur that you are to come back to Bath, pretending you were somebody else," the man continues. "That was where I saw you again for the first time since you fled the town. I'd been looking hard for you, but I hadn't found you anywhere. And suddenly, there you were. I sat at the back of the Assembly Rooms and saw you strutting on the stage like a peacock, all airs and graces, all lies and falsehood."

"I can assure you, there was nothing between your sister and me," Hawksley interjects. "It was merely a misunderstanding on her part."

"Oh, was it? You gave her a ring. You swore undying love. And you did that which I will refrain from naming in a public place. You are the lowest of the low – a vile seducer!"

"I have only your word for all of this," Hawksley exclaims. "Maybe you are lying. You know I am rich – perhaps you and your sister are in league to fleece me of my money. Oh yes – I see it now. Blackmail is a criminal offence, you do know that?"

The man's face is contorted with rage.

"I care nothing for your money, Godfrey Sharpe. Nothing! And as for my poor sister, she is currently an inmate of Earlswood Asylum, driven mad by your brutal rejection and abandonment."

The man reaches into his inner pocket and brings out a long official-looking white envelope.

"This is a summons to appear before Marylebone Magistrate Court next Thursday morning. On behalf of my sister, who can no longer speak or act for herself, I am suing you for breach-of-promise. If you fail to attend, Godfrey Sharpe, then I swear that I will go to every newspaper in the land and tell them my sister's story. I will furnish them with your likeness. I will ruin you. Nobody will ever do business with you again. And if you attempt to cut and run, I will hunt you down like the dog you are. And when I find you, it will be the worse for you."

He thrusts the envelope into Hawksley's hand and melts back into the shadows of the night.

For several minutes after the encounter, Hawksley does not move. He stares into the middle distance, stunned by what has just happened. Then he seems to reach a decision. Stuffing the letter into the pocket of his coat, he sets off purposefully towards the bright lights of the Strand.

***

Sunrise comes slowly, imperceptibly, like the ticking

of a clock face, the fog lifting to meet it. Marianne Corvid feels her eyes and ears working in the pale dawn before she is even thinking properly.

Her heart beats the blood awake. She throws back the coverings and stands in her night-gown in the freezing cold room, pushing back her hair, kneading the ache out of her shoulders before lighting the gas-lamp, which hisses and murmurs like human voices.

Marianne opens the lid of the clothes chest. Inside is a mirror. She stares down at her reflection. Her eyes are like a reducing chamber. If she looks into them long enough, she will become as small as her own reflection. She will diminish to a point and vanish.

She notices the hollow in her throat under which a necklace should hang. It has been a long time since she wore jewels for pleasure. She doesn't have any jewellery now. It is all gone, all sold.

Somewhere in the white distance, church bells chime. She dresses, packs her bag with what she needs for the day ahead, then leaves the empty house. She is not looking for a way to escape the past. The past is in everything she does, that obsession to love and be loved, which is now merely a reservoir of love gone sour.

The streets are crowded with people coming into the city to work, but she finds that if she looks at them in a certain way, they shift around her. It feels almost physical, in the way that memories can seem physical. Even the quality of light seems to change.

She walks on. The present becomes occluded. She is two people, separated by the years. One of them is lost. The other is what she has become, what she is now. She blinks, and the two coalesce and suddenly she finds herself here, where she knew she would inevitably end up, under the plane trees with the ebonised dust blowing in the air. Waiting for the future to arrive.

***

Frederick Undercroft's bedroom door has been shut for the past week. But today the master of the house finally emerges, weak and pale but dressed in his business suit. He descends the stairs, slowly, holding tight to the banister rail, and makes an unexpected entrance in the dining-room, where Georgiana is just finishing her breakfast.

She glances up, her eyes widening.

"Good morning, Frederick. Should you be up and dressed?"

He slides into a chair, indicates to the maid to pour him a cup of coffee.

"I can hardly go into work in my nightshirt."

"Is that where you are intending to go? You do not seem in quite a fit state."

"My state, fit or unfit, is no concern of yours," he snaps, gulping down the bitter black brew. "There is work to be done, clients to see. And letters to write. Important letters."

There is an expectant pause. He stares at her meaningfully.

"What letters?"

"It is my intention to write to the detective police. I want the case reopened. Lying up there has given me ample time to think it over, and I believe I have new evidence that I wish to lay before the detective inspector."

"What is this evidence?"

He looks across the table at her, his face stony, his eyes settling on her. His lips and cheeks are as pale and precise as waxwork.

"I am not going to tell you. Suffice to say that I now

believe that more than one individual was involved. I know who they are and I will give the names of these individuals to the authorities."

"What names?"

He does not answer.

She looks away.

"They will not believe a word you say. You are clearly mad."

His smile is vulpine.

"Ah, you'd like to think that, wouldn't you? But you are wrong. I have never been saner in my life. By the end of the day, the matter will be back in the police's hands. And there is nothing that anybody, especially you, can do to stop me."

He staggers to his feet, and lurches unsteadily to the door, calling loudly for his overcoat and top hat.

She sits immobile until she hears the front door closing. Then she, too, rises and makes her way to her room. She sits at her dressing table, trying to work out what to do.

I do not claim to be a good person, she thinks, *but I do not deserve this.*

She dresses herself quickly and without the aid of the maid. Then she slips out of the house and strides determinedly up Haverstock Hill. Reaching the chemist's shop, she pushes open the door, the tinkling bell bringing the young assistant from the back where he has been grinding powders to make pills.

She states her request in a low voice, touching her forehead with a gloved hand, as if in pain. He nods understandingly and hands her a small bottle of ruby liquid. She fumbles in her bag, produces the payment, and goes.

Georgiana walks up to the horse pond at the top of the hill, where she picks up a cab, ordering the driver to take her into the West End. All the way there, she sits stony-faced, staring straight ahead, her mind lost with childhood memories.

She sees her young self, happy, loved and secure. Dreaming her girlish dreams in her little white bedroom, about the wonderful man who will one day arrive to sweep her off her feet. How naïve and innocent she was back then. How sad and disillusioned she is now.

She gets the cab driver to drop her at the top of Oxford Street. There are many pharmacies and chemists in the area. None of them know her, or will remember her, a pale, unenticing woman complaining of a headache.

By mid-afternoon, she has amassed a bagful of small bottles of ruby liquid. She takes a cab back to the house in Downshire Hill, tells the servants she doesn't want any supper, is going straight to bed and is not to be disturbed.

Georgiana climbs the stairs to her bedroom and bolts the door, placing a chair under the handle. Then she sits down on the bed. Her hands are trembling. Her breathing is fast and ragged. She sets the bottles out on the nightstand and begins to uncork them. The pungent smell of cinnamon fills the air.

Georgiana Undercroft reaches for the first little bottle, closes her eyes and downs the contents in one quick swallow.

**

In the late afternoon, Frederick Undercroft sits at his desk. He has no recollection of how he has spent the day. There were documents to sign, there were clients to advise. He supposes he performed the appropriate actions in both cases.

At some points, his lawyer's clerk entered, placed

cups of coffee on the desk, and re-entered to remove them later. All this must have happened, but it is as if he has been an onlooker to events. Now, with the pale afternoon sunshine waning and the light in his room becoming too dim to read clearly, he decides to call it a day.

He puts on his overcoat. In one of the pockets he finds a letter addressed in his handwriting to a Detective Inspector Stride at Scotland Yard. He is tempted to open it to see what he wrote. He does not recall composing it, nor can he work out why he should want to write to this man.

Undercroft leaves his office, the letter in his hand. It is his intention to post it but he cannot now recall where the nearest post box is located. He sets out to find it. On his way, he finds himself cutting through a courtyard in which a marionette show is coming to an end.

The audience is hooting with laughter. To Undercroft it appears that the puppets are being made to fornicate. When he looks more closely, he sees that they are. Bemused, he walks on.

The city closes in around him. He begins to lose all sense of where he is, what he is. His thoughts stammer in his head. All the hours and minutes and days of his life are colliding. Time is suspended. He could be anywhere, or nowhere at all.

***

Frederick Undercroft is not the only one experiencing a baffling sense of loss. Belinda Kite lies awake in Hawksley's bed, unable to sleep. Something is very wrong. She'd arrived at his hotel a few hours earlier to find no tempting little supper laid out by the fire, and a host who seemed dull and preoccupied, strangely indifferent to her chatter.

Usually, Hawksley couldn't wait to hear her talk about her day, what she'd seen, or eaten. Her tart comments on the women she encountered in the street never failed to provoke a wry smile and some compliment on her beauty, wit and intelligence, and how much he loved her for them.

Tonight, however, Hawksley has barely spoken to her, seemed uninterested in her excited description of her new dress, and has not reiterated his promise to take her out to the finest restaurant in town.

When he led her to his bedroom, he removed her clothes detachedly, as if she was just some woman he'd picked up for the night. Worse, for the first time since she went to bed with him, he did not wait patiently for her to climax first, taking his time to arouse her with his kisses and caresses.

Instead, after a few perfunctory strokes of her breasts, he rolled her onto her back and mounted her, spending himself inside her with a groan, then sliding off her without a word.

Now he sleeps, one heavy arm thrown carelessly across her naked body.

Belinda eases out from under his arm and gets out of bed. Tiptoeing over to the chair where he has flung his clothes, she starts to go through his pockets.

She does not know what she is looking for, but she does know that she is looking for something that might give her a clue as to his behaviour. She wonders whether she has been replaced in his affections by another woman. It seems the only logical explanation.

There is nothing incriminatory in his trouser pockets, nor in his waistcoat pockets. Belinda moves on to his jacket. In an inner pocket, she finds a railway ticket to Liverpool. It is dated for tomorrow morning, first thing.

Further exploration elicits a message from the

Electric Telegraph Office, 448 Strand. Dated late last night, it states that a single berth in a first-class cabin has been reserved on the SS Great Eastern, leaving Liverpool for New York in two days' time.

She checks ticket and message carefully, just in case she has misunderstood what she has discovered. She has not. Both are reservations for one person only. Mark Hawksley is leaving London for New York, and he is leaving on his own. He has not told her, nor clearly has he made any plans to take her with him.

For a moment, the perfidy of her lover stuns her. She actually takes a step back, as if he has struck her a blow. Given all that she thought she meant to him, and he to her, such a betrayal shocks her to her core. It is even worse than discovering that he has another woman.

She returns to the bed and stares at Hawksley's sleeping form. He does not move. Once again, the old despair of being abandoned by those she trusted and loved begins to rise up inside her, but she pushes it down. Now is not the time for such thoughts, she tells herself. She needs to think clearly and act quickly.

Belinda crouches down and feels under the bed until her hands close on the cash box. Gently, she eases it out and with catlike tread carries it into the other room, setting it down by the door.

She puts on her clothes. She does not look round. Part of her wants to, but she doesn't let it. Instead she tucks the cash box under one arm and walks out of the room, out of the hotel, and out of Mark Hawksley's life forever.

Some time later Belinda Kite steps down from a cab. Giving the driver instructions to wait, she lets herself into Number 11, Cartwright Gardens. At this hour, the place is in darkness; the servants are all either out or in their own rooms. Even so, she knows she must move fast. She has not got much time.

But before she prepares to gather together her few belongings, there is one last important thing to be done. Belinda makes her way to the basement kitchen and helps herself to something from a kitchen drawer.

She goes up to her bedroom. Hanging from her wardrobe is the new dress. It is perfect, the stuff of dreams. Her dreams.

All her life Belinda Kite has dreamed of owning a dress like this. In the darkness of the boarding school dormitory, in the loneliness of her abandoned childhood, always standing in the shadows, she had watched other girls, far less pretty, less accomplished, waltz in and out of her life in their beautiful dresses.

She feasts her eyes upon the cream puffings, the bronze velveteen flounces and the delicate lace embroidery of the dress that was bought and paid for by her false seducer. Just as she has been bought and paid for, and now discarded, her heart ripped in two.

Then Belinda lifts the beautiful dress from the hanger, rolls it up and stuffs it into the grate. Striking a match, she drops it onto the material and watches as the dress is consumed by fire until there is nothing left but blackened ash.

***

Darkness falls. A solitary man walks towards the lights and bustle of King's Cross Station. Look more closely. Do you recognise him? He passes through the sooty brick archway, his shoulders rounded, his unbrushed top hat pulled down low. This much you see. What you cannot see is the darkness that fills his head like cold ink, the tendrils of it dragging at his mind.

Like a moth drawn to a flame, Frederick Undercroft

heads towards the warmth and lights of the concourse. He has a sudden urge to be amongst strangers going about their everyday business. People who do not know him, who do not wish him harm.

It is 6.20 pm and the station is unexpectedly busy. There is a palpable air of excitement mixed with expectation. Everyone seems to be heading towards the same destination. A leaf caught in an updraft, Undercroft follows them.

He arrives at a certain platform, finds himself borne along in the middle of a crowd of men and women. Many of the men carry cameras. They hurry down the side of the platform until they are close to the end, where they start setting up their equipment.

"What is going on?" he asks.

"The Flying Scot is coming in," he is told. "Ten hours from Edinburgh Waverley, and she's due in a couple of minutes. Never late."

He stands at the edge of the platform staring up the line. He sees two yellow lights glowing like vengeful eyes, far away still but coming closer, closer. He hears steel upon steel, the thrumming of rails, the rhythmic churning of the engine.

Then the gigantic green behemoth is in sight, smoke billowing from its chimney, steam hissing from its sleek sides as the driver applies the brakes.

Undercroft takes a step forward. He smells acrid smoke, feels the power of massive pistons moving remorselessly up and down. The great heart of the train is beating, beating. He takes another step.

A sudden cry. A screech of brakes. A shout from the crowd. But the mighty machine moves on until it comes to rest at the wooden buffers. Too late. The crowd surges forward. Too late. The fireman jumps down, slips between the footplate and the rails. Too late. Far too late.

As the crowd surges forward, and the porters and guards rush to the platform to stop anybody alighting from the train, a black-clothed and heavily-veiled woman separates herself from the excitable throng and walks calmly back down the platform towards the now unmanned barrier. She makes her way out of the station and goes to find a cab.

***

Detective Inspector Stride sits at his desk and surveys the pile of paperwork. Despite his new *file-it-on-the-floor-and-forget-it* system, the pile seems to have grown again. He picks up the top item – a letter addressed to him personally – heaves a sigh, and opens it. As he reads the contents, the frown between his eyebrows gets deeper. When he has finished reading, he goes to the door and calls for Cully.

"Am I going mad, Jack?" Stride asks, handing him the letter.

Jack Cully scans the contents.

"It doesn't make any sense."

"I'm reassured. I thought it was me."

"It's just a string of meaningless gibberish – though it appears to be signed by Mr Frederick Undercroft and is written on his official legal note paper. Some sort of hoax?"

Stride shrugs.

"Who knows? Get someone to take it round to his office and see what he has to say about it, will you?"

There is a pause. Stride looks up.

"Is there a problem?"

"Mr Undercroft won't be in his office today."

"I see. So where will he be?"

"In the police morgue. Apparently, he fell under a train at King's Cross station last night."

***

At the coroner's inquest on the body of Frederick Undercroft, evidence will be presented as to the extremely agitated state of mind of the deceased in the days leading up to his death. A report from his clerk and a garbled letter addressed to Detective Inspector Stride of Scotland Yard will be produced to corroborate this.

The presence of small, but not insignificant amounts of arsenic in his body will be attributed to the chemical being used in the manufacture of the vibrant Arsenical Green dye used to colour the green wallpaper in his bedroom. (New research, recently published in scientific journals, has thrown unexpected light upon the malign effects of inhaling and ingesting even slight residues of the chemical over a long period of time via this unfortunate choice of decorative material.)

The final report on the death of Frederick Undercroft, lawyer, will state that he was apparently the victim of a tragic accident, though given the mitigating circumstances, an open verdict will be declared.

The role of the unknown black-clad woman who had followed him from his office to the station, and of the unknown black-gloved hand that pushed him into the path of the oncoming train, will not be considered as a major contributory factor.

***

A wintry day in Leeds is pretty much the same as one in London. Same dark streets, with an icy wind whipping round the corners and catching you unawares. Same acrid smoke-filled air; same soot-blackened buildings.

Same hum and thrum of machinery, same clip-clop of horses' hooves and cacophony of street vendors' cries. Same pale watery sunlight casting shadows, and same pale underfed people huddled into their clothes against the winter cold.

Here, in a nice house on the outskirts, Josiah Bulstrode, boot and shoe manufacturer and (much to his surprise) now an engaged man, butters his toast with vigour and takes big crunchy bites.

He breakfasts alone, the black armband on his jacket bearing witness to his recent loss. The fire splutters in the grate. A carriage clock ticks madly on the mantelpiece.

The small and slightly erratic servant girl, who has been hired to replace the more reliable servant girl who has gone back to her mother's house since Sissy's death, sidles in cautiously.

"Um ... a letter has arrived, Mr ... master ..."

"Hand it over, Lizzie Lou," Josiah says with a resigned sigh.

She does. He frowns.

"Now then ... Who could this be, writing to me from there?"

Josiah slits open the envelope with the butter-knife and pulls out a banknote. Then another banknote. Then some more.

He upends the envelope. Banknotes flutter out like white birds released from captivity. A couple of bright guineas roll into the centre of the table, coming to rest by the butter-dish. Right at the bottom of the envelope, he finds a tiny piece of paper upon which is written:

There is no Dominion Diamond Mine Company. It was all a fraud. Here is your money back. A Well-Wisher

"Well, now, this is a mystery," Josiah says to the wide-eyed and speechless servant.

He scoops up the notes and rescues the errant guineas.

"You see all this? Somebody has done me a good turn, Lizzie Lou. I don't know who it was, but I thank them from the bottom of my heart. Indeed, I do."

***

It is early evening, a few days after Josiah Bulstrode received his letter full of banknotes, and in the tiny rented terraced house in London, Jack Cully puts down his copy of *The Police Gazette* and glances across the hearth at his beloved wife.

"You look very tired, my dear," he says. "I've noticed it for some time. Is anything wrong?"

"Yes, Jack, I am very tired," Emily Cully agrees with a sigh. "But there is nothing wrong."

She sets down her sewing and comes to sit on his lap, which is very pleasant. Then Emily bends forward and whispers in his ear, and Jack Cully, street-hardened and not one to give way to emotion easily, suddenly finds his eyes filling with tears.

"When?" he asks.

"Sometime next spring."

And he kisses her and holds her, very gently, very tenderly, as if she is the most precious and priceless and wondrous object in the whole world. Which, as far as Jack Cully is concerned, she certainly is.

***

Next spring, when the Cullys will be blessed by the safe arrival of a beautiful baby girl, whom they will name Violet, the Bois de Boulogne in Paris will also witness the arrival of a beautiful new stranger, whose emerald green eyes and hair the colour of falling Autumn are perfectly offset by the fitted riding dress, clinging so tightly to her provocative curves that her lovely figure is plain for all to see.

She will be observed driving a smart modern phaeton with a pair of perfectly-matched white ponies and an adoring tiger pageboy standing proudly behind her, ready to help her down whenever she chooses to alight.

If you follow the phaeton, and many young *gallants* do, you will observe it pull up at the door of one of the biggest mansions in the Rue de Ponthieu, where *La Belle Anglaise* lives in the best suite of rooms. Nobody knows from whence her wealth originates, but it is widely acknowledged that she is immensely rich.

It is rumoured that she has a wardrobe stuffed with silk dresses from Worth, and that her *cabinet* contains a seat padded with swansdown. It is also whispered that she never removes her beautiful diamond necklace, not even when she is taking a bath.

Finis

Thank you for reading this novel. If you have enjoyed it, why not leave a review on Amazon or Goodreads, and recommend it to your friends?

30246175R00160

Printed in Great
Britain
by Amazon